VERDICT OF THE COURT

Hoogan 5/17

MH

VERDICT OF THE COURT

A Burren Mystery

Cora Harrison

This first world edition published 2014
in Great Britain and 2014 in the USA by
SEVERN HOUSE PUBLISHERS LTD of
19 Cedar Road, Sutton, Surrey, England, SM2 5DA.

British Library Cataloguing in Publication Data

Harrison, Cora author.
  Verdict of the court.
  1. Mara, Brehon of the Burren (Fictitious character)–
  Fiction. 2. Women judges–Ireland–Burren–Fiction.
  3. Murder–Investigation–Fiction. 4. Sieges–Fiction.
  5. Burren (Ireland)–History–16th century–Fiction.
  6. Detective and mystery stories.
  I. Title
  823.9'2-dc23

ISBN-13: 978-07278-8378-0 (cased)

All Severn House titles are printed on acid-free paper.

Severn House Publishers support the Forest Stewardship Council™ [FSC™],
the leading international forest certification organisation. All our titles that
are printed on FSC certified paper carry the FSC logo.

MIX
Paper from
responsible sources
FSC FSC® C013056
www.fsc.org

Typeset by Palimpsest Book Production Ltd.,
Falkirk, Stirlingshire, Scotland.
Printed and bound in Great Britain by
TJ International, Padstow, Cornwall.

This book is dedicated to my friend and former colleague Judith Harper because she likes Mara's scholars and picked out Enda as a particular favourite. She, like me, knows the satisfaction of hearing about former pupils' successes and the feeling of sadness when a particularly gifted young person does not carry the promise forward into adulthood.

Acknowledgements

As always, thanks are due to my agent, Peter Buckman, who works so hard on my behalf; to my editor, Anna Telfer, and the team at Severn House who cheer me with their appreciation and stop me making terrible errors; to my family and friends who put up with having bits of Brehon Law inserted into most conversations and to my dog, Lily, who is my faithful companion during the hours of writing and who stops me overdoing my journeys with Mara through the Burren by firmly putting her paw on the keyboard and indicating that it is time for a real walk.

One

Qudachc Morainn
(The Testament of Morann)

'Let him (the King) not elevate any judge unless he knows the true legal precedents.'

One of the most important decisions that a King must make is in the appointing of a Brehon (judge) to administer justice in the kingdom. A Brehon must be a person of virtue and integrity as well as having a deep knowledge of all things pertaining to the law.

There was a light frost over the landscape when Mara, Brehon of the Burren, set out from that kingdom to spend the Christmas of 1519 at the King's court. It made everything look incredibly beautiful, she thought, as she stood holding the reins of her horse and waited, looking across the landscape, while her five scholars fastened their satchels to the sides of their ponies. She had lived at Cahermacnaghten on the western edge of the Burren ever since her birth forty-six years ago but she never tired of the view from the gate. She looked lovingly over the stone-paved fields where the limestone glistened in the early morning sunshine, its silver-whiteness contrasting with the red berries of short, stunted holly bushes that grew here and there in the grykes or cracks between the giant slabs of stone. A tiny wren had been pouring out its winter song from the feathery twigs of a juniper tree but just as Mara had climbed onto the broad back of her new horse, six majestic swans flew overhead, the vibrant throbbing of their wings silencing the tiny bird until they passed on their way towards one of the seasonal lakes in the valleys. A minute later the swans had disappeared; the wren had taken up his song again and a red-breasted robin chirped from the stone wall of the enclosure, almost touching the hand that she had placed on the gate pier. In the distance the flattened cone of Mullaghmore Mountain was an exquisite shade of palest blue, slightly paler than the cloudless sky above them.

'Wait, everyone! I've forgotten my throwing knives. I've forgotten my throwing knives, Brehon,' shouted nine-year-old Cormac, the youngest scholar at the Cahermacnaghten School and Mara's son by her second marriage to King Turlough Donn, lord of three kingdoms in the west of Ireland: Thomond, Corcomroe and Burren. The King had other sons by a previous marriage and Cormac had been destined to become a lawyer like his mother and her father before her, but at the moment his throwing knives were his most important possession. Mara sighed slightly as she watched her son racing back across the paved yard towards the scholars' house in the Cahermacnaghten Law School. What did he expect to do with them at a Christmas feast? she wondered. It had been her intention that Cormac would qualify as a lawyer, and then as professor, even perhaps take over the school at Cahermacnaghten from his mother, but, though clever and quick to learn, his interests were those of his warlike father and he would, she knew, prefer to be a soldier. This was not something that Mara wanted for him. There were enough of the O'Brien clan already jockeying for the high position of *tánaiste* or heir and she had no desire to see her son amongst them. By his last wife, Turlough already had grown-up sons and a grandson of seventeen, as well as innumerable nephews and cousins.

Ten years, thought Mara. Ten years ago, on Christmas Day, I was married to Turlough Donn O'Brien. The marriage, which had been followed six months later by a son, had been a successful one. Each lived their own lives, coming together as frequently as they could, but also enjoying the liberty to follow the path laid down for them; the one as king of three kingdoms, and the other in maintaining law and order in the smallest of these kingdoms, investigating crimes, drawing up contracts, teaching a school of young people to follow in her footsteps – Mara's life, like Turlough's, was a happy and fulfilling one.

Normally her scholars would return to their own families for Christmas and she, her husband and her son would spend

Christmas together, alone except for servants, but this year was special. This Christmas was the twentieth-year anniversary of Turlough Donn's accession to the leadership of the powerful O'Brien clan. On this day in 1499 he had been inaugurated on the mound of Magh Adhair, the white rod of leadership placed in his hand and he had sworn to protect his people and to be a true and just leader. He had carried out those promises well, thought Mara, his reign was a peaceful and successful one and he had defended his people against the assaults of neighbouring chieftains and against the insidious influence of the English king – King Henry VIII – who would have liked to have the whole of Ireland under his rule and to impose English law and English customs on a people to whom they were alien.

Turlough was a good man, a good soldier, a good husband and father, she thought affectionately, as Cormac, her son, and his son, came running back from the scholars' house brandishing the set of throwing knives slotted into a leather belt, far too long for his narrow waist, but his prize possession. If young Cormac grew up to be as good a man as his father she would be satisfied. The schooling would do him no harm, but it looked unlikely that he would want to be her inheritor. Her position of maintainer of the law was a worthy one; but perhaps not one that suited her son's nature. Her father had been Brehon of the Burren, and the fact that she was an only child had probably tempted him to allow her a place in his law school. Later he grew proud of her brains and when he had died just after Mara's sixteenth birthday, when she had already qualified as a lawyer, he had bequeathed the law school to her. She had rapidly taken her examinations to become an *ollamh*, or professor, and then had qualified as Brehon, or judge and magistrate, and had maintained law and order in the Kingdom of the Burren ever since, hardly ever stirring from that one hundred square miles of limestone, flowers and sweet grass. A happy life and a satisfying one, she thought. But now she had to attend the festival and to leave her kingdom for a few days.

'And if any problem should arise that Fachtnan cannot deal with or if he is incapacitated in any way,' said Mara to her farm manager, 'just send immediately over to the Brehon of Corcomroe. Either he or his assistant will deal with it.'

'Don't worry, Brehon,' said Cumhal. 'Nothing will happen over Christmas. Everyone will be too busy feasting and enjoying themselves quietly with their own families.'

'But there might be a crime at Bunratty Castle,' said Cormac hopefully as they rode away from the massive walls that enclosed the law school on the western boundary of the Burren. 'There'll be hundreds of people there and they'll all be drinking and strong drink leads to fierce fights; the King told me that; he told me to steer clear of mead for that reason.'

'Our Brehon won't have to deal with it, though; that will be for Brehon MacClancy to solve,' said Domhnall, Mara's grandson. Fourteen-year-old Domhnall was the eldest scholar at the law school, and although Cormac was his uncle, in reality Domhnall was a figure of authority in the law school and all of the other boys obeyed him without question. His word was law in every respect and although a very peaceful boy himself, his best friend Slevin, less than a year younger, was quick with his fists to punish any disobedience.

Mara smiled to herself as her argumentative son subsided without a word. Domhnall, she thought, with a slightly regretful glance at her son who was busy making sure that each one of his throwing knives was slotted into position, Domhnall was the scholar who would make a good Brehon and a good head of the law school when she felt herself too old for the position. Of course he was quite right – any crime, any disturbance, any trouble that occurred at the King's court at Bunratty would be for Brehon MacClancy to deal with. She could relax and enjoy a week of leisure and her scholars would love the crowds and the excitement and feasting that would take place at the most splendid castle in Ireland, according to Turlough. And if there was a tiny regret in her mind that she and her husband and her son could not spend Christmas quietly together in her beloved Burren, well that regret was quickly banished. Mara had never been inclined to waste time grieving for the unattainable.

The short winter day was almost over by the time that Mara and the five boys arrived within sight of Bunratty Castle.

She had been a little worried when the light had dimmed by the time they crossed the Six Mile Bridge and they descended onto the path that wound through the marshes towards the city of Limerick. However, they only had another few miles to go and Bunratty Castle, standing on a small promontory overlooking the River Shannon, was visible even from this distance. It looked as though every window was illuminated. The castle was a large one, with four towers built around a central block, each tower culminating in a small flag-bearing turret. The main building had two large halls, private apartments for guests of honour and in addition about twenty-four private sleeping places within the four towers. Mara sighed at the thought of all the guests with whom she would have to make polite conversation. The boys, however, she knew, would have a wonderful time and all of their families had been delighted to give them the opportunity of spending Christmas at the King's court. Cormac, in particular, was wildly excited, not just at the prospect of seeing his father whom he had not met for months but because on his last weekend visit in the early autumn he had made two new friends while visiting Bunratty. One of Turlough's comrades, Maccon MacMahon, chieftain of the MacMahon clan, was there at the time. He had brought with him his two youngest children, ten-year-old twins, who were being fostered by Brehon MacClancy at his ancestral castle at Urlan. Maccon MacMahon would, of course, be present for the festivities and Turlough had sent word to Cormac that the twins had been invited as well. Mara and everyone at the law school had heard a lot about these twins – Cael and Cian were their names, apparently, and according to Cormac, they had, all three of them, great '*craic*' together climbing around the leaded turrets and pelting the good-natured cook, Rosta, with hazel nuts for ammunition and taking instruction from him on how to cook fish pie and how to kill the salmon in the river by the use of throwing knives. There were also whispered stories of underground passages and raids on houses in the village around the castle and all in all, Mara had an uneasy feeling that it might not be going to be a restful Christmas if these two were as wild as Cormac's account of them implied. Brehon MacClancy was a widower who spent most of his time at Bunratty Castle so the twins had probably got a bit out of hand, she thought. There was, apparently, no formal law school at Urlan Castle, but it had been a custom, from time immemorial, for the MacMahon children to be fostered by one of the MacClancy law family.

The minute they arrived at the stables a pair of red-headed boys burst out of the door to the castle, came flying down the steps and across to the courtyard to greet them. They were dressed completely alike, with short madder-red woollen cloaks and knee-length *léinte* whose linen had probably started the day snowy white but now were stained with smears of earth and of grass. Not really identical twins, thought Mara, studying them as they and Cormac went through an ecstatic greeting ceremony. Both had red-gold hair, both had fair skin covered in pale tan-coloured freckles and both had pale blue eyes, but Cian had a nose that already was aquiline and would, probably, in his adulthood, be of a considerable size, whereas Cael, the taller of the two, had a small and neat nose.

'Look up,' said Cael with dramatic emphasis and obediently the law-school party raised their eyes. Outside the front entrance to the castle was a tall oak tree, and from a branch about twenty feet above the ground dangled a figure with a rope around its neck, a large figure with an enormous stomach, dressed in a threadbare cloak with hood drawn over the head; stuffed with straw, reckoned Mara spotting a few stray stalks on the ground below. The face and eyes were roughly drawn with charcoal on a piece of white linen and a flowing white beard and giant pair of moustaches of sheep's wool, as well as the hood, hid most of the features. A legal scroll, bound in linen tape, protruded from the edge of the cloak and even without this it was obvious to anyone who knew him that this was a crude attempt at a likeness of the venerable Brehon MacClancy.

'Did you do this?' Mara eyed the pair sternly and they both giggled and avoided the question.

'It's great, isn't it? We've been firing knives at it from the top of the north-western tower. It's good, isn't it, Cormac?'

Thinking that she would do her best to keep Cormac away from them during their stay, Mara beckoned over a stable boy. He looked to be about sixteen, she thought, sturdy and well-grown. He had been grooming a restless stallion with an adroit determination which she admired and was now hanging up the brushes and leathers.

'Could you climb that tree and cut down that nonsense before it offends anyone?' she asked and when he nodded with a grin, she held out her hand to Cael.

'Give me your knife.'

'Not my knife! That's a throwing knife. That rope will blunt it!' The defiance was unmistakable and Cael backed away, slotting the knife back into the belt.

'Give me that knife,' said Mara steadily. That tone of voice always worked on the Burren, but somehow it didn't seem to be effective with the red-haired twins.

'No!' yelled Cael and Cian added his voice and went so far as to stick out his tongue.

'That's their father,' said the stable boy, grinning widely. He nodded in the direction of the castle steps where a middle-aged man came briskly down, skipping every second step in a youthful fashion. Mara had met him once, she thought, but not for some time, and she noticed that a large round bald spot had appeared on the crown of head of red-gold hair which she remembered.

'Ah, Brehon,' he said affably. 'The King sent me to welcome you. He is just changing his dress – we've been riding. I see you've met my two rascals.'

'We were having a discussion about removing that,' said Mara crisply, indicating the swinging figure dangling from the branch.

To her surprise and fury, Maccon burst into an enormous laugh, the sound pealing against the stone walls all around.

'By the lord, that's good. It's him to the life.' He said the words with warm approval and the twins smirked.

'We've been using it for target practice, Father,' said Cian in the tones of one who knew that he could not fail to please.

'That's my knife through his heart,' said Cael.

'And mine through his neck – that's just as good – that

would kill him immediately – and there would be a fountain of blood,' said Cian.

'*Iontach!*' exclaimed Cormac looking up with admiration at the knives inserted into the dangling figure in the oak tree.

'I think it should be removed before it causes offence,' said Mara firmly. She was tired after her long journey and had no great affection for Brehon MacClancy, but right was right. A man, and especially a Brehon, should not be exposed to ridicule in that fashion. In any case, badly behaved children always annoyed her.

Maccon ignored this. His attention was on a figure coming through the gate.

'Fionn,' he called, 'come and see. Look at what my two scamps have made! Guess who!'

Mara knew Fionn O'Brien well. He was a cousin of Turlough's – a hanger-on, she thought of him, someone whose people passed him over in favour of his younger brother and who had spent the next twenty years trying to pass his time by visiting more fortunate relations. Last year he had married a daughter of one of the MacNamaras – an only child – and had inherited a castle at Cratloe and some land with her. Mara had not met his wife but hoped that she was satisfied with her bargain. Not to her surprise, Fionn found the swinging effigy of Brehon MacClancy to be very funny also. Mara decided that the most dignified thing was to walk away as soon as possible.

'Let's go and greet the King,' she said to her scholars. She had meant to make them attend to their own ponies, as they did back at the law school, but felt that it was bad for them, especially Cormac, to witness the amusement at the rather unpleasant prank of Maccon MacMahon's twins. She hoped that someone would have the sense to remove it before the elderly Brehon of Thomond caught sight of it, but decided that it was really none of her business.

Two

Críċ Gablaċ

(ranks in society)

The lowest grade of king has an honour price of 42 séts and he has direct control only over his own kingdom. A king who has control over three kingdoms has an honour price of 48 séts and can be called a great king.

The highest king in the land has an honour price of 84 séts. He rules over a province and can be described as a king of great kings.

The castle of Bunratty, seat of the court of the O'Briens, Kings of Thomond, Corcomroe and Burren, was the largest and finest in the whole three kingdoms. Unlike most castles it had two main halls – the great hall, where the King and his family and particular friends, as well as the most important members of his household, could dine and then below it the main guard hall, where the rest of the household could feast and dance and listen to music. The food for the main guard hall was cooked in the separate kitchen house within the enclosure, but the King's meals were served in the great hall from a small pantry and buttery which had a hatch into the fifty-foot-long room, and that was where they feasted that night of Christmas Eve. There were only twenty of them to dine with the King that evening so they were all seated at one table which stretched across the width of the raised platform at the top of the hall. It was a magnificent room, one stone wall hung with an elaborately stitched tapestry, purchased by Turlough's uncle from a French ship. The floor was paved with marble tiles and during daylight hours the room was full of light from five twenty-foot-high windows, facing south, east and west, that were set into recesses in the depths of the thick walls. Now, on this winter's evening, the hall was lit by candles and by the enormous fire where a whole tree trunk, balancing

on iron supports above fast-blazing smaller logs, sent out light
as well as heat to the whole hall.

'Murrough did not come,' said Mara in a low tone to Conor.
Murrough was Conor's younger brother.

'I sent a message by young Raour, but he refused to
come. He is very high in the favour of the King of England,
Raour said.' Conor spoke in a low voice in Mara's ear. There
would be little apprehension that Turlough could hear the
words above the tumult of voices and laughter and shouted
remarks, but Mara could understand why Conor, a sensitive
young man, made sure that his remarks reached her ear only.

Murrough, a couple of years younger than Conor, had been
Turlough's favourite son but had been banished from the
kingdom of the Burren and from his father's court when he
committed a heinous crime. Turlough, a man of strong affections, had by now forgiven his son and blotted out from his
memory any wrongdoing of the handsome young man, but
Murrough preferred to remain in London and to court King
Henry VIII. He had reappeared once and had done his best
to induce Turlough to accept King Henry's proposition of
'surrender and regrant' which would have entailed the surrender
of his three kingdoms and his title of king and *taoiseach* to his
clan in exchange for an English earldom and the regrant of
most of his land. Mara smiled to herself at the memory
of Turlough's rage and then grew serious as she took one look
at Conor's white face and emaciated form. Conor was
Turlough's heir, the *tánaiste*, but Conor was a sick man plagued
by recurring bouts of the wasting disease which consumed his
health and the clan would have been very happy to accept the
vigorous and warlike Murrough, physically so like his popular
father, in his place.

And if that happened, thought Mara, it might be one more
nail in the coffin of Gaelic Ireland and would certainly mean
an end to Brehon law and all that she believed in so intensely.
Though sorry that Turlough did not have both his sons with
him to celebrate his twenty years of kingship, she was glad
that Murrough stayed in London. And Conor had rallied
before and could surely rally again. His disease was lingering
but he was better than he had been ten years ago. She turned

to Aengus MacCraith, the poet, who was seated across the table from her and began to discuss the ancient *feiseanna* of the past and their possible revival at the time of the horse fair at Coad. She kept that conversation going for a while until Conor had regained his cheerfulness and wanted to talk about his son Raour, recently returned from fosterage and looking to be a very promising young man with none of his father's constitutional weakness. In fact, thought Mara, the young man could do with losing some weight. However she was sorry for Conor and praised his son enough to satisfy the proud father. And then he turned to Fionn O'Brien's wife and made the same remarks to her. Raour was obviously the light of Conor's life at the moment, the hopeful promise of the future. Aideen looked bored, arched her very black eyebrows, sighed, sipped from her glass, but Conor still continued, relating anecdotes about Raour's prowess with the spear, his ability to judge a horse, his astuteness in business matters, his ability to master any stallion in the land. Mara smiled to herself, wondering how long Aideen, as a childless woman, would stand this outpouring of praise. It would be different if she, like many others, could wait for a gap in the conversation, and then insert a few anecdotes about her own children.

And then she realized that Aideen was not in fact listening to Conor, but had her eyes fixed on the bottom of the table where Brehon MacClancy sat. What had attracted her attentive gaze in that direction? The Brehon was old, not attractive, not even a very pleasant man. Conor, for all his faults of partiality towards his own son, was an agreeable and a pleasant dinner companion.

Mara sipped her wine, made light conversation, listened and thought her own thoughts until they had reached the second course of the elaborately cooked meal.

The toasts to Turlough's health and to another twenty years of reign had been numerous, but these were informal. The formal praise came when Seán Brody left his place at the table and went to stand beside his harp. Aengus MacCraith joined him, and, had, to the accompaniment of the harp, sung and spoken of the great love that all in the kingdom bore to

Turlough Donn, descendent of the great High King, Brian
Boru. Turlough, a modest man, had signalled to Rosta to serve
the next course.

And that was when Brehon MacClancy, sitting at the bottom
of the table, suddenly exploded.

'Ye all sit there and ye nod your heads and ye smile,' he
said maliciously when Aengus MacCraith finished and cheers
had risen to the rafters. 'Everyone loves the King; that's what
all the poets say, but I know better,' he continued, gazing
around, as knives ceased to work and Maccon MacMahon,
sitting a few places down the table from the King, paused in
his selection from a tray of roast goose.

'I know that there's one of ye here, one whom the King
trusts and loves, and who declares his love for the King on
all occasions, there is one person here tonight who is secretly
cheating him and when Judgement Day comes then the
name of that person will be revealed and the King will
know the truth. And don't think that I won't inform him
of all the scandals and evil-doing that go on in this place,
too.' Brehon MacClancy gave a triumphant sound which
was half a grunt and half a suppressed giggle. Mara wondered
whether the man's wits were becoming addled with age.
Why this public expression of malice? Perhaps he had seen
the hanging effigy and that had angered him into this display.
Perhaps it was aimed at Maccon; after all he was a great
friend of the King's. And Maccon, she thought severely,
should keep those badly behaved twins of his under control.
She looked at the Brehon's assistant, Enda, who had once
been a scholar at her school, but Enda's eyes were averted
from her and were fixed studiously on the polished oak
surface of the table. One finger was tracing a circular motion,
perhaps around a knot in the wood, and his slim young
body seemed stiff with tension, as if awaiting some further
revelation from his master.

But Brehon MacClancy had finished. He beckoned impatiently to Rosta, the King's cook, to bring him some of the
goose, and the conversation resumed.

There was an uneasy note in the voices, though. The harpist,
Brian MacBrody, endeavoured to break the tension by

strumming a few notes from the strings of his instrument and beckoned to Mara's grandson and the eldest scholar at her school to come across to try out his harp, telling him how the instrument had been made from one piece of wood as the front was carved from a branch protruding from the tree trunk which formed the back of the harp.

'Feel those strings,' he said to Domhnall. 'What do you think that they are made from?'

'Brass,' queried Domhnall. He was a very well-mannered boy, but his attention was focused on the roast goose.

'Gold,' said the harpist triumphantly, but his eyes were not on Domhnall, but had gone across the polished boards and were looking intently at the elderly Brehon.

And so was, noticed Mara, Maccon MacNamara. She began to think about the man. One of Turlough's best friends and *taoiseach* of Clann Baiscinn from the western tip of the kingdom; his lands lay only a few miles away, further west and just where the huge River Shannon entered the sea after it had passed through the city of Limerick and passed the Castle of Bunratty, perched on its promontory. Maccon was a great man for boats and he and Turlough enjoyed fishing together. Mara had met him on previous occasions, but this was the first time that she had met his three children – the eldest, like her deceased mother, Mara guessed, a beautiful dark-haired girl of about sixteen and two red-headed twins not much older than her own son Cormac. He had been hilariously funny earlier, telling stories about narrow escapes that he and Turlough had when their net got tangled in the weir and teasing his daughter about being in love. A nice man, probably, even though he should have shown himself a bit more authoritative with those twins, she thought. However, she told herself forgivingly; perhaps he spoiled them because he saw little of them and because they had no mother. Otherwise she had always liked him; a man who was a good companion to her husband who was a fun-loving, easy-going ruler. But now Maccon was silent and his eyes were apprehensive as he glanced across at Brehon MacClancy. It would be worrying if the Brehon had something to disclose about Maccon. Turlough would be most upset if one of his best friends had betrayed him.

Mara allowed her glance to wander around the table. There was certainly a feeling of uneasiness among the guests seated around the long table spread with so many splendid dishes. There was a long silence, a silence when people looked at each other, looked at the elderly Brehon and then back at their platters again. And then, too quickly and too loudly, Fionn O'Brien, Turlough's cousin, called up from the bottom of the table.

'Turlough, let's go hunting tomorrow. That marsh at the back of the castle is full of birds. I swear I heard a bustard outside my bedroom window. Rosta, you'd cook bustard for us, wouldn't you, if we managed to get a few for you?'

'One would be enough, my lord; these things weigh nearly as much as this young gosling here,' said the cook readily. He poked Cormac in his skinny ribs and chuckled. He had once been a foot soldier in Turlough's army, but an injury to his leg had made him lame and he had turned to cooking. He was a great favourite with Turlough and quite at home with all the company and Cormac was so taken by his mastery with pots and pans that he had informed his mother on his return from his last visit to Bunratty that he thought he'd rather be a cook than a lawyer.

Turlough laughed uproariously at the mild joke from his cook and the mood changed. Everyone seemed to have a story to tell about bustards, or a method of catching the huge birds, and Mara relaxed. She watched Enda, though. She was worried about him. It had seemed a wonderful position, nine years ago, for a seventeen-year-old boy to become an assistant to the Brehon at the King's court, but now she wondered whether he had done the right thing. By now, with his brains and his qualifications, he could be holding a position such as she held, dealing with all the legal matters, solving crimes, keeping the peace between neighbours. Even in a kingdom as small as the Burren, the satisfactions of the job were immense and Enda could open his own school to train boys. She resolved to have a talk with him afterwards – this business of waiting around to fill dead men's shoes was not good enough for one of her cleverest scholars. She was not the only one who looked at his downcast face, she noticed. Maccon MacMahon's pretty sixteen-year-old daughter kept stealing glances at him and then blushing and looking away.

'If you can kill two or three bustards, then I'll have the feathers for a cloak,' said Ellice, the wife of Turlough's eldest son. She was ageing quickly, thought Mara. Nine years ago she had been a very pretty girl, but now she had a sour and discontented look. Her husband, Conor, suffered from poor health and she probably did not have much fun out of her life, being tied to a sickbed for long periods every year. Still she might be better now that her seventeen-year-old son, Raour, was back from fosterage. There was talk that the young man might replace his father as heir to Turlough if Conor continued to suffer from these continual fevers. He was certainly a fine, sturdy-looking fellow, thought Mara and she resolved to have a chat with Turlough about him. A king had to be warlike, had to be a leader of his people and the delicate Conor who coughed and shivered his way through every winter would not be acceptable to the clan. Turlough was now over sixty years of age, and the clan would be looking attentively at his appointed successor. It was important to groom a man for the position of king. If Conor agreed to step aside and allow his son to be elected as *tánaiste* in his place, then the youngster could live with Turlough and be educated into all the subtleties of friendliness, good manners, good humour and a thorough understanding of his fellow men which had made Turlough such a very successful ruler over three kingdoms.

It was just as she was considering the question that Brehon MacClancy spoke again.

'I'm an old man now,' he said heavily, 'and some of ye like to make a game of me.' He glared around the table and Mara felt her heart sink. She should have stayed and made sure that the offensive effigy had been removed. She had been tired, but if it had been her own territory she would not have allowed that to deter her. No, she acknowledged to herself, she did not like Brehon MacClancy and had just used the presence of the children's father as an excuse to go away. Now the elderly man was going to allow a piece of childish spite to prod him into disturbing Turlough's peace of mind in the midst of the celebrations of twenty years of successful kingship. Perhaps she could talk to him after the festivities were over, could suggest that he prepare the King for anything which would concern a near relative or close friend, make sure, perhaps, that he had firm evidence for the accusation. She watched him carefully now as he chewed his way through a mouthful of roast curlew and was devising an innocuous remark when suddenly and disgustingly he spat out what remained in his mouth and shouted out:

'I can see your eyes on me; I know you'd like to kill me, you'd like to stick a knife in my back, but I'll tell you something; whenever you are around I'll have my eye on you and I have a fine strong lock on my bedroom door so don't think that you'll follow me up there. You can just sweat in your guilt until the moment is right to inform your king and the people of the kingdom about your treachery.'

And then he got to his feet unsteadily, thrust Enda, who had risen also, back into his chair and stumped out of the room. The company around the table fell silent, listening to his heavy footsteps going up the spiral staircase of the south-east tower to the bedroom which was reserved for him whenever he stayed at Bunratty Castle. The remaining guests looked at each other and looked away and Rosta called to his kitchen boys to bring in the third course of the meal.

Mara turned to Maccon. 'Are both of your sons destined for the law?' she enquired.

'Both,' he said, looking puzzled and then laughed. 'I have only one son, Brehon; just this fellow, here,' he said, tousling Cian's hair. 'Cael is a girl, but she likes to dress up as a boy; she and Cian have always been together and she enjoys what he enjoys. As good at throwing a knife as any boy, aren't you? Shona doesn't approve, do you?' He looked across at his eldest daughter and she hoisted her shoulders and pouted but made no remark. She, also, had been fostered by the MacClancy family at Urlan Castle, Mara seemed to remember.

The strange thing was that her face, which had flushed a

rosy pink earlier, when she had chatted with Enda, was now a stark white and her eyes were wide with apprehension. Only the children at the table seemed unconcerned by Brehon MacClancy's threats.

Three

Uraicecht Becc
(little primer)

A physician has an honour price of seven séts. He is expected to apply herbs, to supervise diet and to undertake surgery. There will be no penalty for causing bleeding, but if he cuts a joint or a sinew he has to pay a fine and he will be expected to nurse the patient himself.

A banliaig, woman physician, is a woman of great importance to the kingdom.

Enda hovered at Mara's side when they came out of church on Christmas Day. She had been looking for an opportunity to talk with him and instantly dropped Turlough's arm and moved a little aside.

'Come and look at my new horse, Enda,' she said. 'My dear old mare has gone into retirement now though I still use her on a few short journeys. This new fellow is splendidly strong. He hardly noticed the journey between here and Limerick.'

The stables were a good choice. No one had taken a horse out as the church was only a four-minute walk from the castle so the place was quiet and deserted – even the stable boys were enjoying a chat near the well where most of the inhabitants of the small village around the castle gathered to exchange news.

Despite the privacy Enda seemed reluctant to come to the point and spent such a long time discussing the horse and his breeding that Mara grew impatient.

'Are you happy here, Enda, working with Brehon MacClancy?' she said eventually breaking into a rambling discussion about Spanish blood.

He flushed vividly. 'To be honest, I'm not,' he said. 'I haven't been for the last few years.'

That surprised her. Enda, she thought, had always had a

good opinion of himself. She was astonished that he hadn't moved on to another post as soon as he had found the present one unsatisfactory and said so immediately.

'Not so easy,' he said cynically. He gave a quick look over his shoulder. There was no one near, but oddly he still hesitated.

'Come on,' she said. 'You know that you can tell me.' He had been such a brilliant boy, burning with intelligence and with assurance. He was still very good-looking, but somehow the burnish had gone from him and his blue eyes held a wary, defensive look which seemed to dim the perfection of their jewel-like intensity of colour.

'I've applied to various clans all over the west and the midlands – every time that I heard of a death or of a move,' he said after a minute, 'but it has never seemed to work. No one was interested in me.'

That surprised her; hurt her also, that he had not turned to her when in trouble. Her quick wits immediately recognized the problem. She spoke quickly and impulsively without taking time to think.

'Why didn't you send a message to me; you silly boy?' she said and then she stopped. There was an implication behind her words and it was not one that she should, under normal professional rules, have given voice to.

However, the words had been spoken and Enda nodded his head drearily.

'I was going to; for the third position that I applied for; when Seán Barrett and his son, at Tirawley, were both killed in a raid – I told Brehon MacClancy that I would not trouble him to write a reference for me – that I would ask you – I'd begun to suspect that he was not saying anything very good about me . . .'

'And what did he say?' Enda had, of course, been correct in informing the Brehon that he was not going to ask for what her housekeeper, Brigid, called a '*spake*' but nevertheless, Mara felt that he had been imprudent. A word with the King, a social visit to the Brehon at the Burren, an opening of his heart in confidence to a former *Ollamh* would have been the way she would have tackled the matter. But, of course, that was probably the woman's way; Enda, as a young man, was more inclined to go headlong into the fray.

'He was furious,' said Enda. 'He abused me, told me that I was a ne'er-do-good, that I would never be fit for anything other than to run errands, that he would certainly hesitate to recommend me for anything. He told me that he would tell the *taoiseach* at Tirawley that I was certainly not fitted for the post. He advised me to study more, to try to learn a little of the law, to study the Triads, and then he walked off.'

'The Triads!' Mara was bewildered. Enda had been such a clever scholar, with a wonderful memory. He had learned most of the Triads off by heart before his ninth birthday. These pithy, three-line summaries of the law were easily memorized by the young at a time when their memories were at a height, and were normally retained for the rest of their life.

Enda smiled slightly at her expression and then shrugged his shoulders. 'I do nothing here – just listen to Brehon MacClancy. He never even tells me anything about the cases that are coming up on judgement day, never shows me his notes or discusses his verdicts. The only way that I am involved is when he sends me to summon people to court – and he could use one of the stable boys for that,' he finished. There was a note of depression and finality in his voice which worried Mara more than if he had shown anger and resentment. She faced him resolutely.

'Listen, Enda,' she said firmly, 'you mustn't sit down under this. You have brains and you have ability. It's now nine years since you left my law school; you are a qualified *Ollamh* – you took and passed that examination two years after you left me. You should and could pass your examination to be a Brehon as soon as possible. Come back to me and you can study for it. I haven't too much to do at the moment – Fachtnan does so much of the teaching of the younger children – and you know, Enda, I would love to have an advanced scholar again. I still miss Shane – we sharpened our wits on each other, but, of course, he is back in the north of Ireland now and will take over from his father next year.' She saw him wince at that – Shane had been a youngster of thirteen when Enda had left her law school with very high marks in his qualifying examination to be a lawyer. Now Shane would have a position among the venerated Brehons of Ireland, while Enda would still be an errand boy.

'Do come to me, Enda; give this up! It can be easily explained. You want to put your whole attention into this final qualification. King Turlough will soothe matters over so that no offence can be taken.'

However, he shook his head. His face flushed a dull red and for a moment there was a glow in his eyes. 'I need to stay here for the moment, Brehon,' he said hesitantly. He looked at her in an embarrassed way.

'I know,' she said, jokingly, but inwardly she was conscious of a slight feeling of annoyance. 'You're in love. It's that pretty girl Shona MacMahon, isn't it?'

He nodded. 'I have been studying,' he said in a burst of confidence. 'Not the Triads, but the hard stuff. I sneak his books away when he is dozing after his dinner. I'm certain that I could sit the examination in front of any Brehon in Ireland, except Brehon MacClancy himself, and that I would pass. And if . . .' He stopped, eyeing her rather uncertainly, and then said with an air of indifference, 'The physician, Donogh O'Hickey, keeps warning him that the sound from his heart is very bad. Its beat is irregular. He told Brehon MacClancy yesterday that if he allowed himself to get into any more passions then he could throw a fit and drop down dead at any moment.'

'I see,' said Mara. She was conscious of a slight feeling of distaste. Enda, as she had suspected, was waiting for dead men's shoes. She didn't approve, but she could see the sense of it. If he did inherit the position of Brehon, then Maccon MacMahon, with the King's approval, would probably be very happy to have his daughter betrothed to a young man with whom she was, fairly obviously, in love. Enda, from the time that he was fifteen years old, had always been prone to fall madly in love with various girls. It was probably time that he was married and this would be a suitable match. She would not meddle, she decided virtuously, and then smiled to herself. She would, of course; it was after all a question of one of her boys and she had known Enda since he was eight years old. She could never

divest herself of maternal feelings towards those who had spent
their childhood in her care. Perhaps a word in the King's ear
would be a good idea, she thought. He should be keeping an
eye on his household.

'Well, don't forget that the offer stands,' she said lightly. 'We
would love to see you again at Cahermacnaghten. Brigid would
go mad with joy. She likes nothing better than to have one
of her boys turn up. Well, we'd better go back and join the
others.' She led the way out of the stable without waiting for
his reply and noted that the pretty girl, Shona, was lingering
under the oak tree, from which, yesterday, the effigy of Brehon
MacClancy had dangled with knives glinting from various
parts of his straw-stuffed body. The girl was looking well this
morning, she thought, and wondered whether she had just
imagined the white face yesterday when Brehon MacClancy
had made his pronouncement. Still it was unlikely that a girl
of that age, just out of fosterage, had a secret of any particular
importance.

She did not walk with Enda, but parted from him with a
reassuring nod and a pat on his arm. Then she went across
the bailey to join the physician, Donogh O'Hickey, who,
standing below the steps up to the castle's main entrance, was
solemnly and patiently feeling the muscles in the arms of four
young people. She had almost said four young boys – there
was no doubt that the two MacMahon twins looked like boys.
Not even for the sacred ceremony of Christmas Day Mass had
Cael deigned to put on the longer *léine* of a girl, and with her
cropped hair and her short cloak, as well as the manly hose,
she looked just like a boy.

'This one has the best muscles,' said Donogh, pointing
to Art.

'I thought he would,' said Cormac enthusiastically, while the
twins scowled. Her son was, thought Mara, quite disappointed
that his muscles had not been deemed to be the best, but his
loyalty to his foster-brother, Art, reigned supreme in Cormac's
life. 'Art is always working on the farm belonging to his mother
– he's always carrying loads of hay and dragging hurdles around
for sheep enclosures.'

'Belonging to his father you mean,' snapped Cian. The boy

was annoyed and still kept his arm in the position where his muscles showed.

'No,' said Cormac with surprise. 'It's Art's mother that owns the farm; his father owns the fishing boat. Art does the rowing in that. No wonder his muscles are so good,' he said seriously to the physician and then with a quick glance at Mara, he said mischievously, 'I'm forced to spend my nights and days studying, so that is what makes my muscles weak.'

Mara ignored this. Art, she thought, did just as much study as Cormac, but he was an industrious child. Cormac was happy to wander around with his wolfhound puppy or chat to the farm workers in the evening, while his foster-brother went over to help his parents on the nearby farm.

'Your pupil, Nuala, sends her greetings,' she said to Donogh. Nuala, the physician at the Burren, was almost a daughter to her and she knew that the girl had been very grateful for the teaching that she had received from the elderly physician. There had been a time when she thought the thankfulness would overspill into a match between Nuala and the old man's son, but in the end Nuala had turned to Fachtnan, the playmate of her early life and the object of her youthful adoration. It had been and was still a happy marriage, but Nuala, she knew, felt that she owed the O'Hickeys, both father and son, a great debt of gratitude for all that she had learned from the family. She watched the affection come to his eyes and hoped as hard as she could that Brehon MacClancy's malice was not going to implicate this kind man. And yet, she remembered that he had worn a strained look at that unpleasant moment yesterday.

'Tell me how Nuala is getting on,' he said as he walked beside her up the castle steps.

'Very well,' she said promptly, 'combining motherhood with work; still a great student; always trying to find out something more. The people of the Burren think highly of her. They have great trust in her and that is what everyone needs in a physician.' And in a Brehon, she thought. Without trust, doubt and dissension step in and matters are settled with a knife or sword which could have been solved at the place of judgement.

'I always hoped for a match between my wanderer of a son and Nuala,' said the physician with a sigh as he pushed open the heavy front door, glancing upwards, momentarily, as everyone did, at the murder hole above. The castle at Bunratty had never been stormed, but the murder hole remained, ready for the defenders to pour boiling oil down onto the attackers.

'One can never plan these things,' said Mara. Privately she thought that the solid, reliable presence of Fachtnan and his lack of knowledge of medicine was probably a very good thing for Nuala. She was too serious, too inclined to be obsessive about her work. Married to another physician, the girl would never relax, she thought, as she said aloud, 'Come up to the solar with me and I'll give you all the news. I was going to ask you if you had any ideas about getting scholars for Nuala's school. She has a great desire to set up a school for young physicians, just as I have a school for young lawyers.'

'I thought that she already had a pupil,' said Donogh O'Hickey, with a quick sidelong glance at Mara.

'That's right,' said Mara readily. 'But he is almost ready to qualify and she would like a group of young people to instruct. She is a very good teacher,' she went on earnestly. 'I remember her explaining to my young scholars how deaths such as Roman Claudius and King Henry I of England, who both died after eating a hearty meal supposedly poisoned by an enemy, might just have been caused by the food itself. Claudius who was supposed to have been poisoned by his wife had just eaten a dish of mushrooms,' said Mara with a reminiscent smile. 'Nuala told the boys how a poisonous fungus that looks just like a mushroom could have accidentally got into the dish, and the first of the many Henrys might well have been poisoned by the dangerous innards of the lampreys, so that rather than having a surfeit of them, or being poisoned by his nephew Stephen, as the story goes, he might just have been a victim to a careless cook. She is a wonderful teacher – the boys were testing poisonous fungi on trapped bluebottle flies for weeks after. She makes everything very interesting to them. I always get her to talk to them about the medical aspects of Brehon law.'

'So she is still keen on the idea of a school.' Donogh O'Hickey gave an indulgent smile.

'That's right,' said Mara immediately. 'And she has two little girls who will be trained up in the ways of medicine.'

'Girls,' said Donogh O'Hickey, making a slight face. 'What a pity that she did not have a boy.'

Mara bit back a sharp report. It was amazing, she thought, that someone like Donogh O'Hickey, who knew that Nuala was probably the cleverest, the hardest-working and the highest-achieving of any of his scholars, would still think like that. She thought thankfully of her father, who had made the best of having no son and had trained his daughter to be a lawyer.

'Tell me, how are things going here?' she queried politely. 'Brehon MacClancy does not seem in too good a mood. Is there something wrong?'

She had not expected him to tell her anything very much out here where people were passing continually and she was not surprised when he shrugged his shoulders and then began to talk hurriedly about the meal which was to be held to celebrate her arrival. She wondered what was going wrong in this castle that both he and the Brehon appeared to be tense and on edge. I must ask Turlough about it, she decided. But in the meantime she would try and get some more out of the physician so she invited him to join her in the solar for a drink. They could talk privately there, she thought.

'I must just make sure that everything is in order for the boys,' she said by way of excuse. He would have expected her to go straight to the great hall, but a private conversation there would be impossible.

By the time they went up the stairs, the majority of the castle guests were going for a midday meal in the great hall. As she passed the great hall, Mara could see Rosta in the small kitchen beside the hall rushing to and fro, firing orders at his helpers. This was a very busy time for the King's cook, but the look on his face told her that he was enjoying himself immensely. He was a man who loved his art and loved to display what he was capable of. Although the Christmas night banquet would take place in six hours' time, the meal being carried in looked every bit as elaborate as the feast last night.

'There's something in the solar for you, Brehon, if you

would prefer it,' he called out, seeing her pass his small kitchen. From the doorway of the great hall a malevolent face peeped around and then withdrew. Brehon MacClancy was used to being the only one bearing that title and he resented Mara's use of it. She had, from the start, however, resolutely set her face against being known as 'queen' – her status, she reckoned, was that of Brehon, and only in private life was she the wife of a king. Brehon MacClancy would just have to get used to it – in just the same way as if Brehon MacEgan, or any other Brehon in Ireland, had visited the castle.

The solar was part of the King's private suite of rooms at the top of the castle and a staircase in the north-east tower led up to them. There was an elaborate bedchamber with a magnificently curtained bed, a fireplace, a clothes rail as well as a beautifully carved hanging press, some chairs and a door that led to the garderobe where there was a board covered with a green cloth and the opening to the shaft leading to the moat was plugged with a cushion in order to prevent any smells arising. Above this room were another couple of bedrooms, used for the King's children when they were young, but now occupied by the law-school scholars.

Beside the bedchamber was the King's solar – a smaller version of the great hall, furnished with a table, already spread with some cold meats, some baked apples, baskets of bread rolls, and a flagon of wine. A fire was burning brightly in the six-foot-long fireplace. There was no one there and the candles were not yet lit, though some light came through the 'squint' looking down into the great hall where Turlough and his friends were talking loudly and enthusiastically about a hunt on the following day. St Stephen's Day was traditionally hunting time and it looked as though, with the frost, it would be an ideal day for the marshy land around Bunratty Castle. Mara smiled to hear her husband's voice boasting about a bird that he shot from an impossible angle – he sounded rather like nine-year-old Cormac, she thought as she peered down, unnoticed by the crowd. She withdrew and inserted a taper into the blazing fire on the hearth and went around the room, carefully lighting all the candles within arm's reach before saying quietly:

'What's the matter with Brehon MacClancy, Donogh?'

The physician shrugged. 'Nothing that he can't cure by abstaining from over-eating and over-drinking.' He also spoke very quietly, almost in her ear, although the heavy oaken door was firmly shut and the noise from the hall below would drown any voices.

'I don't mean his health – that is not my affair. He seems to be upsetting everyone, especially some of the young people. He seems to love upsetting them and giving malicious inform- ation . . .' She hesitated there. Perhaps she had no right to enquire into Enda's affairs – after all he was a man of twenty- six years and had left her law school nine years ago.

The physician was looking at her strangely. He moved away from the hearth and over to the table. He sat down, poured out some wine into two goblets, and nibbled at a bread roll before saying thoughtfully: 'He told you about Shona, then; he swore not to mention it to anyone, but I suppose he thought that he could trust your discretion.'

'I'm more concerned about Enda,' she countered. Shona, daughter of Maccon MacMahon, one of Turlough's friends, was none of her business and she decided that it was prefer- able to talk about Enda than to trick the physician into thinking that she knew something to Shona's disadvantage. It did explain the girl's white face yesterday, though.

'Enda was one of the brightest scholars that I ever had,' she continued, looking at the physician earnestly. 'If you can imagine Nuala, or your son, Donogh Óg, hanging around, running errands for a physician, but having no opportunity to practise all that they have learned, well then, you can imagine what I feel about Enda. But don't mention to anyone that I spoke of this; I don't want to make a bad situation worse,' she added quickly.

Donogh O'Hickey frowned heavily, drank some wine and munched some more of the bread.

'I know what you mean; I've been worried about him. There have been times when he looked at the end of his tether. Not a patient nature, I would imagine.'

'No.' Mara smiled as she thought of Enda's adolescence. He had been one of the most troublesome, but at the same time one of the most rewarding, pupils that she had ever had.

'I'd like to help him, but don't want to interfere,' she said after a minute.

'Put out of your head any notion of trying to talk to Brehon MacClancy,' he advised. His voice sounded alarmed. 'There is only one thing that you can do to help matters.' He eyed her carefully before continuing, 'You can use your influence with the King to get the man removed from office. He is unfit; some of his judgements have been harsh; in a few cases people have appealed the verdict over his head and King Turlough, God bless him, has softened the fine.'

'How did that go?' Mara was a little appalled. Turlough had never mentioned these occasions to her. 'How did Brehon MacClancy take the overturning of his verdicts?'

'He pretended to accept it, but he had a face on him that looked as though he could commit murder. Brehon MacClancy is no man to cross.'

Mara thought about this but decided that she did not wish to discuss the matter any further with Donogh. She was surprised and slightly hurt that Turlough had not mentioned the disputed verdicts with her, but, knowing him, it was, she supposed, possible that it all gone right out of his head and would be classified, if he retained any memory of it, as a spot of bother that had been dealt with and should now be forgotten. She wondered, in a slightly suspicious way, why the physician wanted her to tackle the question of Brehon MacClancy. Did he feel at all threatened by the Brehon?

'What an odd little girl that child is, the twin belonging to Maccon MacMahon,' she said impulsively. 'Why does she think that she has to dress as a boy and pretend to be a boy?'

'You didn't do the same when you were her age?'

'Why no, I didn't,' said Mara, surprised at the question. 'No, I think I was quite happy to be a girl. I felt unique, perhaps, but I felt that being a girl and being a foremost scholar at the law school made me quite interesting. I suppose that I was an impossible child at Cael's age – always wanting to be better at the law than my father's other scholars; but I didn't want to pretend to be a boy.'

'Perhaps, though,' said the physician gently, 'you had a father who cared and loved you and was proud of you. I wonder could the same be said for Maccon MacMahon.' He got to his feet with the haste of one who feels that he has said too much.

'Let me leave you to yourself now, Brehon.' He cast a look down through the hatch at the riotous crowd below. 'At least nothing is spoiling the enjoyment of my lord the King on this special anniversary for him. Let's hope that the night passes peacefully and that you solve the problem of your young friend before your visit has finished,' he said as he went out of the door.

Mara sat for a while, sipping her wine and nibbling her roll. Tomorrow, she thought, I will speak with Turlough and then perhaps I will tackle Brehon MacClancy myself. That man should not be allowed to spoil the life of a young man setting out on his career. Had he, she wondered, some sort of hold over Enda, some piece of youthful indiscretion which might make the young man reluctant to assert his rights – something that had been said, or done which would deeply offend King Turlough?

Brehon MacClancy's words came back into her mind: '*I know that there is one person here tonight who is secretly cheating him and when Judgement Day comes in seven days' time then the name of that person will be revealed and the King will know the truth.*' What was meant by that, she wondered? Of course, it might mean nothing – just a hook to take the poet, Seán MacBrody, out of the picture and put the Brehon as the centre of attention. He had gone on to make more vague threats about knowing scandals and evil-doing; that might have caused even more uneasiness.

All in all, it was not a comfortable atmosphere and Mara hoped that Brehon MacClancy might retire early to his bedchamber and leave the King to enjoy his celebration without that old death's head at the feast.

Four

Duties of the King
(Ancient Poem of the Gaels)

If thou be a king thou shouldst know the prerogative of a ruler, refection according to rank, contentions of hostings, sticks, quarrels in an alehouse, contracts made in drunkenness; valuations of lands, measurement by poles; augmentations of a penalty, larceny of tree-fruit; the great substance of land-law, marking out fresh boundaries, planting of stakes, the law as to points of stakes, partition among coheirs, summoning of neighbours, stone pillars of contest, fighters who fasten title.

From a king must come the extent of protection; the right of the fine, up to the sixth man, in movables and land. Valid is every neighbour-law that is contracted by pledges and secured by fines consisting of séts. Greater or smaller is the value of penalties. The penalty for breaching a boundary fence: from a bull-calf to a heifer-calf, from that to a yearling beast, up to five séts it extends.

Let fines be forthcoming on the fifth day after the offences, according to the law of neighbours. What single ox shares liability with the drove? What overleaping by a single piglet shares liability with the herds? What are the drivings carried out negligently for which final responsibility is not enforced? What are the concealed drivings forward? On which man grazing-expense does not fall? What are the unauthorized stalkings which deserve immunity? What are the larcenies from houses which do not entail a penalty?

Mara surprised herself by really enjoying the night's festivities. Everything was very informal. Villagers and clansmen mingled freely with everyone, people passed up and down the stairs between the main guard hall and the great hall, and Turlough, suddenly tired of the praise heaped on him, announced that he wanted no more speeches or poems about him – let everyone eat and drink and sing and dance and laugh was his command and that was the way that evening went. Instead of two elaborate banquets, the food and drink were arranged on the table on the raised platform of the great hall or on tables pushed to the sides of the main guard hall and the guests sampled from both floors.

'Have some of the lampreys,' said an elderly woman to Mara. 'They do them well here; put vinegar on them. And spice, too – cinnamon, I've heard tell.'

'I think I'll just stick to the salmon,' said Mara apologetically, heaping some applemoy sauce on to her platter. She loathed the taste of lampreys, eel-like fish, and her housekeeper, Brigid, had a great prejudice against them, saying that she would never eat them unless she prepared them herself as there was poison in the sac and they had to be very carefully cleaned out. Still, lots of people were eating them here and they seemed to be very popular. Bunratty was a great place for fish as two rivers, the immense River Shannon and the tiny River Raite, met here before joining the ocean a little further west.

'You're the King's wife, aren't you?' said the old lady in a friendly way. 'I haven't seen you before; I don't live around here, but I'm the mother of the King's carpenter. He's a lovely man, your husband, God bless him.'

'And a very handsome man,' said Mara laughing as Turlough joined them, a flagon of ale in his hand.

'Say *God bless him*, don't you know that it brings bad luck from the fairies if you praise someone and don't call down God's blessing on them,' scolded the old woman, while her son, who appeared at her elbow, blushed for his mother.

'God bless him,' repeated Mara obediently, though she wondered where the fairies stood in the hierarchy around God. She looked around for Enda to share the joke with, but there was no sign of him. Brehon MacClancy was sitting by himself in one of the window recesses, moodily staring into his goblet, but his assistant was nowhere to be seen. He's probably dancing with Shona down in the main guard hall, thought Mara, feeling pleased that Enda was steering clear of the bad-tempered old Brehon. She left Turlough exchanging witticisms with the old lady, who had come all the way from Cratloe to join in the celebrations, and moved across the room to where a well-built lad was standing with dish of chicken and pork in one hand and huge slab of white bread in the other. He had been looking across at her from time to time as though hoping to catch her eye and now she recognized him as the boy who had taken her horse when she arrived and she went across and greeted him.

'What happened to that silly figure of Brehon MacClancy?' she asked.

'I took it down as soon as they all went in, but I'm afraid that the Brehon saw it – the old Brehon, I mean,' he said hastily and Mara gave him a nice smile for his courtesy and wondered whether she would still relish compliments when she was seventy years old – probably, she decided. So Brehon MacClancy had seen the work of the two little rascals; well, it couldn't be helped. She had done her best.

'They're holy terrors,' said the stable boy in a lowered tone watching Cael doing a sword dance with her father's sword, which was almost as big as she was. 'You never know where they are or what they're up to. They slip in and out like a pair of eels. You wouldn't believe it, Brehon, but that little fellow,' he pointed to Cael, 'brought that sword over when he heard that it was me that took down that thing and he threatened to stick it in me if I didn't give him back his knives that minute. Really violent, he was.'

'Send for me if you have any trouble with any of them, including my own fellow,' said Mara with a nod towards Cormac, who was walking on his hands while swaying to the music of the drum.

'Ah, he's a very nice little *buachail*,' said the boy hastily. 'He's been in and out of the stable petting the wolfhounds. He was telling me about his own puppy, Smoke, and how obedient and well trained he is. He misses him terrible, so he says.'

Cormac's wolfhound puppy was, thought Mara, reasonably well trained if you held a piece of meat in your hand and gave him an order. Otherwise he was the wildest, most disobedient, badly behaved dog that Mara had ever possessed. She was struck, though, by the fact that Cormac had told the stable boy about how lonely he was for his half-grown puppy and had not told her, nor his father.

Just as she was turning that over in her mind, the church bells struck the hour of midnight. The captain of the guard banged on a shield hanging from the wall and held out his goblet. Everyone quickly filled up, got to their feet if they had been sitting, held out theirs and then the toasts to Turlough began, wishing him a long life and a happy one; a healthy heart and a wet mouth; all the wealth of the sea and the land to come to him and his; that the sun would shine on him; that the road would rise up before him and that he would die surrounded by those that loved him.

And then the musicians lined up at the front of the great hall. The *bódhrain* drums started to thud, the fiddles were plucked and the *rince fada*, the long dance, began with the line of dancers stretching to the very back of the hall. Three times they went around, sunwise, and then down the great hall, out of the door, down the spiral staircase where only the young and the agile managed to keep the dancing steps going and then all passed into the main guard hall and the musicians went up to the gallery. For a few minutes it looked as though none could move; the main guard hall was just too crowded. On this Christmas night of 1519 there was a huge number of relations, friends, clan leaders; all had gathered at the court of Bunratty to celebrate their King's twenty years of rule over the three kingdoms of Thomond, Corcomroe and Burren. But after one dance the King, his family, his close friends, his personal guests and his immediate household, his harpist, his physician and his poet returned to the great hall and continued to dance and to talk there with room to move. The harpist relaxed with a goblet in one hand and a pastry in the other. Now a set of pipes provided the music for the young and the agile in the great hall.

But Brehon MacClancy had not joined the merry crowd, Mara noticed when she returned. He was still sitting by himself at the table recess. When she re-entered the room she saw him hold out the flagon to the cook in a wordless gesture and Rosta filled it from a larger flagon of mead which he was bringing in from the buttery to place on the table at the top of the room. The man would soon be drunk, probably was already drunk, thought Mara and then shrugged her shoulders. It was none of her business and at least he was quiet and disturbed no one. She went to join in the dance, whirling around, hand in hand with Turlough, marking the time, while feet stamped and pipes blew their shrill notes.

When they finished she saw that Conor, Turlough's eldest son and, at present, his heir, was sitting by himself in the window recess opposite to the one where the Brehon had taken up his position. He did not seem to be looking at the dancers, at his wife, his son or not even his father, but stared steadily across the hall at MacClancy.

'How are you, Conor?' Mara went and sat beside him at the table. 'Raour is looking well, isn't he?' She had deliberately not asked about his own health – he must be sick of the subject. He was now approaching the age of forty, she reckoned, a man who had lived his life in the shadow of his popular, successful and warlike father, not strong enough for warfare, not able enough for administration. A disappointed man, she guessed and knew that one part of his troubles was probably his conviction that his younger brother, Murrough, would have by now been the choice of the clan if he were still living in Thomond.

'Come and dance with me,' she coaxed. 'That jig was too energetic for me but this is a nice, slow reel.'

He was reluctant, but too well mannered to refuse her. Ellice, his wife, was whirling around in the arms of Brian MacCraith, her dark eyes excited and her sallow skin warmed to a deep rose colour by the excitement, the exercise and the heat of the great hall. Enda and Shona, Maccon MacMahon's daughter, had been sitting in the window recess behind the table but now rose and came to join the dance. This was a popular reel. Everyone, except Brehon MacClancy, was now dancing. The long table had been cleared of all remains of food and the door closed behind the last of Rosta's assistants.

Another half-hour and then I can go to bed, thought Mara, conscious of slightly aching feet and a head that was spinning from the rotation of the reel. She sat down and watched the rapid movements of those dancing the jig. She had arranged with Rosta to serve soup and new bread to the guests an hour after midnight. After that, she hoped, most of Turlough's guests would seek their bed chambers and the royal couple could do the same.

Five

Ɑn Seɑnchɑs Ɱór
(The Great Ancient Tradition)

There are two fines that have to be paid by anyone who commits a murder:

A fixed fine of forty-two séts, or twenty-one ounces of silver, or twenty-one milch cows

A fine based on the victim's honour price (lóg n-enech — the price of his face).

In the case of duinethaide, *a secret and unacknowledged killing, then the first fine is doubled and becomes eighty-four séts.*

It was young Cormac who discovered the dead man. While most of the King's guests had given up the dancing and wandered around the hall, drinking and eating and greeting friends, the younger ones had continued to skip energetically up and down. Cael, her brother Cian, Cormac and Art had given a marvellous display, forming a complicated interlocked foursome, clicking the iron tips of their boots on the white and red marble tiles. When this had finished, Cormac had gone into the recess to cool his hot cheeks against the cold glass of the tall window there.

'The Brehon is dead! He's definitely dead. Look at his eyes!' he screamed. His shout was loud enough to make the drums falter, enough to stop the footsteps of the dancers, and enough to still the pipers at the top end of the great hall. Instantly Mara gathered up the skirts of her splendid court dress and dodged through the crowd of shocked faces. In a moment she was beside her son.

The Brehon lay slumped in the dim light of the window recess at the back of the great hall at Bunratty Castle. His long iron-grey hair and one side of his huge pair of moustaches were soaked in sticky, honey-coloured mead and a goblet lay over-turned on the small wooden table that stood in the window recess. It was a secluded corner – away from the energetic dancers and away from the focus of the harp playing the accompaniment to the poets and ballad singers and of the pipers who played the dance music that followed it. Brehon MacClancy had been sitting there for most of the evening, not joining in the merriment, not listening to the praise of his King, but drinking steadily and undisturbed by all. That is, thought Mara, by all except one person. Sometime in the last half-hour, someone had come over and stuck a dagger under his shoulder blade.

Mara stayed there for a moment, gazing down at the face of the man who had predicted his own death twenty-four hours previously. And yes, Cormac was right; Brehon MacClancy was dead. And not dead from failure of an elderly heart, but murdered. Even in the dim light of the window recess something gleamed. Mara moved behind the chair and bent over the body. A long, slender knife protruded from one shoulder blade.

She was joined by the King's physician, Donogh O'Hickey, but she hardly needed to glance at him to confirm the evidence of those dull eyes, normally alight with sharp wits and malice, but now fixed and staring. She reached out and touched the hand which lay outstretched on the table. It was still warm and pliable. She looked across at Donogh O'Hickey and saw him copy her action, testing the temperature and bending the fingers gently.

'Not long dead; less than an hour. I saw him ask for a drink when we came back. About half an hour ago, that's right isn't it? And the hand bears that out, I would think, is that right?' she queried and almost before he nodded, Mara turned to deal with the crowd that was pressing forward.

'Stand back everyone.' She spoke quietly, but her clear voice was filled with authority and the crowd took a step backwards. She had, of course, no formal authority here in the Kingdom of Thomond, but she had been Brehon of the Kingdom of the Burren since she was twenty-one years old and twenty-five years of investigating, judging and punishing crimes had given her the confidence to deal with every eventuality.

'Go and stand by the door, Enda,' she said in a low voice
to the young man who had appeared by her side. It was only
when he had quickly done her bidding that it occurred to her
that Enda was the person who should be giving the orders,
since he had acted as an assistant to the Brehon for nine years.
However, he had no independent experience of conducting
an enquiry and this was going to be a very difficult and sensitive
affair. In any case, it was too late to take back the command
so she waited quietly by the body, watching her five remaining
scholars, led by her fourteen-year-old grandson Domhnall,
leaving the floor of the great hall and coming to join herself
and Cormac. Unlike most of the guests they did not exclaim
or question and this pleased her. It showed, she thought, their
maturity. They just stood silently, looking down on the body
and waiting for her instructions. Swiftly she made up her mind.
She would apologize to Enda later on, but now she had to
control this situation and make sure that the guilty person did
not escape. She gave a swift glance around the hall. Her husband,
King Turlough Donn, was approaching, his eyes wide with
disbelief and his face aghast. Tomás MacClancy had been
Brehon for the whole of Turlough's reign and it was a terrible
shock to see him slumped, dead, across the table on this night
of celebration.

'Someone stuck a knife in him,' he said. 'Not far in, is it?'
He reached across as though to pull it out, but she seized his
hand quickly. She said nothing but she hoped that he would
understand that the evidence could not be tampered with. It
was odd, though, she thought, looking more carefully at the
knife. He was right. The knife was not far into the Brehon.
A large section of the blade was still visible. It looked as though
someone with very little strength had driven the knife into
the man's back. Not much blood, either, though perhaps the
dark-coloured mantle masked it. She bent down and touched
it. Some blood, but definitely not soaked in it. Of course, she
thought, Brehon MacClancy was very elderly. He must now be
about seventy years old. Perhaps he died instantly of the shock
as the knife pierced him. It was odd, though. As she peered at
the knife she reckoned that only half an inch of blade had
penetrated the skin and flesh.

'Come,' she said to Turlough. 'Tell them that they must
remain until I can question them. No one must leave this room
until I give permission.'

With him at her side she had double status – Brehon and
wife of the King. She faced the crowd who had instinctively
shrunk back against the wall. Her mind was working fast. It
would, she thought, have been just under an hour since
midnight. The bells had rung. Then came the toasts, following
these the main crowd of revellers had retired downstairs to the
main guard hall to drink and dance the rest of the night away
– she could hear the thump of music still which showed that
the revels continued down there. Traditionally the merriment
in the main guard hall continued as long as they pleased. Later
on most of them would sleep either there in front of its large
fireplace or in the captain's quarters, or go back to their own
small houses scattered around the enclosure which was fortified
by a ten-foot-high wall and had a moat filled with sea water
encircling it. The King's guests had gone down with them
after the toasts – all of them except Brehon MacClancy – but
they had returned quite soon.

But Brehon MacClancy was not dead at that stage. Mara
clearly remembered that he had asked for a drink. The cook
Rosta had seen that everyone had what they needed and then
he, too, had retired to the kitchen with his assistants, closing
the door of the great hall firmly behind him. The elderly
Brehon was still alive then. Mara remembered looking down
at him, wondering whether he would demand another drink,
before Rosta went out.

Those who were left in the great hall were all of the King's
particular guests – and, thought Mara, these guests were those
who had heard the words of Tomás MacClancy yesterday
evening when he had promised to expose the wrongdoing of
one of them.

'Did someone see who pushed the dagger into the Brehon's
back? Any of you noticed that happening?' roared Turlough
and for a moment she felt irritated. What a silly question! If
someone did see that about an hour ago and kept quiet about
it then they would be unlikely to come out with an account
just now in front of everyone. She gave a slight sigh as she

thought of all the careful questioning that she would have used to seek the truth, slowly and carefully, in the way that a good cook would peel the translucent layers from an onion in order to expose the succulent centre. Just as she was thinking about him, there was knock on the door. It was pushed open and Rosta arrived on the scene holding a large ladle in his hand and followed by two of his assistants carrying an enormous iron two-handled urn which, according to her instructions, would be full of soup. This was to signal the end of the eating and drinking and merriment for the night – in the great hall, though some might go down and join the revellers in the main guard hall. Rosta did not appear to notice the slumped figure of the Brehon and the appalled faces of the guests. Mara made a swift decision. Her scholars were tired and were eyeing the soup with appreciation, but now while memories still were active she had to take notes.

'Get my satchel from our bedroom,' she said in Cormac's ear and saw a flash of almost incredulous pleasure flash from his large green eyes. He wasn't, she thought, used to being chosen from the ranks of the law scholars and she had picked on him because he was fast, observant and often in and out of their bedroom, playing wrestling games with Turlough on the huge four-poster bed.

'Go ahead and pour the soup, Rosta,' she said aloud. 'And then you and your assistants can depart. The King has something to say to his guests, here. Could you and your assistants go down to the main guard after you have finished.'

Rosta looked puzzled, but did her bidding in silence, using his ladle to fill the small wooden bowls stacked on the table. She moved slightly so that she would conceal the dead body for the moment and Domhnall moved also, the others following him. They stretched like a guard across the window recess and waited in grim silence until the door had closed behind the cook and his assistants. Then Mara went over to Turlough.

'My lord,' she said formally, 'I think it would be best if you announced this sad death to the rest of your guests. They will not wish to continue with the merriment in the face of the terrible event. Tell them that they can then disperse to their sleeping places, unless anyone has information to give to me.'

Hastily and before Turlough could assure her that no one would be too upset at the death of the Brehon and that it was a shame to cut short the night's fun, she moved away and went back to her scholars.

By the time that Cormac had come back she had arranged the boys in pairs: Art with Slevin; Finbar, who was not too sensible on occasion, with the reliable Domhnall; and Cormac himself with Enda. She hoped that all would think that this was because Cormac was the youngest and so was placed with the assistant Brehon, but at the back of her mind she had a tiny doubt over whether Enda might not be involved in this killing and Cormac, she knew, would speak out loudly and clearly if there were any attempt to tamper with any of the evidence. Her heart hurt to think this of Enda, but she had to use her logical brain at this stage, not her heart. The young man had much to gain from this opportune death.

Aloud she said: 'Brehon MacClancy was killed by a knife plunged into his back at some time during the last half-hour. Did anyone come in or go out of this room at that time?' She waited for a moment, but heads were shaken. 'Or see anyone go in or out?'

Heads were shaken again, but Cael said in a high, clear voice. 'I saw something.'

All eyes turned to the urchin-like figure and her elder sister Shona took a step towards the child.

'Yes,' said Mara. She could have wished that this had been said to her in private but everyone was looking with intense speculation at Cael and it was probably best to hear what she had to say in public.

'Just a bat, one of those big bats,' said Cael hastily and her father gave a hearty laugh. Cael smirked and looked at her brother for approval. A few people smiled, but there was an air of tense preoccupation on most faces.

'I see,' said Mara coldly. By now each of her scholars had a pen and a sheet of vellum and Domhnall was busy mixing ink from the powder they carried in a small leather bag, and some water from a flagon. Rapidly she told them the questions to ask – this would be a quick, simple investigation into everyone's memory of the time since their return to the great hall just after midnight.

'It's especially important to check whether anyone went towards the window recess or whether they saw anyone linger in that area,' she said emphatically. 'And remember to ask everyone whether they observed Brehon MacClancy, and if so what they noticed about him.'

She arranged for them to use the four remaining window recesses, all of which were furnished with small tables and benches, as places in which to ask their questions. Slevin and Art would interrogate the three professional men, Aengus MacCraith, the poet, Brian MacBrody the harpist and the physician, Donogh O'Hickey, she decided. To Enda and Cormac she assigned Conor, his wife Ellice and his son, Raour. To the tactful Domhnall and the well-mannered Finbar would fall the task of taking evidence from the notoriously touchy Fionn O'Brien and his heiress wife.

'I'll do the MacMahon family myself,' she declared just as Turlough came back into the room. He cast a hurried glance at the still body in the corner and said in a hushed whisper: 'Should I send someone to wake up the priest?'

'Yes, of course.' Mara was embarrassed that she had not thought of that. Of course it should have been her first thought. There was something she remembered about a man's soul not leaving his body until half an hour after death. The priest should have been sent for instantly. It was surprising that no one had thought of it. It seemed to show that there was not much interest in Brehon MacClancy's place in the next world from the crowd who had feasted so merrily in his company this past night.

'I'll have a word with Rosta – get him to send one of his lads down to the priest's house in the village – you won't need any of them, will you? None of them have been in the room for an hour or so.' Turlough seemed glad to get out of the room and away from the solemn faces and didn't wait for an answer before rushing away. Mara crossed over to Donogh O'Hickey, who had just given his evidence to Domhnall, and Finbar and said in his ear:

'When the priest has finished giving the last rites then I'd like to talk with you about the cause of death.'

He nodded. There was a thoughtful look in his eye as he glanced across at the dead body slumped across the table but he did not go near it, nor, she thought, had he shown much interest when the body had been discovered. For a moment she wished that she were back in the Burren and conducting this investigation there where her word was the law and where her first thought was always to send for Nuala and watch the girl conduct a detailed and thorough investigation into the cause of death. Still there was no use in wishing for what was not possible at the moment, she thought, as she sent Cormac with a polite request to Maccon MacMahon.

Maccon MacMahon had little to say. He had wandered down the room at one stage, he thought – just to look at the finely carved wall bench near the door leading to the stairs. He thought he had looked across at Brehon MacClancy on the opposite side of the hall, but couldn't give Mara any information on what the man was doing, or whether he was sitting upright, or sprawled across the table at the time. He had no idea how long it was since he had gone to look at the bench, but thought it might have been quite soon after they had returned from the hall below. Mara dismissed him to his soup after a few minutes and thought that oddly, this murder might be quite difficult to solve. There had been twenty people in the room where the crime was committed, probably nineteen witnesses – and some seven of them were sharp-eyed and sharp-eared children. However, the light was very dim – half of the candles had expired and had not been re-lit, many of the guests had been drinking heavily, the continuous music had meant that dancing broke out from time to time. It was a pity that the hatch to the buttery and to the kitchen had been closed; otherwise Rosta or one of his assistants might have noticed something of importance.

Shona had even less to say than her father. She had been listening to the pipes, had danced a little, drank a little wine, kept an eye on the twins, who were flying up and down the hall . . .

'And did you dance with someone?' interrupted Mara. The tunes that the pipes had played were suitable for solitary dancing as well as couples but she was surprised when Shona said, very firmly, 'By myself.'

'And did you talk to Enda?' queried Mara. Directness would work better with this girl, she thought.

Shona thought about that for a moment and seemed about to deny it, then saw Mara's expression and turned a shake of the head into a slight nod.

'For a while,' she said.

For a long time, thought Mara. She had noticed them again and again, sitting side by side on the window seat at the top of the room, well away from the laden table and quite as private, if they kept their voices down, as though they were in a room of their own.

'And what did you talk about?' asked Mara.

'That is private,' said Shona with dignity.

'Nothing is private when it's a murder investigation,' said Mara firmly. 'However, whatever you tell me now will remain private unless it has anything to do with the crime that has been committed.'

Shona hesitated and then after a minute's thought, she gave an artificial smile. 'It was nothing, really. I'm just so sick of the twins listening to everything that I say that I went to a place where they couldn't stand behind me or creep up on me without my noticing. I really can't remember what we were talking about. I think it might have been about King Turlough and what a wonderful King he is,' she said sweetly.

The bit about the twins is probably true, thought Mara, but she doubted whether either of the young people had wasted their time talking about Turlough when they had the far more interesting subject of themselves to discuss. Still while they were in that position they could not have murdered Brehon MacClancy. But how long had they sat there for – and could one of them moved while the other pretended to talk to someone half-hidden by the half-closed window shutter?

'And did you notice anyone approach Brehon MacClancy?' asked Mara.

Shona was on her feet almost before she shook her head, 'No, Brehon,' she said firmly.

'Sit down again,' said Mara. She waited until the girl

reluctantly lowered herself onto the stool again before saying, 'So you were fostered by Brehon MacClancy, is that right? How did you get on with him?'

'Very well,' said Shona and then rather spoiled the decisiveness of her answer by saying, 'I didn't see too much of him, to be honest. His sister looked after us.'

'And the legal business? Who looked after the affairs of Urlan Castle and the lands around when Brehon MacClancy was at Bunratty?' queried Mara.

A smile softened Shona's beautifully cut lips, but she compressed them instantly. 'His assistant was usually there to deal with anything that came up.'

'I see,' said Mara. So the ageing Brehon, perhaps jealous of his position, of his relationship with the King, got Enda out of the way on the pretext that he could look after anyone in the Urlan area, about eight miles away from Bunratty. A beautifully wooded area, Mara remembered and guessed that the pair might have had some idyllic times together before Shona's fosterage ended.

'And has there been a marriage fixed up for you?' Usually fosterage for a girl ended when a marriage contract was drawn up – in fact it was normally the business of the foster-father to arrange this.

Shona faced her courageously. 'Yes,' she said, 'there was talk of a marriage with a nephew of Brehon MacClancy, but I don't think that will happen now.' She glanced across at the dead body in the window recess opposite and then gave Mara a challenging look.

'I see,' said Mara. This time she did not prevent Shona leaving her, but gazed after her thoughtfully for a moment. Shona's younger sister was very skilled with the use of a knife – what about Shona herself? Did Brehon MacClancy's absence from the castle where the MacMahon children were being fostered mean that Shona also ran wild? 'Send your brother and sister over to me, will you?' she called after the girl.

Cael and Cian wore determinedly tough expressions when they lounged over. Everything in their bearing seemed to be calculated to warn Mara that they were not impressed by her status and authority. She pointed towards the bench on the other side of the table and allowed a long silence to elapse before she addressed them. A tough pair, she thought. Most children of that age would be starting to look uncomfortable by that stage but Cael and Cian just stared at her appraisingly. She stared back but to her surprise they were the ones who spoke first.

'How old are you?' asked Cael.

'How long have you been a Brehon?' demanded Cian.

'Why do you wear your hair like that?' asked Cael.

'Do you enjoy your work?' was Cian's next contribution.

'Why do you talk like that and keep ordering everyone about?' Cael seemed to think that was a good question. A triumphant look shone in her eyes. They had probably forestalled the sort of questions that adults usually asked them.

Mara sat back in amazement. She tried to look stern but then felt her lips pucker. She could not help herself and decided to make the best of matters. She put down her pen and laughed. The twins' saintly expressions became somewhat uneasy and they looked at her suspiciously.

'Do you know,' said Mara confidentially, 'I think I might have made a mistake about you.' She allowed a silence to fall before adding with an innocent expression, 'I thought that you looked clever and I imagined that you would be a great help to me.'

They looked at each other and then Cael looked across at Cormac, who was writing down something said by Turlough's daughter-in-law, Ellice, and jerked her thumb, saying, 'Like him?'

'No, not that sort of work, more like secret spies. The King of England has secret spies so why not a Brehon in Ireland? I thought you might be good at that as you can slip in and out of places quickly without being noticed.'

They exchanged another glance. 'Would we get paid some silver?' demanded Cael.

'You would have to speak to the King about that,' replied Mara firmly.

There was another silence and then an almost imperceptible nod passed between the twins.

'All right,' said Cael. She appeared to be the leader of the two, but Mara addressed herself to Cian. 'I have to test you first,' she said solemnly. 'It's no good taking you on unless you prove that you will be useful to me.'

'Try us.' Cian squared his shoulders and sat up very straight.

'And then you'll have to draw up a contract,' warned Cael.

Mara looked at her with respect. 'I can see that you've studied the law,' she said admiringly, 'but first of all the test. Now, you were the last of the dancers to come back up the stairs, I remember; was Brehon MacClancy alive at that stage?'

'Alive; he farted,' said Cian without hesitation. He watched Mara for signs of shock.

'Dead people can fart, birdbrain,' said Cael. 'Dead cows do, anyway. What you should have said was that after he farted, he looked at the flagon and said, "*Excuse me*," to it. He was dead drunk.' She looked triumphantly at Mara.

'Good.' Mara kept her face serious and businesslike. 'And now for a more difficult question,' she added. 'Could you give me a list of all the people who went up and spoke to him during the hour after midnight – before Cormac realized that he was dead, I mean.'

The twins eyed each other with discomforted looks and Mara's heart sank. If this sharp-eyed pair, who knew everyone in the room so well, had not noticed anyone, then the mystery of MacClancy's death might prove very difficult to solve. Her own scholars had yet to be questioned, but she knew them well enough to guess that if they had seen anyone approach the window recess they would have whispered the information to her. This was not the first murder investigation that they had taken part in.

'I just saw one,' said Cian eventually and Cael glared at her brother.

'One is enough to be going on with,' remarked Mara, trying to keep her voice even.

Cian looked nervously at his sister and then whispered in her ear. A slow smile spread over Cael's face.

'Lover boy!' she exclaimed and then, with a straightforward-ness that Mara admired, she said, 'I didn't see anyone. You tell her.'

'I saw Enda,' said Cian. 'You know Enda – the Brehon's

assistant. He went up and whispered in his ear. Well, I think that's what he was doing, anyway.'

Mara's heart beat uncomfortably fast. For a moment she wished that she had never come to Bunratty and was back in the Burren, but that moment passed. The truth had always to be uncovered. If Enda had done this deed then he would have to confess to it and abide by the punishment that the law would inflict. If true, she thought sadly, it would mean the end of his career as a lawyer. No man, or woman, who broke the law in such a serious matter could be allowed to sit in judgement over others. She looked keenly at Cian.

'Are you telling the truth?' she asked.

'I don't tell lies,' he said, affronted.

'Only cowards tell lies,' put in Cael. 'We're afraid of nothing, afraid of no one so we don't tell lies.'

'But there can be other reasons to tell lies,' said Mara seriously. 'I've known people tell a lie in order to injure someone they disliked. Perhaps you don't like Enda because you think that Shona, your elder sister, is fond of him.'

'Or perhaps you don't want to believe Cian because Enda used to be one of your scholars,' snapped Cael.

'That, indeed, could be possible,' admitted Mara. 'But I hope that I would test the evidence against my greatest enemy as vigorously as against my greatest friend. How long was it before the discovery of the dead body, before Cormac shouted, that you saw Enda go up to Brehon MacClancy, Cian?'

'Two tunes back.' The answer came very readily and Mara acknowledged, with a pang, that his words had a ring of truth about them.

'Why didn't you see this?' She turned with an accusing air towards Cael and was interested to see how the girl looked first taken aback and then thoughtful.

'What were they playing then?' she asked her brother.

'The jig; the "Hey",' he said, without pausing.

'That's why,' said Cael. 'I was standing under the wall cloth on that side of the room for that tune. Some dust fell out of it when I was hopping up and down. I wouldn't have been able to see the window recess where the Brehon was swigging the mead.'

It began to sound more and more likely to be the truth, thought Mara. The jig had a fast tune, and unlike the reels where the men and women, boys and girls, partnered each other, holding one hand and swinging around, the jig was mainly danced by individuals, each clicking their heels in time to the music and dancing by themselves. The music was fast and furious and people moved around, seeking a new space, or dropping out in order to refresh themselves with a drink.

'You've been very useful to me,' she told the twins. 'Don't say anything to anyone about our arrangement; and I will remember to discuss it with the King,' she put in quickly as she saw Cael open her mouth. 'But,' she went on, 'do think back over that time – less than an hour – and perhaps you could make me a list of the tunes. That would be a great help in jogging memories. I'm not very musical so it's not something that I can do for myself – and you know everyone there.' She got to her feet. The priest seemed to have finished anointing Brehon MacClancy's body with the holy oils; her three groups had finished their interviews and were sitting with the sheets of vellum scrolled up, waiting for her arrival. Art, she noticed, as she came across the room, was yawning heavily and Slevin had dark shadows under his eyes. She greeted the priest, said a few conventional words in answer to his exclamations of horror, managed tactfully to send him back to his house and bed, and then she stepped into the centre of the room. All murmurs of conversation ceased almost instantly and all turned towards her.

'As you all know by now,' she said, 'Brehon MacClancy has been unlawfully killed here tonight. Under the law of this kingdom, unless the person who did the deed confesses it within twenty-four hours, I will count it as *duinetháide* (a secret and unlawful murder) and the fine of forty-two *sét*s, or twenty-one milch cows, or twenty-one ounces of silver will be doubled to eighty-four *sét*s, or forty-two milch cows, or forty-two ounces of silver. I will start my investigations tomorrow morning and until this crime is solved, no one present in this room during the last hour shall leave the grounds of Bunratty Castle. But for now, I would like everyone to retire to their own room and to avoid discussing the matter in public.'

The die had been cast; she had taken the investigation of this crime into her own hands and it would be for her, not for Enda, the assistant Brehon of the kingdom, to conduct the case. She avoided his eyes, telling Domhnall to collect the scrolls of evidence and then to escort the scholars to their sleeping place. The legendary King Cormac had advised his son, Cairbre, not to have an indulgent man as his judge; she, Mara, could not show any indulgence towards Enda until she had cleared him of all complicity in the murder of a man whom he hated and who had wronged him.

Six

Cain Oigillne
(The Law of Base Clientship)

'For what qualifications is a king elected over countries and clans of people?' asked Cairbre.

'He is chosen,' said the King, 'from the goodness of his shape, and the nobility of his family, from his experience and wisdom, from his prudence and magnanimity, from his eloquence and bravery in battle, and from the number of his friends.'

'You didn't mean that about no one leaving the castle grounds; did you?' Turlough had, with unusual tact, delayed his protest until all, except for Donogh O'Hickey, the physician, had filed out of the door of the great hall and gone to seek their sleeping places. Conor and his wife occupied the south solar and its adjoining bedroom; the others had rooms in one of the four towers that were attached to the central block. It was a luxurious castle and there would be no hardship for anyone to stay there a couple of days longer than they had planned.

'Hopefully, it won't take too long,' she assured him.

'But what about the hunt tomorrow? Everyone is looking forward to that.'

Mara sighed slightly. She had noticed lots of muttering as they filed out. Fionn and Raour had their heads together and Maccon was earnestly pouring whispers into the host's ear. The poet and the harpist, both men in their prime, had been urgently whispering also.

'Well . . .' she began.

'The women can stay and keep you company,' said Turlough obligingly. 'I'm sure that they will be a great help to you in the investigation. You wouldn't keep the young lads at home, would you? They'd be very keen. And Enda, he'd like to come.

But most of the women wouldn't like those marshes – they'd get their gowns wet. You could talk over the case with them. Ellice, now, she's sharp as a . . .' He stumbled, not liking to use the normal comparison *sharp as a knife* about his daughter-in-law. 'And then there's Fionn's wife,' he went on, 'and Maccon's eldest daughter, and Donogh – you're not too keen on chasing through the marshes, are you, Donogh? You can stay with Mara.'

'I think, my lord, that the murder must take preference over the hunt,' said Mara. 'But, of course, it may well be that a confession will have been made, or else the identity of the guilty person proved before your breakfast is over tomorrow morning,' she added and was amused to see his face brighten. He had a great belief in her cleverness and efficiency.

'You go up to bed,' she said comfortingly. 'I'll follow you in ten minutes. I just wish to have a word with Donogh first.'

When the physician had finished, she decided, she would summon the captain of the guard and have the body carried into the nearby church and locked inside it. A messenger would have to be sent to his sister and to the servants and workers at Urlan Castle – the burial would take place there, though it would, of course, be obligatory for King and court to attend the funeral.

She glanced through the scrolls while Turlough was making his farewells to Donogh, and while he was examining in a fascinated manner, once again before he left, the knife in the man's back. There was little of use to her in her assistants' written accounts, she realized with dismay. Conor had been sitting on a cushioned bench on the dais for most of the time; Ellice had danced a little, wandered around the room, and eaten, drunk, chatted. Raour, their son, had danced for most of the time, and had talked with Turlough about hunting – he wasn't sure whether he had gone down to the end of the room, but thought that he hadn't. Couldn't remember whether he had noticed the Brehon or not. Fionn O'Brien and his wife were equally vague.

There was, of course, one person's evidence missing from those scrolls, thought Mara as she gave Turlough a hug and promised to come up to the bedroom as soon as possible.

Tomás MacClancy's young assistant, who might well hope to inherit the position of Brehon of Thomond, had not been interviewed. Tomorrow she would have to talk to Enda before doing anything else, she planned, as she went across to the window recess where the physician was standing, yawning over the corpse.

Strange that Donogh O'Hickey didn't show the slightest sorrow, not even shock, thought Mara. After all law, medicine, music and poetry were, as someone said, the four pillars that held a king in his place. These two men, the Brehon and the physician, must have had quite a bit to do with each other – they were of the same age and had served King Turlough Donn and his two uncles before him, for almost thirty years.

'What do you think was the cause of death, Donogh?' she asked.

He looked at her with surprise. 'The knife in the back, of course,' he said. 'It's obvious, isn't it?'

Mara looked down at the protruding knife doubtfully. Before she could say anything, though, the door opened and a great gust of wind swept in, drawing a billowing cloud of smoke from the burning logs.

'Oh, I'm sorry, Brehon. I didn't know that you were still here,' said Rosta. 'The King came into the kitchen to say that he was on his way to bed so I thought that we could clear off the table.'

Mara did not answer for a moment. She was staring down at the table where the body of the old man still sprawled in that undignified pose. Whether it had been the wind that swept in, causing the fire to smoke and the candles to flare and flicker, or whether it would have happened at that moment in any case; that she did not know. But the knife had fallen from Brehon MacClancy's shoulder blade and tumbled into the fold of his cloak. Turlough had been right – it had hardly penetrated the flesh.

'Yes, Rosta, you go ahead, you won't disturb us,' she said then and shook her head quickly as the physician stretched his hand towards the knife. Her mind was whirring with thoughts as they waited in silence for the table to be cleared. One of the boys had opened the hatch leading to the kitchen and they placed the loaded trays, one by one, on the wooden counter behind this and soon they all disappeared back into the small kitchen.

Mara waited after the door had closed behind them. She looked curiously at O'Hickey. Turlough, her husband, no physician, but a practical man who had seen death throughout the numerous wars and skirmishes throughout his lifetime, had remarked that the knife seemed to be inserted very shallowly. Why had Donogh not noticed this? She picked up a candle from a nearby shelf and holding it in her hand she lowered it until the flame illuminated the back of the corpse. There was little to be seen. The man's clothes, the cloak, the tunic, the *léine* all served to obscure the entrance pathway of the knife. But could any knife that delivered death have fallen out so easily? Or could he have swallowed or eaten something poisoned? She picked up the goblet of mead, sniffed, but could come to no conclusion. Still, poison was unlikely. After all what was the point of the knife if poison was the real weapon?

'He must be stripped and examined,' she said decisively. 'The basement will be the best place for that.'

'My apprentice has gone to his home in the north for Christmas; it will take days to get him back.' Donogh O'Hickey stared at Mara in dismay. 'We can't keep the body for as long as that. Could we get Nuala over from the Burren?' he queried.

Mara thought about this. Nuala worked terribly hard and had been looking very pale. Her assistant, Peader, had gone to visit his mother in Scotland so Nuala would be reluctant to leave her territory when a serious accident might occur. It could not be justified to take her away when her absence might mean that a man could bleed to death or a woman die in childbirth. Surely there were other physicians in the large kingdom of Thomond. Why was Donogh so reluctant to investigate this death properly?

She went to the kitchen hatch, knocked on it and when Rosta appeared, told him to send the captain of the guard to her.

'Oh, and Rosta, could you lend me a box and a clean linen napkin,' she said. 'It doesn't need to be ironed or starched.' Rosta, she knew, was very proud of the starch which he made from the roots of the cuckoo flowers and she could see by his dismayed face as he handed her the crumpled object, which one of his assistants had taken from a large basket, that he didn't think it was fit for the wife of his King.

'That's perfect,' she assured him, 'and just that small box over there, that's all that I need. Tell the captain that his men should bring a litter and perhaps a rope so that the body can be carried safely down the steps.'

The safest thing on that spiral stairs, she thought, as she returned to the window recess, would probably be for one of those strong men-of-arms to sling the body over his shoulder and take it down to the cellar like that, but that might be considered to be discourteous to the dead man and could even be against some obscure rule of the church. She bent down to pick up the knife and slightly recoiled. A slightly fishy smell seemed to emanate from it. She looked down at it, feeling puzzled. She had expected a smell of blood, but not of fish. Holding the napkin to shield her hand she picked up the knife by its handle and held it to her nose. Yes, it was fish – rotten fish, she thought.

And yet the knife itself with its long blade and its deadly sharpened edge was no kitchen knife. It was a warrior's knife, a knife that was meant to kill.

Meditatively she placed it into the box and closed the lid. This knife, she thought, had been inserted into the body of an ageing and malicious man. But was it the instrument of his death? She glanced across at Donogh O'Hickey. Another ageing man, she thought – not malicious – at least, she amended, she didn't think so; but getting old, getting tired, wanting an easy life, wanting an easy answer to a problem.

It was not Mara's way and she prayed that no matter how old she became, it would never be her way. Let me wear out on the task, not rust away, she sent up a brief prayer and wished that she could see into the future.

When the captain of the guard and his men arrived she was courteous and determined with them. The body had to be taken to the very low temperature of the basement. It needed to be guarded from rats – whether by means of a cage or of a human guard and a terrier dog, she suggested, she would leave that in the hands of the captain. The physician would need to work on the body on the following day before the burial could take place. She gave him no time for questions, just smiled warmly at him, expressed King Turlough's gratitude for his prompt appearance and for the efficiency of his arrangements and watched the slow and difficult conveyance of the body down to the freezing depths of the basement beneath the castle – damp, cold; and a sad end, she thought, for a man who had held a position that was the envy of most of Gaelic Ireland.

And then she went back up the spiral staircase to the King's bedroom on the north-easterly side of the castle.

'You're frozen,' said Turlough, reaching out for her. He got out of bed and went across to the brazier and took a lidded flagon from it. Carefully he poured some liquid into a wooden goblet with elaborately carved handles and gave it to her. It was delicious – a Spanish wine, but softened by sugar, hot and perfumed with spices. She took a sip, undressed quickly and slipped in beside her husband. Only now, in comparison with the heat that came from his large body, had she realized how very cold she had become. She would think about this murder tomorrow, she decided.

Seven

Urcailte Bretheman
(The Forbidden Things of a Judge)

A judge shall not come to a decision before the chaff has been blown from the corn; that is to say, all evidence has to be carefully sifted.

No one person should influence a judge; all must be equal before him.

He must not be slow or negligent in the seeking-out of the facts.

He must never accept bribes or show favour.

He must never allow his knowledge of the law texts to fade.

He must not make up his mind too quickly, but must challenge all his decisions as if he were his own enemy.

He must never utter a lie at a public judgement.

Mara was up before most, but when, once washed and dressed, she went into the solar beside their bedroom she found that Rosta and his assistants had already been in and there was a breakfast of newly baked bread and cold meats and cheeses laid out on the long table in front of a blazing fire. There was milk as well as ale in flagons on the table and she poured herself a goblet of it – fresh this morning, she thought – and with a hunk of bread and butter in one hand and the creamy milk in the other she went over to stand by the heat of the logs and looked down into the great hall from the hatch by the fireplace.

Breakfast was spread on the ten-legged table there, also, but the platters seemed unused, the baskets of bread were still piled high and the goblets were neatly arranged in three rows of six in the centre of the table. As Mara watched, munched and drank her milk, she heard the door open. Someone came in, walking quietly and lightly up to the top of the room, stood for a moment surveying the breads, cheeses, cold salmon and slices of meat and then turned away and went towards the fire.

It was Enda and at the sight of him, Mara abandoned the rest of her breakfast and slipped quietly out of the door, taking care to tread as noiselessly as possible on the stone flags of the spiral staircase.

As she rounded the last bend she saw Rosta leave his kitchen. He did not see her, but went into the great hall.

'What about an egg?' he was saying when she opened the door. 'I've got some lovely fresh eggs – I could fry you a couple in an instant. Nothing like it if you've had too much to drink the night before – settles the stomach.'

'No, no thanks, Rosta – I don't feel like anything.' He sounded subdued, thought Mara. Neither of them had noticed her so she closed the door behind her silently.

'You're not upset about that old *francach*, MacClancy, are you, lad,' said Rosta in the cajoling tones that he used to Cormac when the boy was in a bad mood.

Enda made no reply, but kicked one of the logs in the fireplace, sending out a shower of sparks that flew up through the air and then subsided into small blackened morsels on the hearth.

'He's no loss,' said Rosta emphatically. 'And let me tell you this, lad; whoever did the deed, did you a service. He was no friend to you. I heard him with the King talking about you and I can tell you I was hard put not to drop some hot fat down the back of his neck.'

'Oh, I'm not mourning him,' said Enda indifferently. 'Just a bit off form – too much to eat and drink; I'll try those eggs, Rosta. Perhaps they'll do me good.'

'Come into the kitchen and eat them straight from the pan,' said Rosta coaxingly. 'I always say to the lads out there that we get the best of it – food straight from the fire. Nothing like it! Come on, now; come into the kitchen and have a couple of eggs and you'll feel better.'

Mara opened the door, and then closed it with a bang. It would appear as though she had just entered. She didn't want Enda to feel that she was spying on him.

'Did someone say something about eggs,' she said cheerfully.

'I'll bring one straight up to you, Brehon,' said Rosta

agreeably, but Enda started at her entrance, flushed and then turned his head away.

'No – straight from the pan; that's what my cook, Brigid, always says,' lied Mara. Giving neither man the opportunity to say anything she led the way into the kitchen, astonishing various boys who were scurrying around. One was holding by a long handle a flat circle of iron decorated with twisted spirals and as Mara watched, he poured some creamy liquid from a flagon over the hot surface. It immediately crisped and Mara gave a genuine cry of delight.

'Wafers!' she exclaimed. 'Oh, I'd love a hot wafer, instead!'

She had hardly said the words when Rosta seized a pair of tongs, transferred the wafer to a trencher of coarse brown bread and offered it to her.

'Rose-water, whites of two eggs, well beaten, add a bit of honey, some flour and even a fool like Seánie here can turn out something fit for a King's wife,' he said rapidly. 'Would you like a lump of butter with it, Brehon?'

'No, it's perfect as it is – Enda, do try a wafer,' said Mara. It might better for him than fried eggs, she thought. He had a white look about his mouth and his eyes were deeply shadowed as though he had not slept. She made sure that he had four of the sweet, tasty morsels and that he swallowed some ale before saying casually, 'Well, I must go. Come with me, Enda. I will be glad of your help and advice.'

He flushed at that and she felt mean. It was, however, essential, that the truth was found and found as quickly as possible. A murder in the King's own castle would be a destabilizing matter in the three kingdoms. News of it would leak out rapidly and then rumours would start. For Turlough's sake, as well as for the sake of the law by which she lived her life, this murder had to be solved and the solution presented in public to the people of the kingdom.

'Come with me,' she said to Enda once they had come out onto the stairs. The cold struck her as they emerged from the heat of the kitchen, and she regretted that she had not brought her cloak, especially as she knew that where she was going would be even colder. Still it could not be helped. Impulse had ruled her and she had learned that it often led her in the right direction. *Carpe diem*, the Latin proverb that she made her scholars memorize, was a part of her philosophy of life: seize the moment – another as good may not come along.

She chatted amiably as they went down the stairs, but noted how silent he was. The captain of the guard was voluble in his explanations – Mara guessed that he had not expected her so early. Once the body had been securely locked into a lead-lined box, he told her, they had not thought it was necessary to have men stand on guard, though they had taken up her suggestion about . . . He unlocked the door to the basement as he spoke and an ecstatic terrier, with a fringe of rough hair obscuring his eyes, shot out, his long ragged tail wagging so hard that it set up quite a breeze. There were no dead rats around and the dog seemed bored and lonely, responding gratefully to her petting. Certainly the box looked uninjured so Mara nodded and praised his idea and decided that the dog deserved his liberty and a good breakfast and that the body could remain there until Donogh O'Hickey arrived to examine it. She made an arrangement with the captain of the guard that a couple of his men would be available to help the elderly physician – the captain said grimly that he had a couple of lads in mind who would be well served for their behaviour last night by being given that duty. Mara glanced covertly at Enda when he said that, but there was no trace of a smile on the young man's face. He looked deeply troubled and had an indecisive, hesitant look about him which surprised her. Enda, no matter how difficult, or how rebellious he had been during his turbulent teen years, had never looked or sounded unsure.

'I'm frozen; let's go up to the solar and warm ourselves,' she said when they came back up the steps. The icy chill of basement reeked of damp – she wouldn't be surprised if the river came into the room at high tide, she thought, remembering that they were only a few miles from the sea and that both the Shannon and the River Raite would be tidal at their junction beside Bunratty Castle.

'I'm surprised that you didn't ask him to open the box,' said Enda curtly as she closed the solar's door behind them. Luckily neither Turlough, nor any of the scholars, had made an appearance yet, so they had the place to themselves.

'Why are you surprised?' Mara knelt on the floor beside the fire and tossed on a few small logs onto the glowing embers beneath the thick logs lying across the fire irons. She held her cold hands out to the flames and did not look up at him. Nevertheless she was aware of his tension. His voice had been strained and over-loud.

Enda gave a brittle laugh. 'Well, you know the old story, don't you? If a murderer stands beside the man that he has killed, then the wounds open up and bleed. Brigid was a great believer in that. You'd have solved the case if Brehon MacClancy had begun to bleed in my presence.'

Mara sat back and looked up at him. 'There would have been three present,' she said evenly. 'There would have been you, me, and the captain of the guard – and the little dog, of course. Which of these is supposed to have murdered him?'

'You know what I mean,' said Enda impatiently. 'Don't treat me like a child. You don't need to humour me and joke me out of a bad mood. I'm not one of your scholars now.'

That's wrong, thought Mara, once a scholar, always a scholar. She knew that her emotions were engaged here, but there was nothing she could do about that – nothing except to control them. This crime had to be solved. She was determined about that.

'Are you confessing that you were the one who killed him, Enda?' she asked, keeping her voice steady and even. She glanced up at him again and then returned her gaze to the fire. She would give him a moment to think over the situation, she had decided, but as the silence lengthened her heart plummeted to the soles of her shoes.

A moment later a sound roused her. The door to the solar had opened and closed. He had gone. Seriously worried now, she got to her feet and went to the doorway, but he had disappeared around the corner and she decided that she would not lose her dignity by chasing after him. Sighing deeply she picked up the flagon of ale in one hand and tucked a basket of buttered rolls under her arm, went into the bedroom and woke up Turlough.

'I need your help,' she said as she took off her shoes and gown, slid in beside him and warmed her cold feet on him.

It took her a while to get him back to the subject of her worries, but once he had gulped down a pint of ale and crunched his way through a few bread rolls he considered the problem.

'I thought that knife wasn't too far in,' he said triumphantly. 'You wouldn't let me look, but I could have found that out for you.'

'It must have been only barely in, because a draught from the door seemed to have knocked it out,' said Mara. This still puzzled her.

Turlough shook his head decisively. 'Couldn't have been that; it was just the muscles all relaxing or something – happens before it stiffens. If you'd seen the number of dead bodies that I have you'd know that they keep on changing, just as live bodies do. They get flabby, then they stiffen – I'd say that you won't be able to get poor old Tomás out of that box now, he'll be as stiff as a poker, and then they get flabby again. You'll have to wait for that before he can be undressed or anything. Should have done it last night. Why didn't you ask me?'

'I didn't think of that,' confessed Mara, feeling annoyed with herself. 'I'm so used to summoning Nuala as soon as anything happens and then she just takes charge and I get on with the brain work. After a few hours she has everything ready to tell me all about the corpse and the reason for death and things like that.'

Then she thought of something and turned a puzzled face towards Turlough.

'Why didn't Donogh think of all that? Nuala has such a high opinion of him. She says that he taught her so much. Why didn't he warn me?'

'Getting old – old and forgetful – cantankerous, too – never used to be like that. Big change in him, gradually coming on – hard to say when it started – not too keen on Tomás – two of them had a great shouting matching one day – I had to take them apart and say: "Now look here, lads, we can't have the Brehon and physician quarrelling" . . .' Turlough's words came between gulps of ale and bites of his bread roll, but Mara understood and her heart sank. It almost seemed as though she would have to manage without all the efficient medical details that she become accustomed to. Once the brain started to go in an elderly person like Donogh O'Hickey, there was no stopping the downward decline. Still, she told herself, the cause of death is only one of the clues – the real problem is who had a strong enough motive to kill him. That's what I have to solve.'

She got out of bed and pulled on her gown and shoes, neatened her hair by rebraiding and coiling it at her neck and then went out of the door and up the narrow winding staircase until she reached the long room under the roof. Here had slept Turlough's sons – two of them now dead, one of them in England, only the delicate Conor left with his father. Now it was occupied by her scholars. All except Domhnall were fast asleep so she tiptoed over and sat on the end of his bed. Even in the dim light she could see that his eyes were wide-awake and thoughtful.

'I've been thinking about the murder,' he whispered. 'I think that we need to do something a bit more, more, well sort of more scholarly – we're just asking them if they can remember anyone talking to Brehon MacClancy, but half of them were drunk and it's too difficult to remember something that was completely unimportant at the time.' He stopped and looked at her with an air of slight deprecation – he was a boy who was very respectful of her status and she guessed that he didn't want to appear to criticize her handling of the affair.

'I think you're right,' she whispered back. 'We'll discuss it after you've all eaten.' She looked at the sleeping boys. 'Allow them to wake of their accord, but you get up whenever you like. There's plenty of breakfast ready in the solar and more in the great hall.' She gave him a nod and left him.

He was right, of course, she thought. Unfortunately finding who had gone near Brehon MacClancy last night was not the same as finding who had murdered him. People would be reluctant to admit to approaching him, reluctant also to incriminate friends or relations. Add to that the very bad light, the incessant moving and the continuous drumming and piping which numbed the senses and distracted the mind; any evidence would have to be carefully tested. It appeared to Mara that these enquiries were going to be tedious and perhaps, in the end, unfruitful.

But there was another line of enquiry.

Murder, when it concerned a secret killing, was usually the last step in a perilous or dangerously tempting situation. As far as she knew any private fortune that Brehon MacClancy possessed would go to his nephew, with, probably, some provision for his elderly sister.

And Brehon MacClancy's nephew was not present last night when his uncle was murdered in the hall in the presence of his King, his King's relations and friends, his fellow members of the King's household – before their very eyes. Nor was the elderly sister.

This meant that the man had not been murdered for gain or greed. Probably he had been murdered because of anger occasioned by a past deed, or more likely for apprehension of what he might do. In all probability, thought Mara, as she walked down towards the solar, Tomás MacClancy had been murdered because someone feared that malicious tongue of his. He had sworn to uncover some deed in the presence of the King, to destroy the King's trust and love in one of the guests.

Mara stopped for a moment and looked out of one of the arrow loops on the stairway and saw two figures walking through the trees near the church. Even from this height, she recognized instantly Enda's bright gold hair, and the hooded figure beside him, was, she felt sure, Shona MacMahon. As she watched the smaller figure stopped, seemed to bury her face in her hands for a moment and then to turn and clasp the tree trunk. Enda immediately encircled her with his arms and they withdrew into the shadows.

Not just the usual courting, she thought, but a pair of very troubled young people, giving and seeking comfort. She grimaced slightly and continued down the narrow, winding steps. What was going to be the outcome of this Christmas Day murder, she wondered as she pulled up the latch and pushed open the door of the solar. Then she stopped in surprise. Turlough was there at the table munching his way through a second breakfast – he was sprawled on the cushioned bench, but standing rigidly, one on each side of the fire, were two figures.

'Visitors for you,' said Turlough with a jerk of his thumb.

'On private and confidential business,' said Cael, looking hard at Turlough.

He took the hint immediately, rose with a grin on his face and said, 'I'd better go downstairs, hadn't I, and see what the rest of my guests are up to? What do you think?'

Neither of them smiled or moved. They were quite a serious and intense pair of children, thought Mara, looking at them with interest. Neglected, too – perhaps their elder sister should be looking after them instead of walking through the trees with Enda. Cael had chopped her hair even shorter – now it hung just barely below her ears and neither appeared to have changed their *léinte* for days. They had been grubby when she arrived – and she had put that down to ordinary childish play, but they had remained grubby through the celebrations. She wondered whether they had proper night clothes, whether anyone ever made sure that they washed and changed, or whether they even combed their hair. Brigid, old as she was by now, would sort them out quickly, she thought. Then feeling a certain respect for their self-sufficient intensity, she turned a serious face towards the twins and asked them deferentially whether they wanted to sit down.

'We've got the list of tunes for you,' said Cian, holding out a grubby piece of vellum. The script on it was fluent, well formed, although both of them, she had noticed when watching them drink, were left-handed. It was well spelled, also, so their early education had not been neglected. There had been, according to it, six dances after the King's guests had come back into the great hall and each one of them had the name of the music placed beside the numeral and, in a bracket after it, the type of dance. Domhnall, thought Mara, had been thinking along these lines and this would form a good basis for a more thorough investigation.

'That's not all, though,' said Cael. She looked grimly at Mara and then unbuckled the leather belt that she wore. It was studded with knives, each sheathed in its leather holster, eleven of them, counted Mara, but there was one of the dozen slots without a knife.

'That's right,' said Cael with a nod as she saw Mara's eyes go to the empty space.

'She threw two of hers into Brehon MacClancy's body – the one we made, the one swinging from the rope,' said Cian. 'I threw one, also, but she only got back one of hers.'

'We tortured the stable boy,' said Cael with relish.

'But he swore by all that he held holy that he had sent the three knives over to the castle.'

'It was my one that went into his chest, into the chest of the straw effigy – that was the one that is missing – my best knife. So . . .' finished Cael, watching Mara's face.

Odd, thought Mara. She had only noticed two knives in the dangling figure. However, she said nothing. It was possible she had been mistaken. Mara went across the room, picked up the box from its place on the carved court press and opened it. She said nothing, but held it out and the twins reacted immediately.

'That's it,' said Cael triumphantly.

'Definitely,' said Cian.

'You see that scratch on the hilt – I did that when Cian and I were throwing it at a bird. We wanted to see which of us brought him down.'

'Don't touch,' said Mara moving the box away from them. 'That's evidence now.' An idea occurred to her and she said casually:

'I suppose that one of your knives is kept for cleaning fish, or do you use all of them?'

There was a moment's silence. Cian, observed Mara, just looked puzzled, but Cael eyed her narrowly. She could have sworn that the girl caught in her breath.

'My throwing knife to gut fish!' she exclaimed then and looked at Mara with contempt.

'What's the difference between gutting fish and killing something, or someone?' asked Mara with an innocent air. 'Have you been fishing?'

'No.' The answer was uncompromising but probably the truth as her brother did not contradict the statement. He looked as though he was thinking hard and an annoyed look came over his freckled face.

'You know what it means, of course, Cael,' remarked Cian. His voice sounded slightly sulky. 'It means that you are the prime suspect for the crime of committing a murder.'

His sister's face lit up.

'I hated him,' said Cael with satisfaction.

'You wanted to help Shona, didn't you,' put in Cian.

'And Enda,' added Cael with a smirk. 'Don't forget dear Enda.'

'You just wanted to get rid of Brehon MacClancy to help the world,' said Cian with a flourish.

They both stared at Mara in a challenging way and she nodded her head with the air of one who is not too impressed.

'Yes,' she said, 'but there are other suspects.'

'You,' said Cian. 'Because of the satire.'

'That doesn't make her a suspect – it was the *file* wrote the satire about her. That's not her fault. He just did it for a joke,' Cael assured Mara. 'He never thought that Brehon MacClancy would seize it and refuse to give it back.'

Mara's eyes narrowed. A satire on her; this was the first that she had heard of it. She wouldn't have minded – no, probably she would have been immensely irritated, she told herself with a flash of honesty, but in public she would have had the self-possession to take it as a joke. Turlough, however, had a straightforward simplicity and he would have been furious. It would be no wonder if the poet, Aengus MacCraith, had been sick with anxiety when the Brehon maliciously confiscated it. She would have to go through the Brehon's papers. Once she had finished with the twins she would send them to summon Enda and ask where MacClancy had put his notes. There would have been a judgement day arranged for the sixth of January, she remembered, so the cases should have been listed. In the meantime, she would see how much more information she could get from the twins.

'Why should your sister, Shona, want to kill Brehon MacClancy?' she asked in a respectful tone.

'Because he was stopping her marrying Enda,' said Cian quickly.

'I see,' said Mara. There would be more than that to it, she guessed. The marriage would not have been favoured by the girl's father, unless Enda had better prospects. In any case, if the fosterage had ended, then it was not for MacClancy to say who she was to wed. She turned her mind to a different matter.

'Where did the stable boy leave the knives?' she asked.

'Don't ask me, I'm a suspect,' smirked Cael.

'And I'm her twin brother,' remarked Cian. 'I have family loyalty.'

'Unless you can put aside personal affairs you are of no use to me,' said Mara firmly and they both capitulated immediately.

'He says he gave them to someone to put them in our room,' said Cian. 'He's a hopeless witness because he can't remember who he gave them to – one of the guard, he thinks.'

'And where's your room?'

'Right on the top of the south-eastern tower.'

'I see,' said Mara. So the twins shared a room. She had imagined that Shona would have had her young sister with her in the much more luxurious quarters known as the priest's room. Maccon MacMahon was in the old chapel – when Turlough had become King he had shown his devotion to religion by rapidly causing a small church and a priest's house to be built in the grounds and moving the priest out into these quarters and leaving himself with two beautiful rooms for favoured guests.

But the room that was occupied by the twins was a small room at the very top of the spiral staircase, just under the flag post. Would a member of the guard have gone to the trouble of taking the knives all the way up there, she wondered, or would he have passed them on to someone else. Or even taken them and put them down somewhere. It might be quite hard to find out what happened to them.

'We found them on a window loop at the bottom of the tower,' admitted Cian, 'but one was missing. There's someone outside your door,' he added in a hushed whisper. 'Take cover!' He snatched a knife from his belt, crept over to the door and opened it with a flourish.

'Oh, it's only you,' he said with disgust as the widely opened door revealed the figure of Domhnall with hand outstretched to knock.

'I've had an idea, Brehon,' said Domhnall ignoring, in his dignified way, the badly behaved twins. 'I was thinking that I could get a piece of board from the carpenter and use it to make a chart. We could write all the names of the adults across the top of the board and perhaps the parts of the room along the side . . .'

'Do it for everyone during the "Hey Jig" – that's the fourth tune of the evening and that's probably the time that the murder took place,' said Cael in an offhand manner.

'Great idea,' said Mara enthusiastically. 'When all the scholars have had their breakfast, Domhnall, then Cael or Cian will take you to the master carpenter's house and you can see if he has a suitable piece of board for you. If you write with charcoal then the board can be given back as good as new.'

'And it can be wiped clean if the killer forces his way in,' said Cael.

'I thought you were a suspect,' said Cian challengingly.

'I didn't do it – guess why? Because I wouldn't have stuck a knife in his back like that; that's not a good place to kill anyone – just under the shoulder blade. I'd have gone behind and slit his throat. No, it definitely wasn't me.'

'Do you know,' said Mara slowly and thoughtfully, 'I think you two are going to be a great help to me in this investigation.' It was an interesting idea. There were easier ways of killing someone at a feast than sticking a knife into their back under the shoulder blade. She wondered whether it was true that was not a good place and decided that it was. There was a competence and sincerity about the twins' observations which made her believe that they knew what they were talking about, and that they were not lying.

'Let's go and get Cormac out of bed, and the rest of them,' proposed Cian and he and Cael disappeared instantly from the room. Cael had flushed slightly at Mara's praise but had immediately scrubbed her finger tips through her uneven locks of bright-red hair and then tweaked her nose in a business-like way.

'Have your breakfast in peace, Domhnall,' advised Mara, but she knew that he would manage the twins. She went over to the hatch, opened it and glanced down.

Aengus MacCraith was drinking some ale and chatting with Turlough while the cook slid some fried pork and eggs onto his plate. She would join them, she thought. It would be interesting to see the poet's reaction to her presence.

Did those satirical verses still exist? she wondered.

Eight

Bretha Nemed Deinech
(the last laws)

The law regards satire as a very severe attack on a person because it strikes and cuts at log n-enech (literally the 'price of his face' – but meaning the 'honour price'.) Anything that causes a person to lose face, injures that person and recompense has to be paid.

Heptad 33

Composing a satire
Repeating a satire
Mocking a manner of speech
Casting scorn on professional ability
Mocking a person's appearance
Making public a physical blemish
Giving a nickname that endures.

'Here's the person that we all want to see,' said Turlough boisterously when Mara came into the great hall. All faces turned smilingly towards her. It seemed, she thought, still like a merry festive gathering, not a hall where last night a man, well known to all of these guests, had been murdered in the presence of his friends and neighbours.

'What can I do for you, my lord?' she queried pleasantly.

'It's just that Maccon has to go home tomorrow morning,' he said. 'We really do need to have the bustard hunt today.'

'I'm afraid that you will all have to be patient for a while longer,' she said smoothly. It was no good, she thought, wishing that her husband had a bit more sense than to tackle her in public like this. He was who he was. 'I can make no promises – no confession of guilt has been made and my investigations have produced several possibilities.' She allowed that sentence to hang and was pleased to find that the hearty, bloodthirsty expressions of the eager faces turned towards her changed to surreptitious and slightly guilty sidelong glances at each other. Fionn O'Brien, Aengus MacCraith, Raour and Maccon suddenly became very interested in fresh helpings of eggs and bacon produced by the obliging Rosta and she moved slightly back into the window recess and waited with her eyes on Turlough until he had the sense to join her.

'The captain of the guard says that I may borrow two of his men to aid the physician to investigate the body thoroughly,' she said in a whisper. She was an expert at pitching her voice, so she knew that the words had reached the men standing around the table. A whisper, she had found from experience, mostly travelled further than words spoken in a low voice.

She scanned the faces carefully, but they all looked ill at ease and almost furtive. The thought of that dead body stored down in the basement was giving everyone an uncomfortable feeling and she was glad to see that nobody dared to protest about the cancelling of their hunt through the marshy ground after that. She smiled reassuringly at Turlough and left the hall quickly.

'Could you send one of your lads to find Enda for me, Rosta,' she said as he followed her out of the great hall. 'Tell him that I'll be in the Brehon's room,' she added.

Tomás MacClancy's room was always kept for him – indeed, he probably spent far more time in Bunratty Castle than he did in his own place at Urlan. Situated in the south-east tower it was always known as the robing room, as in the past both of Turlough's uncles had used it for that purpose.

Turlough, however, was not a man who liked pomp and ceremony. His view was that his ordinary clothes were in general good enough for all ceremonies and he was strengthened in that belief by his popularity with the clan. He got dressed where he slept and did not require any particular place or particular ceremonies to do with his clothing. The robing room was handed over to his Brehon who found that the impressively carved press, painted dark green, was a useful place to keep the law documents relating to the courts held at Bunratty Castle.

Mara gazed around while she waited and wondered what secrets that piece of furniture might hold, secrets which might point the way to the murderer of Brehon MacClancy.

The problem was, when Enda arrived, that he had no idea where the key might be. Mara's heart sank, but she knew that she had to get that key.

'Go to the captain of the guard and get him or one of his men to search the body,' she said, trying to sound unconcerned though she felt sickened at the idea.

Enda hesitated. He had become very white, she noticed. Despite herself, she wondered about that superstition that the wounds on a dead body would bleed if the murderer stood beside it.

'Wait a minute,' he said. He produced his knife from the inner lining of his tunic and applied it to the lock. After a minute there was a click. Enda grinned – it was, thought Mara, the first time that she had seen that wide grin since she arrived at the castle.

'Nice to be able to open this rather than have it slammed shut whenever I entered the room. It's not often that I've been allowed to have anything to do with this sacred press,' he said flippantly.

The cupboard was a large one, made from oak and with four sections within it. It was neatly arranged with scrolls filling the two bottom sections and a fine collection of law books in the top right-hand section. Beside it was a section labelled 'The Year of Our Lord 1519' and holding boxes, each with a day of judgement marked upon it. They had more judgement days here in Thomond than she did back in the Burren, Mara noticed, reading the exquisitely lettered labels on each box: *Imbolic*, Mid Spring, *Bealtaine*, Midsummer, *Lughnasa*, Mid Autumn, *Samhain* and finally Yule. The Yule box was the one that she was interested in so she took it out and brought it over to the light from the candles on the table. One by one she took out the rolls and unrolled each. They were the finest vellum, the calf skin carefully prepared and bleached almost as white as snow. But there was no writing on them – not even a heading. It looked as though Brehon MacClancy had not prepared for the sitting of the court in a couple of days' time.

And yet he was reputed to be a meticulously careful man. He had often boasted at meetings between lawyers from all over Ireland that he prepared all of his cases weeks in advance and even made a written copy of the evidence from witnesses.

Mara turned to Enda. 'Was this like him?' she asked, indicating the empty pages. 'Not even a list of the hearings.'

'He didn't allow me to know anything about the cases in advance,' said Enda shortly. The momentary flicker of light-heartedness when he had opened the lock had now gone and his face bore a heavy brooding expression. 'The only thing that he said to me last night, and he was rubbing his hands and looking very pleased about something when he said it, was that he had decided to hold the day of judgement on the day after Christmas, and not to wait for the *Little Christmas* as usual.'

Mara frowned in puzzlement. The sixth of January would have been the usual day for a court to be held. The day after Christmas would encroach on the King's festivities.

'Where is the court held normally?' she asked.

'Here at the castle – in the great hall. He, the Brehon, Brehon MacClancy, would sit in the centre of the table with all his scrolls and documents around him. I would sit at the end of the table in case he wanted to send me on some errand or get me to hand him a deed or something. The people would sit on benches in the main hall or stand around by the walls, while the persons in the hearing stood on the dais.'

Mara frowned in puzzlement. Turlough had said nothing to her about a court being held during her stay. She, and her scholars, had been due to return on the fifth of

January. She had chosen the day on purpose so that she would not interfere in the legal proceedings of another kingdom.

'So will a lot of people be turning up to witness a judgement day at any moment now? Perhaps we should send out messages – at least to the village – perhaps to the churches – no good sending to the mills – no one will be grinding corn on the day after Christmas.'

'No,' said Enda with an effort. 'This was not going to be a public day of judgement. When I asked him about that he told me that all concerned would be already at the castle. He was rubbing his hands together and muttering that some people would be very surprised and that the King was going to get a shock and that he was going to uncover secrets and expose what was rotten in the kingdom – that's the way he was talking.'

'And did he tell you who would be concerned?'

'No,' said Enda.

There was something about the brusqueness of the monosyllable that made Mara persist.

'Did he tell you to be there?'

'Of course; I was his servant.' There was something slightly artificial about the deliberately abrupt way that Enda said this and Mara persisted.

'So he told you about the time.'

'Ten o'clock,' said Enda more readily. 'He told me that I would have to hold myself in readiness an hour before that in order to summon everyone.'

It would have been safe to presume that most people would be present within the castle at that hour, especially after the late night, thought Mara. And this question of summoning everyone seemed to indicate that Brehon MacClancy had decided to make a public example of those whom he had intended to prove guilty. Presumably he would have told Turlough the night before – if he had not been killed before that happened, of course.

'But he must, at least, have had a list of those whom he intended to try,' she said aloud.

'He normally had everything written down. Someone

must have taken it and it wasn't I,' said Enda, looking at her defiantly.

Mara did not answer. She picked up a branch of candles and carried it over to the cupboard and examined it carefully. The paint had been thickly applied – fairly recently, she reckoned, judging by the freshness of the colour. But just beside the lock there was a scratch – a scratch deep enough to allow the pale tan colour of the wood to show through. She returned and replaced the candles on the table.

'Let me see your knife,' she said.

He produced it with a puzzled expression and she examined it carefully. No, there was no trace of paint on it now, but, that of course, did not mean that he had not used it the night before, had not cleaned it previously – either early last night or first thing this morning. Enda, she remembered, was housed in the south-eastern tower only a flight of stairs below the room occupied by the Brehon.

Something occurred to her then.

'I suppose that press was locked,' she said. 'It was not that it had stuck or something.'

'It was locked,' said Enda defensively. 'You heard the click, yourself, didn't you?'

It was true, thought Mara, that she had heard a click, but, on the other hand, it would have been easy perhaps to turn the lock backwards and then forwards in order to pretend that it had been locked.

'If someone murdered the Brehon last night then he could have slipped the keys from his pouch and used them to open the cupboard.' It was getting more imperative all the time to have a thorough examination of the dead man and of his clothes. But there was no sign of Donogh O'Hickey this morning.

And if Turlough was correct, then the body would remain stiff for another day or so and it would be impossible to get it out of that box before then. She would just have to proceed with her enquiries. Meditatively she began to stack the unwritten scrolls back into their box and then dislodged one of a different colour – much smaller – parchment rather than vellum, she thought, the quality was not at all so fine. She unrolled it and then took it to the table, flattening it with her hands.

And it was the satire. Cleverly done, she acknowledged, wincing slightly. Not very complimentary to Turlough, also, hinting that she led him by the nose. Aengus MacCraith had observed her closely, copied many of her favourite expressions, contrived to make her sound domineering and a woman well past her prime of life, still pretending to a youth that she did not have, not covering her head with the usual linen but displaying her hair, which he hinted was dyed, to all. The twins had undoubtedly read this, but how had they got hold of it? Once Brehon MacClancy got it into his hands he would have locked it up and surely contemplated showing it to the King on judgement day, or even, she winced again, reading it aloud.

She handed it to Enda with an effort, but was warmed to see a definite look of indignation on his face. He handed it back to her and then said with relish, 'King Turlough will kill him, or roast him alive.'

'I think this is something that we will keep to ourselves. I am the injured party and I choose to do nothing about this.' Mara had come to an instant decision. It was against instinct to destroy evidence, but she could not risk Turlough's hurt and fury if he read this silly satire. She hesitated for a moment. Was Brehon MacClancy's seizure of this document enough of an incentive for his murder at the hands of Aengus MacCraith? She thought not. Despite Enda's words, Turlough was not a man to inflict any savage punishment on one of household. He would have been filled with fury, would have been most upset, but it would all have blown over and they would probably have been best of friends again within months, if not weeks.

Nevertheless it was evidence, so she took a blank scroll from the cupboard and wrote on it,

'*A scurrilous satire was written, allegedly by Aengus MacCraith, on the subject of Mara, Brehon of the Burren. I have read the lines before they were destroyed.*

As witness by hand:

Mara, Brehon of the Burren.

Enda, Assistant Brehon of Thomond.'

She signed the document and then pushed it across to him.

'I'll keep this in case there is need for it,' she said holding the vellum to the fire to dry the ink and then tying it with tape and putting it into her own pouch. She did not look at Enda, but busily arranged the scrolls in the cupboard in neat order.

'Brehon MacClancy changed very much in the last few years, didn't he, Enda? I remember when you went here first that the King said how well you were getting on with him and what high praise he had of you.' She herself did not often come to Bunratty – she preferred, when she was at leisure, for Turlough and herself to spend time in Ballinalacken Castle overlooking the sea and the Aran Islands. However, she had noticed a great change in MacClancy the last time that she had come.

'What happened? What changed him?' she asked then when he did not reply.

'I think that his mind began to go,' said Enda eventually. 'His memory began to get very bad – he would forget people's names, forget things that they said – not the law, he didn't forget that – anything from the past, anything that he had learned when he was young, that was very real to him, but you could tell him something and five minutes later he would forget'

'And how did he deal with this?' Mara had a great wish for Nuala to be present; she was sure that she would understand.

'He got bad tempered,' said Enda. 'And then he would get angry and accuse you of lying to him. He seemed to hate everyone and want to do them harm.'

'And blackmail – do you think that he indulged in that? After all he was going to blackmail Aengus MacCraith.'

Enda nodded reluctantly. 'It gave him a sense of power to find out things about people and threaten them. It made him feel better; perhaps made him feel that he was . . .' He stopped and thought for a moment and then added, 'Perhaps it made him feel more in control.'

Mara nodded. That was the old Enda, clever and astute. She watched him carefully. Had MacClancy blackmailed Enda?

Somehow she did not think so. But someone that Enda loved; now that was a distinct possibility.

'The twins were telling me about the business with Shona,' she said, turning away to stack the law books in a neat pile.

There was a long silence. These books are very dusty; he hasn't used them much for the last few years – thought he knew everything and didn't bother looking things up to check, thought Mara, with one half of her mind, while the other half was tense and concentrated, listening for an intake of breath. She heard nothing, though, and turned to face him. His eyes were very bright and his face was very pale but he looked very directly at her.

'So you haven't found out yet what he was holding over my head.' He almost spat the words out and for the second time in the day he turned away from her and went to the door.

'Wait,' she said imperatively. Enda had been a scholar of hers from the age of eight to seventeen and the tone of voice acted on him like the whistle of a shepherd to his dog. He turned back instantly and she went to meet him.

'We've known each other for a long time,' she said urgently. 'Surely you can trust me. I know that you are in trouble. Tell me, and let us sort it out together.'

For a moment his face relaxed into the expression that she had known so well – half deprecating, half hopeful of forgiveness, and then it hardened. She could see that he was going to walk away and she put out a hand to him in mute protest.

'You don't understand,' he said between gritted teeth.

'I think that I do understand,' she said quickly. 'You are worried about Shona.' She thought for a fleeting moment, anxious to speak before he stormed out of her presence, once again.

'Shona was fostered by Brehon MacClancy,' she said, feeling her way, but endeavouring to sound confident and in possession of the facts. 'I don't suppose,' she went on, 'that, if, as you say, a great change came over his intellect and his personality during the last few years, he was the ideal foster-father for a girl approaching womanhood. I seem to remember that his sister is a woman ten years even older than he, and Shona would not have received much interest, or guidance from her.'

Mara looked at Enda and said with careful emphasis, 'It is possible that in such a situation that a girl like Shona, passionate, warm, loving . . .'

She saw the glow of assent in his eyes and finished, 'A girl like that might have got into some sort of trouble . . .'

. . . might well have become pregnant, born a child to a man who would, in her father's eyes, and also in the eyes of her foster-father and of the rest of the clan, seemed completely unsuited to the daughter of a taoiseach . . . Mara's thoughts ran on as she watched him carefully.

Enda's eyes were now shuttered, the lids dropped down over their burning blue. His hands clenched and unclenched, but he said nothing.

'I think that a young man who truly loved her would understand that what had happened was not her fault, that if all her guardians, those who should have had her welfare at heart, would keep quiet about the past, then a girl like this, with all the good qualities which made her worthy of love, could go ahead to a bright future.'

'But if those that should have been her protectors turned blackmailers . . .' said Enda in a harsh voice which broke over the last word.

'Exactly!' Mara nodded her head. 'I'm not sure what comes next,' she said with great honesty. 'However,' she continued, 'I do understand that if someone whom you love has been badly treated, then a great wall of hate can build up – and perhaps that hate can turn into something self-destructive and evil.' She watched him carefully, but then he turned away. She could see the struggle in his face and then his lips tighten. She had a sudden memory of Enda as a quite young boy, only about nine years old. She had been questioning him about some idiotic behaviour of the scholars which had resulted in the burning down of a tree in the woodland beside the law school. Enda on that occasion had suddenly become very distant, tightened his lips in the way he had done just now and had said, with great dignity: 'It's not my secret, Brehon.'

Then, as now, she had acquiesced in the justice of this

and had told him he could go, and in almost the same words now she said, 'Well, Enda, if there is anything that you feel you can tell me, or anything else that you know about this very serious and difficult matter, do come and find me instantly.'

When he had left she searched the Brehon's press more thoroughly. The scrolls relating to the next judgement day were certainly not there but there could be other clues. She remembered Enda's words about MacClancy collecting evidence and went methodically through the four sections of the cupboard again.

This time she found something that she had missed on the first search. Underneath the rolls of unused vellum, she found a tin box. She thought it contained quills, lying packed in bundles, ready to be sharpened into pens, but when she opened it, she found that there were rolled sheets of vellum and parchment inside it. She pulled out the top scroll and unfolded it. Her eyes widened. The vellum was of superfine quality, but that was not what had startled her.

It was a letter, a letter written in English, not the straightforward English of the people of Galway, but the flowery, multisyllabic English of the King's court. She glanced at the seal at the bottom of the letter and saw that it bore the name of one of Henry VIII's ministers.

'My lord,' it began and then went on to several effusive compliments and wishes for the reader's good health. And then came the bit that made her stare in astonishment. 'I can confirm that your surmise is correct. His Majesty has been pleased to confer the Barony of Moyarta on Turlough O'Brien.'

Turlough! Made Baron of Moyarta! But Moyarta was just one small western portion of the lands possessed by her husband.

And then Mara's mind cleared. Of course, she should have guessed.

The O'Brien lineage from Brian Boru was an ancient one. Time after time she had heard the great names of its chieftains, down through five hundred years to the present day, recited by poet and bard. And each time her mind lost itself among a sea of Turloughs, Donoghs, Teiges, Conors and Murroughs – the O'Briens were mighty warriors but they were singularly lacking in imagination and extremely conservative when it came to naming their children. There were at least ten kings who had been named Turlough which she could recollect offhand, and, of course, they all had nicknames. Her husband was Turlough Donn, because of his brown hair, his kingly uncle had been simply called the *Gilladuff*, the dark lad, and then there had been Turlough of the Chessboard and Turlough Mór – a man of great height – and many others.

So when the grandson of Turlough Donn, Conor and Ellice's eldest son, was born, he was named Turlough through family custom. But after a few years when he showed signs of a plump, broad, heavy figure, he was nicknamed Raour and had been Raour ever since.

Mara stared down at the letter. So Raour, who had been sent to London to invite his uncle Murrough to the celebrations of the twentieth anniversary, had transacted some business on his own account.

Was it the young man's own idea, or had the title been given at the request of Murrough? To be Baron of Moyarta was not a title of any great consequence. Mara guessed that Murrough had a much greater title in mind for himself if the English ever managed to get control of the three kingdoms. However, if his nephew adopted an English title then that would undermine the position of his father, Conor, and of his grandfather, King Turlough Donn.

Turlough, thought Mara, would be furious and extremely wounded if he had heard of what his grandson had done behind his back.

And if Brehon MacClancy told the King of Raour's treachery, then it would spell an end to any chance of the young man being elected as *tánaiste* or heir to the kingship of Thomond, Corcomroe and Burren. Turlough was fanatically hostile to anything English, whether their laws, their way of dress, or their customs – and especially angry at the efforts they were making to extend their influence over Gaelic Ireland and reduce his native country to the status of an offshore island, subject to a master race of England. He would not remain quiet under any action of his grandson that appeared to uphold the English ambitions.

Deep in thought, Mara replaced the document and resolved that she would take this box into her own custody. There was nothing else of interest there: just some bills of sale for copious amounts of salmon – fruits from the river by Urlan Castle, perhaps, she thought – and also an account book detailing payments to a fisherman – probably the one who supplied the salmon. There was nothing in the cupboard which could relate to Fionn O'Brien. Mara had wondered about him. The heiress, the woman who had provided the castle which was now his place of residence, had a tough look about her. If Fionn was to offend her in any way then a divorce would quickly result and divorce under Brehon law, was, as Mara well knew, very easy to obtain if a wife felt ill-used or swindled by her husband. She decided to have a word with Turlough. He was no gossip, but he usually knew what was going on in his kingdom.

Mara placed the box in her satchel, closed the cupboard door and went out of the Brehon's room.

So far, she thought, it appeared as though MacClancy might have been killed by someone who had been a victim of his blackmail. At the moment it appeared as though Aengus MacCraith, Raour, and either Enda or Shona could possibly be the murderer. Leaving out the seven children, there were thirteen others, all adults, moving around and dancing in that dimly lit hall during the time that Brehon MacClancy was stabbed in the back. Conor and his wife Ellice – no motive that she could imagine. Herself and Turlough – no; Turlough had been either by her or within her sight the whole of that time. Maccon MacMahon – unless it was something to do with Shona, she could see no possible motive. Fionn O'Brien might be a possibility – though she could see no motive for his wife Aideen. The physician, Donogh O'Hickey, and the harpist, Brian MacBrody, were men, like Aengus MacCraith, who were part of the four officers of Turlough who lived cheek by jowl with each other. There were possibilities for strain and jealousies to arise between them all, particularly as the dead man seemed to be in such a vindictive and malicious mood. Their names could be added to the list, but at the moment she could not see any further than Raour, Enda, Aengus MacCraith or Shona.

And of these, perhaps Raour had the most to lose.

Nine

Breacha Nemeð Coiseach
(Laws concerning noble or professional people)

A king should have many servants and these should be chosen carefully:
A steward who arranges seating, lying and food for all.
A carver who divides the food and should have a keen eye and a steady hand.
A cook who will guard the king against poisoning.
A cup-bearer whose qualifications are filling, emptying and self-control.

The noise from the solar was attracting the attention of the workers in the kitchen as Mara came up the stairs of the north-western tower. Rosta's chief assistant had a slightly worried look on his face as he stood outside the kitchen and looked upwards.

'Don't worry,' said Mara imperturbably. 'They are just debating legal matters.'

As she spoke the door opened and Cormac shot out and came down the stairs, leaping exuberantly and burst into the kitchen, red-gold hair tousled and green eyes gleaming with excitement.

'Have you got anything to eat, Rosta, I'm starving. Any of those cakes?' he said with the confidence of the petted child of the castle.

'I was thinking that I needed to bring supplies – it sounded like as if there was a siege going on up there. How many of you are there – seven, isn't it?' Without waiting for an answer, Rosta poured some elderberry cordial into a flagon, placed seven goblets onto a tray, and signalled to his assistant to take something out of the iron pot standing on small legs at the back of the fire.

'*Ionach!*' exclaimed Cormac. 'My favourite plum cake! Don't cut it, Rosta. Let me.' He grabbed the sharp kitchen knife from Rosta's hand and bestowed a beaming smile on him.

'And "thank you",' reminded Mara, though she could see how everyone was smiling at the nine-year-old. Cormac, she thought, had all of his father's charm. It was a good thing that he was brought up in the strict discipline of the law school – if he lived here at Bunratty Castle he might grow up spoilt and over-weight. Her mind went to Raour. As the grandson of the reigning King, and the son of a father who had looked for most of Raour's lifetime to be unlikely to live, the clan member who had fostered him may have curried favour with the boy by allowing him to do and to eat exactly what he wished. And to have a title from the English King might have seemed to be a sweetmeat to which he could not say no. The thought of Raour brought her mind back to the time at the Christmas Eve meal when Conor had been boasting about his son to Aideen, Fionn O'Brien's wife. She had noticed, then, the woman's eyes looking apprehensively down the table at the unattractive form of Brehon MacClancy. It had puzzled her at the time, and now it made her think hard and resolve to find out more.

It had to be faced up to – the body of the dead man had to be examined as soon as it was possible. She could not shy away from this any longer.

With a feeling of shame at her squeamishness and neglect of duty, she mounted the stairs, following in Cormac's footsteps and was glad to hear that the angry voices immediately ceased at the sight of what he was carrying.

'Everything all right, Domhnall,' she said in an undertone as the other six picked up the generous slices which Cormac was cutting from the cake made with dried plums.

'It's that girl,' he said explosively. Unusually for him his cheeks were flushed a deep red and his dark hair was untidy. 'She just thinks that she must be in charge.'

Mara concealed a smile. Domhnall normally held an almost effortless sway over the law-school scholars. Cormac was usually the only one who would challenge him and faced with the united front of Domhnall and Slevin he always backed down. Cael, obviously, was made of tougher material. Mara sat down at the top of the table, refused the cake and the cordial, but remained sitting, determined that Domhnall's authority was not going to be undermined by this badly behaved little – *Amazon*, she concluded in her mind, remembering her reading of the Greek historian Herodotus.

'Now could you explain to me what you've all decided, Domhnall,' she said as soon as she saw that he had finished his slice of cake. The twins, a very thin pair of children, had each taken a second slice and she thought that might occupy them fully for the moment.

'I've used ink, instead of charcoal, Brehon, because the carpenter said that he would have to sand it down afterwards, in any case – I borrowed some of the paper so that I could rub out the writing before I returned it to him.' Domhnall, as always, was forward-thinking and methodical.

'But it was my idea,' said Cael with her mouth full of cake.

'We've all worked on the idea,' said Domhnall repressively. 'This sheet of wood is to represent the hall and you can see that I've divided it into three sections – the dais, up here, the portion of the middle of the hall, between the two top windows, is here, and the end portion, between the two end windows, is here.'

'I see,' said Mara. Complicated, she thought, but waited for the next.

'Slevin had the really good idea of using the pieces from the chess set,' said Domhnall with more enthusiasm. 'Explain, Slevin.'

No wonder that Domhnall had such influence over the boys, thought Mara. He had an instinct always to give praise and responsibility to those younger than he. If only Brehon MacClancy had behaved like that with Enda . . . And then she shut down her thoughts quickly. She had been on the verge, she realized, of concluding with the words *then this murder might not have happened.*

'Go on, Slevin,' she said aloud as he stood expectantly in front of her with the box of chessmen in his hand. One by one he took them out and placed them on the dais section of the board, naming them as he went. They had used the white king and queen for herself and Turlough, the black king and queen for Conor and his wife, Ellice. The white bishop was for Enda and the black bishop for Raour. Macon was the white knight and his daughter, Shona, the black knight. The four castles stood for the four professionals: the harpist, the poet, the Brehon and the physician. Five white pawns represented the law-school scholars and two black pawns the MacMahon twins. The set of figures was a large and elaborate one carved from wood, and plated with a thin layer of silver for the white pieces and copper for the black pieces. Each of the figures now bore around its neck a small scarf of vellum where the name was written in tiny but distinct capitals.

'Marvellous,' said Mara with enthusiasm.

'We'll show you how it works, Brehon,' said Domhnall. 'Make sure that you have clean hands everyone.' He waited, effortlessly in command, while the others dipped their fingers into the basin to the side of the fire, and then wiped them on the linen napkin resting on a stool.

'In order of age; youngest first,' he commanded.

It was interesting, thought Mara, that these young people hardly hesitated when they came to placing the figures. There were a few odd things.

Cormac did not remember the position of either of his parents.

Cael placed her father Maccon in the bottom third of the room, but opposite to the window recess where the Brehon MacClancy was drinking.

Only Cian had seen Enda go towards the Brehon.

But all had seen Raour approach him.

'Well,' said Mara, rising to her feet. 'That was extremely interesting. Now I wonder could I give some advice about the interviewing of the rest of the people. I think,' she went on without waiting for an answer, 'it might be best if we bring people in one by one and without making a fuss about it. So Art, could you go and tell Fionn O'Brien that I want a word with him in the solar.'

Fionn O'Brien put himself, predictably, in the top half of the room, standing talking to Turlough during the 'Hey Jig'. He remembered the position of fewer people than did the children – but that was to be expected. Mara herself found it hard to remember what she had been doing during that particular dance, but put that down to her lack of musical knowledge. She was happy to accept the verdict of the scholars who had her standing by the table – drinking, according to Cael.

One by one they came in, and to all outward appearance they were amused and interested by the exercise. Several, though, did corroborate Cael's observance of Enda – Raour went so far as to claim to hear the words when he moved down to check that the hatch between the great hall and the small kitchen was locked.

'Went to see whether Rosta had any decent wine,' he claimed, 'but there wasn't a sound from inside, so I reckoned they had all gone downstairs to the main guard hall.'

'And Enda's words, what were they?' queried Mara.

Raour frowned. 'I think he said something like "*You can't do this,*" but I wouldn't swear to it. There was no reason why I should take notice of it.'

'And what did you think that he meant by that?'

'I thought he might be reproaching the man for getting drunk,' said Raour.

It was a reasonable explanation, but Mara, with the knowledge of that letter confirming Raour's ennoblement at the hands of Henry VIII, was not convinced. There was a guarded look in the young man's eye and she thought that the hand which moved the pieces with their identifying scarves had slightly trembled.

Poised between boyhood and adulthood, he had the sharp visual memory of the younger children and his choices of position almost exactly matched theirs.

Shona, on the other hand, though close in age, declared firmly that she just could not remember. When urged to try, her hands trembled so much that Domhnall politely offered her some elderberry cordial. She refused that abruptly, said that she had a headache and Mara allowed her to depart, gazing thoughtfully after her.

The door had not closed behind her when one of the castle's servants appeared in its gap.

'The physician asked me to see you, Brehon,' he said. 'I was to tell you that he is ill with a fever and has to keep to his bed for the next few days.'

Oh really, thought Mara with annoyance. What an old woman he is to be cosseting himself like this. And no suggestion of sending for another physician. An unpleasant thought came to her mind. If Donogh O'Hickey could not or would not investigate the dead body, she would have to do it herself.

With the help of her scholars she would cross-question all of the guests that were present during that time – less than an hour, she reckoned – when the Brehon, sitting in the window recess, sullenly swilling the mead, while others danced, was secretly and unlawfully done to death. One by one the guests would be interrogated and sooner or later the motive and means would be extracted and the guilty person arraigned and the verdict of the court delivered.

However, when Finbar was despatched for Maccon MacMahon, there was a surprise. Peering over his shoulder with an apologetic expression on his face was Turlough.

'Maccon wanted me to come,' he explained to his wife. 'He wanted me to explain to you that he has urgent business at home. He must leave either tonight or first thing tomorrow morning.'

'No way,' said Cael. 'We're having too much fun – dead bodies, and all that sort of thing.'

'You'll do what you're told,' retorted Macon with unusual severity; he normally treated his two younger children with amused tolerance, while he hardly took any notice at all of Shona.

'You're not in charge here,' retorted Cian. 'She is.' He pointed a grubby thumb at Mara and she suppressed a smile. His words however, made it harder for her to insist on Maccon's presence, on him remaining within the walls of Bunratty Castle, when Turlough, the King, had obviously already acquiesced to his clansman's departure.

'As we agreed, my lord,' she addressed Turlough with careful control, 'it is essential that all guests remain with the castle grounds until the guilty person is found, or confesses.'

'And that could be never,' exclaimed Cael triumphantly.

'May I send Cael and Cian for some more elderberry cordial, Brehon?' asked Domhnall with careful tact. When she nodded, he said carelessly, 'You go, too, Slevin, no hurry.'

Slevin got to his feet with a grin, took up the tray and said to the twins in seductive tones, 'I'll tell you what; let's see if Rosta is making any wafers. I'd love a few; wouldn't you? They're just so good, hot from the griddle.'

A pair of clever boys, my two eldest scholars, thought Mara as the three left the room. Domhnall had understood that she wanted to get rid of the twins, and Slevin had instantly picked up on his intention. She sat back as Maccon, with a frown between his eyes, carelessly set out the figures on the replica of the great hall where Brehon MacClancy had met his death last night. He paused for a moment with the representative of the physician in one hand and then put him at the end of the hall, not too far from where the window recess where Brehon MacMahon had sat drinking. Then, after a moment's hesitation, he moved the figure again and put it by the hatch to the kitchen.

'I'm not sure,' he said apologetically. 'I remember looking at him wondering whether he was going to dance. He hadn't done so during the evening, had just sat by the table, chatting to various people.' He gazed at the few sparse figures that he had positioned and said with a grimace, 'I'm afraid I'm not a very good witness. I'm not very observant, I think. Now about this business of mine, Brehon . . .'

'I'll let you know the instant it is possible for you to leave,' promised Mara and was relieved when the door opened and the three, Slevin and the twins, came in with a tray bearing a flagon of elderberry cordial and a pile of fragrantly tempting wafers. Everyone took the refreshments happily – even Mara partook in order to praise the wafers.

It was only when the tray was cleared the scholars returned to the work. And then Turlough, more by chance than tact, she thought, caused a diversion by demanding to have his turn and he firmly clustered all of the pawns down in the window recess at the end of the hall and said cheerfully, 'I'm suspicious about these youngsters; they were all having a bit of knife practice and one of them went astray.'

Cael and Cian eyed each other uncertainly, but the five law-school scholars, all of them well used to Turlough's sense of humour, giggled almost uncontrollably. Death, thought Mara

charitably, is always a shock. A few giggles would do no harm
and she decided to pretend not to hear. She was surprised,
though, to see how that the twins had reacted with uneasy
glances passing between them. Neither of them laughed and
they seemed taken aback by the reaction of the law-school
scholars.

Maccon, she decided, was not much of a father. He hardly
glanced at his own children and certainly did not appear to
take any notice of their reaction to Turlough's jest. He did
not, however, pester her with any more requests and she hoped
that he had become resigned to staying.

As the day went on she began to feel more and more
puzzled. Domhnall and Slevin had dismissed the others to
run around in the open air and had their heads together in
their room over the sheaf of notes which had resulted from
their elaborate scheme. From listening to the evidence, and
from a cursory glance at these notes, Mara feared that they
were not going to help the investigation too much. Oddly
it didn't seem as though anyone, except Enda, had gone near
to Brehon MacClancy in that time, and somehow she found
it hard to believe that Enda, though driven by love from
Shona and sympathy at her plight, would turn to murder;
after all, even if something had happened, Enda was still
ready to marry her.

Unless, of course . . . now her thoughts went to the
unpleasant, power-hungry old man which the once venerated
Brehon MacClancy had turned into. He would have had power
over Shona and power sometimes led to abuse. If that were
the case . . . Well, then, she thought, Enda's fury might have
known no bounds.

Mara sighed. She thought wryly of Turlough's touching
belief that she might have had everything solved by breakfast
time that morning past.

'I'm not too sure of anything,' she muttered as she left the
room and descended the stairs, 'but there is one thing that I
must do. I must check whether the keys to the Brehon's press
are in the man's pouch, or somewhere on the body, perhaps
attached to a belt.' A shudder of distaste went over her; nevertheless, she went steadily on down the stairs.

A thick mist had arisen, she saw, looking out through one of the small, narrow window loops on the staircase inside the north-eastern tower. Cormac, Art, Finbar together with the twins were chasing around the greensward in front of the castle, Cormac eluding capture by taking to a leafless beech tree with a tall narrow mossy trunk. She could barely see them at first but then the mist lightened for a moment and she stopped to watch with amusement. The twins were the pursuers, armed with lumps of clay from the river, rather than their throwing knives, she was glad to see. As Mara watched, one clay ball splattered against the back of Finbar's best cloak and he sank dramatically to the ground. Cian seized his feet and he was hauled off towards the boathouse on the riverbank. Mara wondered whether she should intervene, but decided to leave them alone. The twins were an odd pair. It was hard to know how much they knew but Mara had an uneasy feeling that they were concealing something – something which might be of importance. She continued on her way, passing the great hall and going down the next flight of stairs, beyond the captain's set of rooms and down into the main guard hall.

All was as usual there. The main guard hall was for the men-at-arms. They ate there, talked, sang, worked there and slept there at night on straw-filled pallets. When Mara came in she saw that the trestle tables for the meals were dismantled and piled up at the sides of the room. A group of guards were talking in front of the fire, another group were sharpening their swords and others were rubbing oil into wooden leather-covered shields. There was a pause in the lively conversation and snatches of song when she came in and the captain came forward instantly.

'Anything that I can do for you, Brehon,' he said, immediately attentive to the King's wife.

'I wonder could you lend me a couple of your men, Captain,' said Mara making a great effort to sound cool and unconcerned. 'I wish to examine the dead body and could do with some assistance. I understand that the physician is ill.'

He made haste to assure her that all the men and anything else that she wanted would be at her disposal. There was an uneasy sound to his voice and Mara understood. This man was responsible for security within the castle and a death during a festival was something which concerned him intimately. She wondered for a moment what relationship he had with the Brehon of Thomond and then dismissed the thought from her mind. Tomás had been killed less than an hour after the return of the King's guests to the main hall. The people in the main hall, the King's relations and his best friends, unlikely as it seemed, were the only ones who could be guilty of the crime.

'If I could just borrow two of your men,' she requested. 'That's really all that I need.'

She thought of asking for one of the trestle stands and its boards, also, but decided that was unfair. In all probability, the table would be taken back and used for dining on later on in the evening. There might be a stone slab down in the basement that could be used.

Without making further demands, she led the way down the stairs to the basement and inserted the key in the lock.

There was a ghastly damp chill that seemed to rush out from the basement once the door was opened. Easy to see how legends about ghosts could arise. However, to Mara's relief, there was no smell of corruption. The two men stood back and she advanced in, trying to hide a shudder as a scampering noise told her that there had been a rat close by. One of the men raised his lantern and she saw the long bald tail disappear through a grating at the far side of the cellar.

'Leads to the river, Brehon,' said one of the men, picking up a stone and firing it in the direction of the grating. 'They used to get rid of prisoners down there in the old days, I have heard tell,' he added. He went across the damp flags that paved the nearest third of the room, his iron-tipped boots striking sharp echoes from the stones. 'It's got a latch on this side,' he said holding up his lantern when they reached the iron grille, 'but you can see, Brehon, that the grid is too small for anyone to put a hand through. They say that King Conor na Srona got rid of many an enemy down through this grating. Used to wait until high tide came and then the minute it began to ebb they would chuck the bodies through and the river would carry them down to the sea.'

'Really,' said Mara. She wondered whether her husband's uncle was really as bloodthirsty as that, or whether the man was just delaying the evil hour when the corpse had to be taken from the lead-lined box.

The captain of the guard, she noticed, had taken the precaution of locking the box, too. It took a long time for it to be unlocked – she suspected that the hand which held the key trembled somewhat, but when at last the lid was thrown back she heard them sigh with relief.

'Stiff as a poker, Brehon.'

'No doing anything with that body for a few hours, Brehon.'

'It's the cold that does it – you remember, Peadar, when we fought that battle in snow – there was one fellow, two days later, out there on the field, still with his arm stretched out and a throwing knife clenched in his hand.'

'Might never unstiffen,' said Peadar hopefully. 'Might be best to bury him in this box – good as any coffin – better than most.'

'Is there any possibility of getting at his pouch?' queried Mara. Perhaps the men were right, she thought, though conscious of her weakness. Perhaps the best thing would be to bury him as he was. Donogh O'Hickey had taken to his bed and was unlikely to rise from it before the body was safely underground. After all, she argued with herself, inspecting the wound would not tell much to an untrained person like herself.

'I'll see if I can get that out for you, Brehon.' Peadar sounded cheerful at that lesser demand and cautiously tried to insert his hand into the fold where the body had been bent in two in order to accommodate it to the short square shape of the box.

It was no good, though. The body was locked into position like a piece of forged iron and there seemed no possibility of getting at the pouch. The men had lifted in the shoulders, head and trunk, and then bent the pliable hips and legs over it.

'No, it's not possible,' said Mara standing back. There was an awful indignity about the way that the body had been

crammed into the box and she felt that she could not bear to
see it again. Peadar's suggestion was probably the right one.
The man should probably be left as he was and buried with
a few ceremonial cloths draped over the cask.

Ten

Óire
(Text on Honour Prices)

Every person in the kingdom has an honour price. This honour price is a measure of status in the kingdom. Women without a trade or a profession take the honour price of their husband or father. Children under the age of seventeen have the honour price of their father. A Brehon has to know the honour prices of all. No judgement can be given, no fine imposed without this knowledge as the first part of the fine is the honour price.

List of Fines:
The honour price of a king is: forty-two séts, or twenty-one milch cows, or twenty-one ounces of silver.
The honour price of a Brehon is: sixteen séts, or eight milch cows, or eight ounces of silver.
The honour price of a taoiseach (chieftain) is: ten séts, or five ounces of silver, or five milch cows.
The honour price of a physician is: seven séts, or four milch cows or three-and-a-half ounces of silver.
The honour price of a blacksmith is: seven séts, or four milch cows or three-and-a-half ounces of silver.
The honour price of a goldsmith is: seven séts, or four milch cows or three-and-a-half ounces of silver.
The honour price of a silversmith is: seven séts, or four milch cows or three-and-a-half ounces of silver, or four cows.
The honour price of a wheelwright is: seven sets, or four milch cows or three-and-a-half ounces of silver.
The honour price of a boaire (strong farmer) is: three séts, or two milch cows or one-and-a-half ounces of silver.
The honour price of an ocaire (small farmer) is: one sét or one heifer, or half an ounce of silver.

'A re those children still out in that fog?' Mara joined the
guards who were standing on ceremonial duty beside
the big front door. She peered out. It was bitterly cold – colder
than frost, even colder than snow, she thought and was relieved
when one of the men shook his head.

'No, Brehon, you've just missed them. They went in. Young
Cormac wanted to pull up the drawbridge, but we told him
to ask the King first.' The man had a grin on his face and
Mara guessed that he wouldn't be surprised if Turlough,
accompanied by a triumphant Cormac, appeared with an
apologetic request for the drawbridge to be raised.

The moat, she thought, was constructed in more warlike
times. It was part of the former castle which had been burned
down, rebuilt, attacked, demolished through a few hundred
years. There had been a time when the clans had all been at
each other's throats, when O'Brien had fought against
MacNamara and MacNamara against O'Brien, and the castle
continually changed ownership between those powerful clans.
It had even been briefly possessed by the invaders from
England. The Norman Thomas de Clare had established his
family there and had built a village around it. The attacks
had gone on with the native Irish trying to repossess the
castle and even its stately hall had seen the shedding of blood
– there was one grisly story when Brian Ruadh O'Brien
sought Norman-English help against his nephew Turlough
Mór. Mara remembered the story, chanted by Aengus
MacCraith on all state occasions.

'After they had poured their blood into the same vessel and
after they had pledged Christ's friendship and they had
exchanged mutual vows by the relics, bells and crosiers of
Munster, the Norman de Clare had Brian Ruadh turn asunder
by horses and within the hall itself, his head was cut off and
his body gibbeted on a tall post outside the castle.'

But now Turlough had managed to get the love and loyalty
of all of the warlike clans within the three kingdoms:
MacNamara, MacMahon, O'Lochlainn, O'Connor, O'Nealain
and MacGorman all gave him fealty and military service. The
enemy now was outside his three kingdoms: the English and
those that they had planted in Irish soil: the Earls of Kildare

and Ormond in the east of the country and the Earl of Desmond in the south. They and their relations were now the enemy of such like Turlough Donn O'Brien who sought to live their lives according to the customs and laws of their Gaelic ancestors.

Mara peered through the mist at the sweep of the moat, at the high wall that encircled the small village, at the drawbridge and the murder hole and smiled at the men.

'I hope you have promised to call Cormac if there is an assault made on the castle,' she said with a smile and they laughed with her, glad of the interlude during the boredom of their spell on guard. How did they occupy the time, she wondered? She had seen the dice in one man's hand, but that must get boring also. She went up the stairs within the north-eastern tower feeling glad that, despite moments like that in the basement of the castle, she had such an interesting occupation that engaged all of her mind. The solar, to her relief, was empty of quarrelling youngsters. She would sit quietly by herself, not think and not try to work matters out; just let ideas and impressions float across her mind and see whether a name came up that would lead her to solving this murder. She went across to the fireplace to insert another few small sections of branches and logs under the glowing tree trunk that stayed alight night and day, suspended across the hearth, resting on iron stands.

Fionn O'Brien, she noticed, glancing down, was in the great hall, talking animatedly with Turlough, though there was no sign of his wife, Aideen. Fionn, she thought, as she went back to draw a cushioned chair near to the fire, was spending a lot of time this Christmas in Turlough's company, eagerly agreeing with everything he said and striving to please and amuse his clan chieftain. Turlough, though preferring the company of his old friend Maccon MacMahon, was good-natured and willing to be entertained.

Where did Fionn come in the complicated family tree of the O'Brien royalty? Certainly he would be descended from the same great-grandfather and this would give him the possibility of being elected as *tánaiste* if anything happened to the King's eldest son, the delicate Conor. The vultures begin to gather, thought Mara. Conor was not looking at all well. His hollow cough sounded continuously through the stairways, and unless summoned for meals, he and Ellice seemed to spend most of their time in their own quarters: the south solar and the bedroom beside it which were positioned at the top of the south-eastern tower. The clan were uneasy; he was not going to be a charismatic, courageous leader like his father, King Turlough Donn. They would not be human if they were not already looking for someone else. A window of opportunity had opened up for other junior members of the clan – always providing that the present King would approve of the candidate and, because he loved him very dearly, that the feelings of his son, Conor, were not hurt by the substitution.

If that someone else were Conor's own son Raour, the probability was strong that Conor would be happy to stand back and to allow the youngster to take his place. But Conor's opinion would matter little to the clan – it was the opinion of his grandfather, Turlough Donn, which would be of import-ance and if Turlough found out about the title of baron which was bestowed by the English King Henry VIII on the young man when he was in London, then wild horses would not get him to consent to the naming of Raour as *tánaiste* and the clan would take seriously an objection from a king as popular as Turlough.

And what about Fionn O'Brien? Was there any reason why he should or should not be a suitable candidate? Had the mali-cious Brehon MacClancy found out anything about him?

Mara's mind was busy with these questions as she sat and gazed into the fire and for a minute the sharp crack from behind where she sat passed almost unnoticed.

A bird's beak, she thought, and then thought again. The short winter's day had drawn to a close and few birds would still be flying free, but would have taken shelter for the night. She was already on her feet when a sharp draught of cold, foggy air was drawn across the room towards the blazing fire. Mara picked up a candle branch from its place beside the fire and walked across the room, lighting another cluster of candles on a small table near the window. Instinctively she avoided the loose tile which gave entrance to the chute descending to the murder hole and put her candles down on the windowsill.

There was no doubt that one of the small panes of glass had been shattered, and no doubt, either, what had shattered it.

Lying on a cushion beside the window was a small lightweight knife. It transfixed a piece of vellum; she recognized it as one of the scrap pieces resulting from the trimming of large pieces to document shape. These were distributed to the scholars and they usually had a few in their pouches. This one bore the word 'HELP!' written in charcoal.

Mara instantly flung open the window and leaned out. The fog was worse, but there was an unmistakable cry of help from across the yard between the castle and the barns and stables. There seemed to be something white fluttering from the apex of the barn roof and once again the cry of 'Help' penetrated the dense fog.

This time she recognized the voice. It was Cormac's, and a secondary less decisive call was probably Finbar's voice.

'Help, we've been locked in!' came Cormac's voice.

Instantly Mara pulled up the tiled board near her feet. The murder hole was dark and smelled of mould and probably of mice or rats, she thought. She didn't hesitate, however, but pitching her voice as well as she could into the dark rounded funnel, she yelled: 'The King's son has been locked in the barn.'

She heard a confused noise of men's voices, but did not wait any longer. Picking up her skirt with one hand she was through the door and clattering down the spiral staircase. When she reached the next level, Rosta emerged from the kitchen, ladle in hand, looking at her with surprise.

'There's something wrong,' she gasped. 'Cormac has been locked in the barn. Get the King.'

And if this turned out to be one of Cormac's pranks, then so much the worse for him, she thought as she ran down the next flight of stairs. And yet, she didn't think so. There had been a note of panic in the voice of her too-courageous son. She did not hesitate when she came to the main guard hall. It would be full of men, but she had already communicated with the men on guard and it was urgent to get Cormac from that barn. As the King's youngest son, he might be thought a bargaining pawn for any enemy.

And if an enemy were to attack Bunratty Castle, this evening of freezing fog, while the Christmas festivities were going on, it might be an ideal time to catch the garrison off guard.

There would be, she thought as she whirled down the last circular set of steps, a guard on the gate at the bridge across the moat, but it would be a perfunctory affair, and there might have been a distraction.

As she reached the drawbridge, she heard a shout. It was Cormac's unmistakable voice.

'He's gone, Brehon,' he yelled at the sight of his mother. 'He's gone. He locked us in the barn and he took the twins.'

Instantly Mara understood. One part of her wanted to go and to make sure that Cormac was unhurt, that no one had injured him, or that he hadn't fallen in his frantic attempts to escape from the loft of the huge barn, but his voice was clear and strong and she could not let his cleverness and quick thinking go for naught.

'Quick,' she shouted to the men that had followed her from the castle. 'Quick, go to the gate. Quick, stop him, stop Maccon MacMahon.'

Somewhere at the back of the crowd, she heard Turlough's voice and then the captain of the guard bellowing orders. They would be getting into fight formation, but she ignored them. This was no attack, she realized thankfully. But at the same time she was filled with fury. That any man would dare to disobey her commandment, would leave the castle when she had specifically forbidden any guests to depart before she gave permission, this brought the energy of youth to her legs and she ran as fast as she could down the little cobbled street between the houses.

There was something on the bridge. She could see the forms through the mist as she rounded the churchyard. An unmistakable neigh came from one horse and then was answered by another. A voice was raised, shouting angrily, and she recognized the powerful bass tones of Maccon MacMahon, now filled with fury. But he was still on this side of the gate. Thankfully, she slowed down and gulped some air into her chest. There were footsteps behind her and Cormac, accompanied as always by Art, caught up with her.

'He locked us in the barn,' said Cormac dramatically.

'Took the ladder away when the three of us were up there,' amended Art, always a stickler for the exact truth.

'And he hit one of the twins when he tried to follow us.' Finbar's voice came in gasps, but he was determined to share the moment.

'And he's a girl,' added Cormac rather confusingly, but with a note of outrage in his voice. He himself was not slow to wrestle with Cael, but it was a different matter for her father to hit her. Cormac at his worst had never been hit by either of his parents as Mara had decided long ago that there would be no corporal punishment in her school. Her scholars, she had resolved, would be motivated to learn for the interest in the law and perhaps out of competition with each other, but not because of fear. And Turlough, of course, was so enraptured by this son of his later life that Cormac could get away with murder so far as he was concerned.

'Tell me later,' said Mara. She slowed her steps to a stately walk. Plenty of men had passed her and were now crowded onto the bridge. The guard at the gate had held. Now it was for her to bring the majesty of the law to bear on Maccon MacMahon, to order him back to the castle and to keep a strict eye on him.

'She'll put him in the dungeon with the rats,' remarked Cormac gloatingly to Art.

'And chained to the ground, down beside the dead body,' added Art with relish and Mara, while suppressing a smile, hoped that the same thought was going through the head of Maccon MacMahon at this very moment.

Maccon was making a huge fuss as they approached. 'I keep telling you that I have permission from the King himself. He will be so angry if he is dragged out here just because you have to be so stubborn and so stupid. Why should the King want to delay me on my important business? He knew that I would only stay for a short time.'

Maccon, thought Mara, was a quick thinker. He had taken advantage of the heavy cover that the fog would have afforded and stolen out. The first flaw in his arrangements had been dislodging the three law-school boys from the twins. His second,

of course, was to underestimate Mara and not to realize that
she would have given instructions to the captain of the guard
that no guests were to be permitted to leave. She marched up
to the group now, and ignoring him for the moment, thanked
the men on the guard for their carefulness, and then gave
instructions to the captain who had arrived at that moment to
escort the MacMahon and his children to their quarters in the
south-eastern tower. For Turlough's sake she would not put
them under arrest in the main guard, but she added in a clear
voice, 'And, Captain, will you have one of your men wait in
the room with the MacMahon.' This, she hoped, would make
sure that Maccon would not prime his children with any false
information.

'Take your hand off me!' Maccon was in a belligerent frame
of mind; the sound of Turlough's voice in the distance seemed
to egg him on to fresh protests.

'Mara,' he began but she swept past him. Like the other
guests he had addressed her as 'Brehon' during the feast and
she was irritated by this attempt at familiarity.

'The captain of the guard will take care of you for the
moment,' she said in an offhand manner. 'And you, Shona,'
she continued. Then she put her hand on Cian's pony and
said to him authoritatively, 'Dismount and lead your pony.' He
did so in silence and Cael copied her twin. She thanked them
gravely and walked in between them, but when she came to
the door and met Domhnall and Slevin, she seized the
opportunity.

'These two young people,' she said, indicating the twins,
'have information that will be of huge importance to this case.
Slevin, will you take the ponies to the stable and ask one of
the lads to see to them. When you have done that, please join
Domhnall. Domhnall, I want you to stand on guard outside
the solar while I am questioning them. Cormac, please find the
King and tell him that the captain of the guard will inform
him about the attempted escape from the castle and then come
back and join us, Cormac. Your evidence will be useful. It
was very quick-witted of you three young scholars to find a
way of informing me what was going on,' she said gravely and
saw them straighten with pride.

Slevin went off with the ponies and Cormac, after a quick request to his mother to keep his throwing knife safe for him, went around towards the south side of the castle, where Turlough, by the sound of his voice, seemed to be surveying the river.

'Come up the solar with me,' she invited the twins, and smiled to herself to see how Art and Finbar flanked the pair as if they were guards in charge of a pair of prisoners.

'What happened?' she asked them when they arrived. Eyeing their white faces and blue fingernails she made them sit beside the fire and handed each a sweetmeat from the dish on the table.

'It was not our fault,' said Cian defensively. 'We were made to go.'

'Forced by duress vile,' said Cael. She eyed Mara. 'Does this mean that we won't get the silver you promised us?'

Mara smiled. 'You just keep on working for me. What did your father say? Why did he suddenly decide to take you away?'

Cael shrugged and Cian copied her. 'Don't know,' she said. 'He doesn't give us reasons. He came out to the barn and we were up in the loft and he shouted to us to come down. Didn't say nothing. Just shouted at us to get on our ponies. He had them ready. He and Shona were already mounted.'

'And then he took the ladder away,' added Cian. 'Cormac shouted down after us: "Where are you going?" and he didn't answer and hit Cael when she tried to argue.'

'Did Shona know where you were going, or why?' asked Mara.

'She didn't say anything to us,' said Cael. 'We don't talk to her much.'

The twins, thought Mara, lived a life that was quite separate from their father and their elder sister. Living in fosterage at Brehon MacClancy's place at Urlan they would see little of their father – probably only during this Christmas festivity had they had any contact with them. Shona, who had been living at home with him during the past year, would be a more fruitful source of information. She got to her feet.

'Let's go and find the others,' she said.

However, when they reached the landing outside the great

hall, Turlough's voice sounded from within. He and Cormac must have gone up the stairs of the south-western tower.

'And I sent my throwing knife through the solar window because I knew that the Brehon would have a fit if any of her suspects had escaped her,' came Cormac's light high voice and Turlough laughed heartily. Mara sighed. That was a mistake to have sent Cormac to his father. Instead of an outraged captain of the guard telling his King about the attempted escape of a guest, a possible suspect in a murder case, a guest who, like the other guests, had been ordered to remain with the castle grounds, what had happened now was that Cormac and Turlough between them were turning the matter into high farce.

Just as Turlough opened the door from the great hall, Rosta limped heavily down from the stairs leading from the King's private quarters. He was carrying a hammer and had a few nails sticking out of his mouth, which he removed at the sight of his King.

'I've just hammered a piece of board over the hole in the window, my lord,' he said to Turlough. 'Nasty night out there, we don't want that mist and cold getting into your room. The carpenter will make a proper job of it tonight while you are at your dinner in the hall. I've sent a message to him. But in the meantime, that temporary job will hold.'

'Good man yourself,' said Turlough. 'Don't know what I would do without you, Rosta. This place would fall to pieces if you weren't here keeping an eye on everything for us.'

What a nice man Turlough is, thought Mara, feeling a rush of affection for her husband. Rosta's face lit up with pleasure and she could see how important the King's opinion was to this man whose life as a fighter was now over, but who brought to his position as cook to the King the same dedication and single-minded devotion he had shown when a warrior.

She turned to her husband with an affectionate smile.

'Perhaps the other scholars could go with you while you are checking your boundaries, my lord,' she said formally and then she added, with emphasis. 'I would like to speak to the MacMahon in a little while by myself and I have asked the captain of the guard not to let him communicate with anyone else until I have a chance to talk to him first.' She looked at Turlough intently and hoped that he would get the point that she didn't want him talking to MacMahon before she had a chance to interrogate the man herself.

Fortunately there was a clamour of suggestions from the scholars, advising where to check for intruders, and Turlough, with a wink at her, took them off.

Mara glanced down at the twins. They were wet, white-faced and downcast. She felt very sorry for them and looked an appeal at Rosta. He nodded cheerfully in reply and encircled each with a large arm.

'Go with Rosta,' she said gently. 'He could do with some help and your wet clothes will dry in the warmth of the kitchen.'

And then she went across to the south-eastern tower and prepared to interrogate Maccon MacMahon.

'Shona, would you wait in your room,' she said when she came in and found Maccon and his daughter sitting listlessly by the fire while the captain of the guard stood stiffly by the door. There did not seem to be much contact between father and daughter. Maccon sat one side of the fire, staring into it, and Shona on the other side, her face buried in her hands. Mara wondered whether she was weeping but as soon as she spoke, Shona looked up, dry-eyed, but white-faced. There was an air of tension and of apprehension about her, but she got to her feet immediately and without a word left the room. Mara could hear her footsteps going up the stairway.

'Would you wait outside,' she said to the captain. She had wanted to interrogate Maccon by herself, but it was, she thought, important for a man who had already defied her orders to know that he was still under armed guard. She waited for the door to close and then looked across at Maccon in silence.

'Could you give me the reason why you defied my orders,' she said after a minute.

He sighed with feigned exasperation. 'But I have already told you, Brehon, that I had urgent business at home.'

'What business?' She snapped out the question almost before

he had time to finish his sentence and was pleased to see how discomforted he looked.

'It's private,' he said after a moment.

'Very suspicious,' she shot back her response.

He bristled. 'Why suspicious?'

'Because I'm sure, with your family connections to a Brehon, you know that anything you tell me in confidence will remain secret. I think,' said Mara, in a reflective tone, 'I, personally, would feel it better to confide, in strict secrecy, some business matter, than to be suspected of murder.'

That shook him. His voice rose in pitch. 'I had nothing whatsoever to do with the murder of Brehon MacClancy – I swear by all that I hold most sacred, I'll swear even by the lives of my children that I had nothing at all to do with that.'

There was a note of sincerity in his voice and her heart sank. She had begun to think, during the last hour, that she might have found the murderer, might with some more probing find the motive and would be able to announce the result. It might, she had been thinking, have something to do with Shona – a revenge killing, perhaps. The flight could have been prompted by MacMahon's pride, his reluctance to confess his guilt in front of his King – and perhaps in front of a woman, she had thought on her way up the stairs – reminding herself that she was not now on her home territory in the Burren where the people of that stony kingdom had accepted a female Brehon over twenty-four years ago and had been content to be judged by her ever since. The people of Thomond might have different ideas and under a show of respect to the King's wife might not like the idea of a woman sitting in judgement over them.

But she could not now hide from herself the instinct that MacMahon spoke with some sincerity. As she gazed at him appraisingly, confident that her face showed only a polite interest, her mind whirled. So why had he been so insistent to leave? Why had he grabbed the twins and taken them from the fun and companionship which they were enjoying so hugely? Even if he truly had urgent business, some sort of deal which he dared not miss, why take them? And why take Shona? Unless he wanted to separate her from Enda, of course.

At that moment there was a gentle tap on the door. The captain of the guard stood there and beyond him was Turlough. He was by himself, so the children had taken themselves off.

'My lord wishes to speak with you, Brehon,' said the captain and without waiting for instructions, he slid in through the open door, joining MacMahon inside and shutting the door firmly behind him. Turlough withdrew into the window recess on the landing and Mara followed him, more curious than annoyed. Turlough had a huge reverence for her work as Brehon and would not have interrupted unless it were something of importance.

'Just thought of something.' His whisper in her ear was loud and would probably carry. However, there was nobody on the stairs so she did not interrupt him, just nodded for him to continue.

'You remember the body?' He waited for her nod before going on.

'*Yes, I do vaguely recollect a body*,' she felt like saying.

'Well, I'd say that it was a *citóg* stuck the knife into him.'

'What! A left-handed person.' All her impatience vanished, but then she was sceptical. 'How on earth could you tell? You only just looked at him and then the knife fell out.'

'I'm sure though.' Turlough was finding the whispering too tedious and had reverted to his normal, battlefield tones. 'Been looking at wounds since I was Cormac's age.'

'I see,' said Mara. She heaved a sigh. 'You're going to tell me now that Maccon is right-handed.'

'That's it.' Turlough beamed at her with such pride in her cleverness that she tried to shake off her annoyance.

'Can you tell me if any one of the guests is left-handed,' she said wearily.

'Just Raour – but of course he had nothing to do with the matter. The boy hardly knew Brehon MacClancy. I'd say that he hardly exchanged more than three sentences with him,' said Raour's grandfather with a touching faith which Mara felt unable to disturb at this stage. She hoped, sincerely, that Turlough would not have to know about his grandson's treachery – probably more a boy's vanity and a manipulation of him by those in charge of Henry VIII's household, she thought. If it turned out that Raour had nothing to do with the murder of Brehon MacClancy, who had noted the evidence of his title, then she would have a private word with Raour, she decided. Probably he might now be regretting matters and could be easily persuaded to give up this empty title and to adhere to his grandfather's belief in Gaelic Ireland.

So Raour is the only left-handed member among the guests at the Christmas supper, she thought, as she nodded to Turlough and turned to go back to questioning Maccon MacMahon as to why he thought fit to disregard her command and leave the castle when he had been told that he should stay.

Though she thought that she had kept her face bland and expressionless, she was aware during the rest of the interview that he was subtly conscious of the change in her. His denials of any motive other than to deal with private business grew louder and more assertive – almost, she thought, as if panic at not being allowed to go had possessed him. She wondered why he was making such a huge fuss about the matter. Why should it be so important that he leave the castle on this very day?

'Rest assured that nothing you say will influence me to permit you to leave before I give the word,' she said with emphasis as she concluded her interrogation. She had almost said *before I have solved this murder* but it had come into her mind suddenly that this was a murder enquiry that might fail. Raour was the only left-handed person among the guests. and yet everyone had placed him as dancing in the lights in front of the pipe players. She herself had noticed him there and had smiled to herself. Heavy though he was, Raour was a talented dancer and was making certain that all would admire him. He had not strayed from the top of the room, beside the table on the dais for the whole evening. It did not seem possible that every single one of the guests, including Mara herself, would have overlooked a move to the bottom of the room where he would no longer be centre of attention and under his grandfather's eyes.

And then she suddenly thought back into the past and her heart plummeted.

Enda had come to her at the age of eight – older than most

of her pupils, but the very talented, very intelligent son of a farmer. She had straight-away noticed the left-handedness and had challenged him to overcome that difficulty and to acquire a script as neat and as legible as that of his right-handed companions. She had made no attempt to get him to use his right hand. He had been taught by the monks at Murrisk Abbey, who had attempted this and then had given up the struggle. She guessed that they had found it best to let him go his own way and to write left-handed. He was a determined boy and had risen to her challenge and soon become one of the brightest and most advanced scholars in her school.

It will break my heart if he has done this stupid thing, she thought.

Eleven

Cáin Adomnán
(The Law of Adomnán)

An offence against a woman is a more serious matter than an offence against a man of the same honour price. In the case of murder the culprit may, according to Church law, have a hand removed as well as paying the honour price of the woman, or that of her husband if she is without occupation. The normal eraic is also payable.

Brehon Law abhors violence against women who are unable to defend themselves.

Mara slept badly that night, and such sleep as she did attain was filled with bad dreams. Towards morning she fell into a deep, heavy sleep and by the time that she opened her eyes from this, she knew that some were already stirring. A sound of hammering came from outside their window, a few shouts from men-at-arms, and then the shrill sound of swords and throwing knives being sharpened against the huge stone that stood outside the front entrance to the castle.

The place beside her in the bed was empty and cold. She sat up abruptly. Turlough was seldom an early riser when he was with her. For a moment she feared that something had happened, but then she noticed the grey light coming through the window and realized that she had just over-slept. She got out of bed, visited the latrine, shuddered at the icy chill that came up from the moat and the river beyond, rapidly replaced cushion and board and having washed her hands in the bowl placed beside it, finished off the rest of her washing with the warm water which stood in a metal flagon beside the fire.

I hate looking untidy, she thought crossly as she braided her hair by touch and thought for the hundredth time that she must suggest to Turlough that a mirror would be an addition to the King's bedroom. She smiled slightly when she remembered Cael's querying her lack of a veil and then suddenly, as she inserted the pins, an idea sprang into her mind. She went to her pouch and counted out some small pieces of silver. There would be a fair in the nearby village to celebrate the eve of the Epiphany and she had planned to give the scholars some spending money before they set off on their journey back to the Burren.

But for the moment she had a better use for some of the money.

Still that interview had to take a background step for the moment. She could no longer shirk this unpleasant task. She had to know whether the murdered man had the keys to his press, or whether they had been stolen by someone.

She also, if she had the courage and the determination, had to resolve the problem of the knife. Did it kill him? And, if it did, why did it spontaneously fall from the wound? Could such a slight incision be responsible for any man's death? Or was there any chance that he had been poisoned? It would have been easier to achieve. But if so, there would be no reason for the knife in the back. Exasperated, Mara twitched her light cloak from the back of the door and draped it around her shoulders.

From the sound of the noisy voices, her scholars, she thought, were having breakfast. She peeped through the stairway wall slot but there was no sign of the physician breakfasting in the great hall. There was no help for the matter, thought Mara gritting her teeth with annoyance at the mental image of Donogh O'Hickey skulking on a sickbed. The body of Brehon MacClancy should now be quite soft and malleable and she admitted honestly to herself that as well as searching for the keys she should also slit the clothing and check on that wound which was so shallow that the knife had just fallen from its slot as the body's fibres cooled. She wished desperately for a competent physician, but it was no good wishing for what she could not have; she had been trained from early girlhood to do her duty whether it was pleasant or unpleasant. She continued down the stairs at a slower pace, deep in thought, and knocked on the door to the captain's room, half-hoping that he was not there, but he opened instantly, with cordial enquiries as to her health, the health of the King and her young scholars. Then he spent a few minutes discussing the music and praising the genius of the cook and eventually wound up by looking at her enquiringly.

'I just wondered whether I could trouble you for the keys to the basement and to the coffer?' said Mara trying to sound matter-of-fact and at ease.

'Oh, so the physician is better,' he stated and then with a worried note, 'There's no one here at the moment but I can send for some men if he wishes for help,' he said.

'No, no,' she said hurriedly. Whatever was to be done down there in the basement, she felt that she would prefer to be alone with her thoughts. There was no way that she was going to undertake an in-depth examination of the body – just a quick look to solve a few queries. In her pouch she carried the throwing knife which had inflicted the deadly wound – the knife belonging to the child, Cael. She had wrapped it carefully in a piece of the oilskin which she used to protect documents from the rain, but when she had taken it out this morning she found that the slight fishy smell had disappeared. Perhaps she had imagined it. And yet the picture came to her mind of Maccon MacMahon and Enda sharing a dish of lampreys and exclaiming loudly over the delicious flavour.

Mara had great difficulty with the lock to the basement. The key was enormous and the lock so stiff that nothing happened when she turned it. Eventually she put her two hands to it and twisted as hard as she could. There was a strange, groaning creak and the door moved back grudgingly, displaying a vast piece of antique ironmongery on its inside. There was a stone lying nearby and Mara guessed that it was often used to prop the door open – she could see a tell-tale groove in the wooden door frame, no doubt a precaution in case a sudden draught slammed it closed. She placed the stone in position, but nevertheless, she took the keys from the outside lock, picked up the small lantern of perforated steel which she carried with her and held it up to the walls until she found a small ledge where she laid the keys carefully. Then she held the lantern aloft again and shone its light towards the centre of the room. But the coffer was not where she had remembered. She shone the light steadily around, moving it along each of the four walls and then around the centre of the room. But she had made no mistake. There was no sign of the box which enclosed Brehon MacClancy's body.

And then, frowning slightly, she moved the lantern again. Something had caught her attention and a moment later she realized what had puzzled her. The gate of iron slats, where she had seen the rat with its long bald tail disappear the last time she had been in the basement, was now no longer latched shut, but was standing wide open.

And that was not all that she saw. The floor at that end of the basement was made from hammered clay and the marks showed up quite clearly – something heavy had been pushed across the floor and had disappeared into the river beyond the iron grille.

Filled with anger, Mara crossed the floor, still holding her metal lantern aloft. The floor continued to just beyond the grate and then it stopped abruptly. Below were the dark waters of the river. She peered down into the water. The tide was full, she reckoned. The last time that she had been here she had smelled wet mud and the rat had disappeared readily through the grille. Rats did swim, she knew, but thought that someone had told her that they did not like salt water. The River Shannon was tidal up to Bunratty Castle and beyond, so surely the water was salt here.

As she stood and glanced around something caught her eye, something just above her head. She moved inside the frame of the metal doorway, and looked upwards. It seemed as though some netting traps were stored there, something for fishing, she thought.

And just at that moment she thought she heard a movement from the room behind her. She spun around, shone the light from her lantern, but there was nothing to be seen. Her skin crawled. A rat, she thought. She lifted the lantern once more. One more glance, she thought, just one more look into the murky depths below her to see whether she could spot the container of her fellow Brehon's mortal remains. And then she would go back and call for assistance. The basement was only a few feet below ground level, but the ground probably fell away at this spot and the lead-lined box, when pushed, had tumbled to the bottom of the river. She had no idea how deep the water was here, but she thought that it would not be worth the risk of trying to retrieve it. The King's Brehon would be buried at sea, and she, Mara, would have to solve the murder of MacClancy without viewing the body once again. She turned back to go towards the door, noting with a puzzled frown that now it appeared to be closed, to be shut so tightly that no light came through it.

Then she heard a drawn-in breath and knew that she was not alone.

And, at that second, something hit the side of her head and shocked her into dropping the lantern from her hand. She overbalanced and tumbled into the water below her feet. At the same moment she heard the metal grille crash closed behind her and there was a sharp click as the bolt was shot home. Sick and dizzy, she fumbled for something to hold on to, but a surge of tidal water swept up, soaking the skirts of *léine*, gown and cloak and she sank beneath the surface. Her mouth filled with water and she tasted the salt. There was a sudden hurried movement just beside her, and for a moment she felt sick with horror as she pictured a shoal of rats swimming vigorously beside her. She struck out violently and instinctively and her hand struck something metal – a cage, she thought, and was shocked to see large eyes looking at her from the violently churning water inside it. She tried to grasp it, tried to hook a finger through the metal, but the outgoing tide swept her helplessly away, leaving her with the impression of silver bodies and wide round eyes. Giant fish, she thought and then realized that it had been a cage full of live salmon.

Mara had never learned to swim, but she had watched her farm manager, Cumhal, teach the small boys of her school. He had waited for a hot afternoon in late spring or early summer, then taken them down to Rathborney, tied a rope around their waist, lowered them into a pool in the Rathborney River, commanded them firmly to kick their legs and flap their arms and under no circumstances were they to even think about sinking. Such was his influence over them that they usually learned to swim that same day.

Now Mara knew that her life was in her own hands and

without hesitation she scooped the water with her hands and kicked frantically. Her head hurt so much from the blow that she felt weak and sick, but she was determined to make her way to the shore. *I cannot and I will not drown.* The words went through her head and she imagined them written on vellum in a fine Carolingian minuscule script with a goose quill dipped in thick black ink made from the bitterest gall.

He's not going to get away with this, she thought, dizzily imagining her murderer – he or she, perhaps, had killed once, and now intended to kill again. One more stroke, she told herself as she felt the bile rising in her mouth and she wondered what would happen to her if she had to stop her frantic splashing in order to vomit.

Sink, that's what would happen. She could not do it. She shut her mouth firmly and thought of her son and of her husband. Cormac needed her. She had given birth to him and she had to fulfil her unwritten contract to care for him, mind and body, until he was grown up. 'Cormac', she used the word like a sacred prayer, visualizing his face and the smell of newly washed hair, remembering his jokes, his courage, his cleverness, visualized his green eyes sparkling with fun, his disordered crop of red-blond hair. She needed to be around until he grew up. She concentrated on her son so intensely that the nausea faded and she began to feel herself move with the vigour of her exertions. Not many women have as much to live for as I do, she thought and wished that the fog was not too thick and that she could see the bank. The light was getting brighter though and she guessed that she had moved out of a tunnel of some sort and into the river that ran in front of the castle.

And then she heard something. Her ears were full of the noise of splashing water and she could not distinguish the nature of the sounds. But it seemed to come from quite near to her.

Once again Mara heard it – a splash as if a stone were hurled into the water. It made her heart stop. Her enemy must be out there, knowing where she was, able to pinpoint her exact position – the murderer couldn't help but hear the wild, noisy splashing which was her only way of keeping afloat. Once again the noise sounded, this time quite close to her ear. A heavy stone, she thought, by the way it hit the water. If that stone hit her head, her struggles would be over. She held her breath waiting. And then she thought that she heard something else. She tried to ease her frantic splashing and spluttering and to listen.

'Don't!' said a girl's voice abruptly. 'Don't throw stones; that's probably a dolphin. I love to watch them. Back at home they come to my whistle. Go inside, Raour; tell my father that you couldn't find me. Don't worry. I'll be in presently.'

'I suppose that you're waiting for your darling Enda.' Raour's voice was quite clear in the foggy air. Had he really thought that the frantic struggles were those of a dolphin, or was there a more sinister reason for the bombardment with large stones? He lobbed a few more in her direction and then she heard him say sulkily, 'I'm not telling any lies for you; your father can go and search for you himself.'

Mara strained her ears. There were no further sounds; she had not heard Raour leave; he could still be hanging resentfully around, trying to take Shona's attention, but she hoped desperately that he had left. I will have to take a chance, she thought, as she felt the weight of her clothes drag her down.

'Shona,' she called softly, but there was no reply. For a moment she panicked – perhaps the girl, after her initial defiance of her father's order, had after all, followed Raour back into the castle. Once again she splashed frantically, and then to her relief heard a soft whistle, almost like a call. The sound was nearer to the water. Shona must have walked down to the river edge. I must take a chance, thought Mara. She could feel her legs, hampered by the heavy folds of cloth, beginning to sink down below the surface. I must and I will get Shona's attention, she thought firmly. Her belief in her own abilities had seldom failed and now it lent strength to the shout as she bellowed out the girl's name. When she ceased she almost expected another blow to the side of her head, but her frantic splashings were the only sounds near to her.

'Wait!' The word was as unmistakable as it was welcome. Mara continued to beat the water, assuring herself that she could survive until Shona ran back to the castle and summoned help. And then, unbelievably, there was the sound of wood against water. Someone was rowing.

There was a small boathouse on the shore with a boat belonging to the kitchen staff there, she remembered. Either Rosta or one of his men used it to take the salmon from the net at the weir. With enormous presence of mind, Shona, instead of running for help, had taken a rowing boat out towards her. Now she could see the girl's back, the dark braided hair and the red cloak.

'Wait,' came Shona's voice again. 'There's a row of stakes here. They use them to tie up the boats at low tide.' Mara waited. She was no longer worried. There seemed to be something very competent and assured about Shona's voice and now that the boat was within her view she could see that it moved steadily and smoothly across the water.

'Can you catch a rope if I throw it?'

Mara gasped out something that she hoped sounded like yes. Catching the rope was more difficult than she had imagined. As soon as one arm ceased its frantic clawing of the water she began to slip beneath the surface and had to quickly resume her efforts. However, on the third attempt, she succeeded in snatching it. She slumped for a moment with relief and then, hearing a voice, lifted her head completely out of the water.

'Hold it with your two hands. I'll tow you; don't worry. You might get water on your face, but you won't sink while you keep hold of the rope.'

Shona's voice was still sensible and matter-of-fact and Mara felt a trust in the girl. Her admiration grew. No questions, no exclamations, just an immediate and practical response. A girl to rely on, thought Mara, as she heroically spat out water after a complete submerging. Clenching the rope with a grip of iron she tried to forget the cold, the awful choking from the water in her lungs, and she concentrated on Shona, willing her to have the strength to manage the boat and to take them both to safety on shore. There were a few bad minutes while the boat had to be turned, Shona using one oar in a wide circle. The movement took Mara off-guard and to her immense annoyance and humiliation dunked her under the surface once more. Why on earth didn't anyone teach me to swim, she thought with irritation and vowed that if ever she had a girl scholar again she would certainly be taught to swim, side by side with the boys.

'Hold tight,' said Shona and once again she spoke in a low voice, almost as though she knew that there was danger lurking.

Mara did not answer. Her mind now had left her present predicament – she had got into the rhythm of gently flapping her feet – her shoes had long gone – and her thoughts now went to trying to put a face to the arm that wielded the club to such deadly purpose and had almost caused her to drown. Someone had overheard her words to the captain, someone had seen her as a threat, had decided to get rid of her quickly – just as the body of the murdered man had been tipped into the river. It would probably have been taken as an accident, she concluded as she clutched the rope, neatly flipped her feet and kept her head well out of the water. A person who had murdered once often did not hesitate to murder again. That had been her experience in the past. It was imperative now that he, or she, be caught and named before another victim was found dead.

Shona was making for the boathouse. She seemed to be expert at the procedure, giving the stone wall one jab with the oar in order to position herself accurately and then gliding in under the roof. Mara hung on to the rope and then when she felt the boat stop, used hand over hand to haul herself inside as well. There was a strong, fishy smell from the water and she could dimly make out the outline of a row of lobster pots.

'I'm holding the boat steady; can you climb out onto the jetty,' came the whisper.

One half of the boathouse was covered over with a slatted floor and Mara presumed that was the jetty. She reached out a hand and pulled herself towards it. After a struggle she managed to get a knee onto the slats and then pulled herself up and stood for a minute streaming with water, using her hands to wipe her eyes and her face. Then she knelt on the flooring and spoke near to Shona's ear.

'I'll never be able to thank you enough,' she said. 'Now is there a way that I can get changed into something dry without causing any fuss? I don't want anyone to know about this.'

Shona's face was invisible under the sheltering roof of the boathouse, but her voice was steady and practical. 'Take my cloak; strip everything off or you will be ill. I'll go up to your room and get you something to wear. If I meet your husband I'll tell him that a clumsy boy spilt wine all over you. I'll be back as soon as I can.'

'I can't take your cloak – you'll freeze,' protested Mara endeavouring to stop her teeth chattering.

'You have to,' said Shona firmly. 'I'll be all right. I'll manage. I never feel the cold. In any case, think of the scandal if anyone comes to the boathouse and finds the King's wife standing there, quite naked.'

And with that she was off and despite her chattering teeth Mara smiled to herself. Who would have thought that the shy, silent daughter of Maccon MacMahon would have so much spirit and enterprise in her? And so much good sense, also. Quickly she stripped off her clothes and seizing a handful of netting scrubbed herself with it and then put on Shona's cloak, bending down over the water to allow her hair to drip as she combed it through with her fingers.

Shona was back by the time that Mara had begun to braid her hair. She had brought nothing complicated – just a thick *léine*, a pair of boots and a very warm, fur-lined cloak with a large hood. She had also brought a square of linen so that Mara could tie it over her head to save soiling the fur with the river water.

'There's a good fire in my bedroom; you can come and change there. I met Enda. He has told my father that I am not well and he will see us safely into the room,' she said, once Mara was dressed.

So Enda was going to be in on this matter, thought Mara, but she did not mind. Her suspicions of Enda had begun to seem ridiculous. After all she knew this boy so well. Could he really have killed Brehon MacClancy just to have inherited the position of Brehon at the court of King Turlough? Murder for a situation was the act of an evil, ruthless person and that was not Enda. And this attack on her had, she felt, made suspicions of him seem impossible. She could not possibly imagine that Enda would try to kill the woman who was his teacher for ten years. Meekly she followed Shona from the boathouse and noted how the girl knew her way so well, going by a path heavily cloaked with a dense hedge of holly to shelter the winter-time vegetables.

Enda was standing by the drawbridge when they edged around the corner. He was apparently gazing nonchalantly into the mist. He raised one hand as Shona gave a light whistle and Mara quickened her pace. Once he saw them he went back into the castle and they could hear his footsteps ahead of them as they hesitated and then at a low whistle, they hurried up the staircase. There was no sign of him, however, when they reached the door to Shona's bedroom and once inside the girl turned the key in the lock. Spread across the bed were a few piles of Mara's clothes, taken from her clothes chest, and there was a large linen towel warming by the fire and a bowl of rose-scented water ready on the wash stand. Shona had efficiently organized everything in the time that it had taken Mara to remove her wet clothes in boathouse.

'Wonderful,' said Mara, shedding the cloak and seizing the towel. Back home at the law school she had a bathhouse, where the water in the iron tub came from a deep well and a charcoal burner heated the water. She longed for it now but did her best with the small basin of water provided. At least, she hoped, it would enable her to get rid of the fishy river smell from her skin and hair.

'Take your time,' said Shona. 'No one will come.'

'What if your father comes?' asked Mara. 'Perhaps we should have some story ready for him.'

'My father is under armed guard,' said Shona grimly. 'In any case he won't press me on any point at this moment. He knows that it would be dangerous to do that.'

Mara raised her eyebrows with a smile, while her mind worked fast. 'You've got him well under control, then,' she said lightly. She did not look at Shona but kept her head bowed down to the heat of the fire as she scrubbed her hair with the thick linen towel. There was a long silence after the remark and when she lifted her head and reached for the comb she cast a quick glance at Shona.

There was a very strange expression on the girl's face. Not the smug expression of a well-loved daughter who could wind her father around her thumb, but a bitter expression of fury combined with sadness. Mara's heart was moved with pity for her.

'What is it?' she asked softly.

There was a long pause. Mara could see that Shona was unsure. She opened her mouth as though about to speak and then closed it again. Her eyes looked down and she fidgeted with her fingers, sliding a ring of silver to and fro.

'I can't say,' she said eventually. And then quite suddenly her eyes looked straight into Mara's and there was an expression almost of terror in them.

'I hate being a girl; I feel so powerless. I wish that I didn't have a family. Cael thinks that she can escape by pretending to be a boy, but as soon as she starts to look attractive then all of that will stop and she'll have to do what she is told, she'll be at the mercy of any filthy beast that desires her,' she said, the words tumbling over each other.

Mara nodded. 'There are some men like that,' she said softly. 'Men that like to get a woman in their power. The law gives protection against such men; punishes them.' She watched Shona intently.

'The law can't restore a reputation once lost,' said Shona bitterly. 'A girl . . .' She hesitated and then went on, with an attempt at sounding indifferent and detached, 'If a girl, as a child, has been raped and has had a child, then she is damaged goods if her secret gets out. No amount of silver can compensate for that.'

'True,' said Mara. She bent her head over the stone hearth and allowed her hair to hang down as she combed it in the warmth of the fire. 'What happened to the baby,' she said without looking around.

'It died,' said Shona in a dull voice.

The mother was too young to bear a child, thought Mara, her heart filled with such fury against a man who would do this to a girl placed under his protection that she felt she could gladly have murdered him herself. A lot was now explained. Cael's insistence on being a boy, her incessant practice with her throwing knives, her hatred of Brehon MacClancy, all this now made bleak sense.

'And your father?' she questioned. What kind of man would allow this to go on; would still leave his two younger children in that man's care? She got up from her kneeling position and went across to the mirror and began to braid her hair.

'I hate him,' said Shona bitterly.

'Did you try to tell him . . .' Mara paused and then added casually, 'about Brehon MacClancy.'

'He believed him; he told my father that I had disgraced myself with a *cú glas*, with a man of the roads.'

'I think that you should have tried to tell your father the truth,' said Mara decisively. 'I think . . .' But then she stopped as Shona said slowly and bitterly:

'And have the same thing happen to Cael – that's what he threatened. He said that it was all my fault, anyway, that I had enticed him, worn pretty dresses, that I was a . . . a . . .'

Shona stopped and Mara looked at her with pity. Probably there was no real relationship with her father – in any case she may have been very young, very young, pregnant and bewildered – shamed by the baby that she was carrying. And the threat to Cael may have been a real one and not one that the sister, who would have been returned to her father and probably married by the time that Cael became attractive to Brehon MacClancy's perverted taste, could have prevented. Mara decided to move away from the subject. Nothing could be done about the past; the future was what counted. The girl had been stiff with apprehension for the whole of the visit and it had not diminished after the death of Brehon MacClancy two days ago.

'What's worrying you, just now?' she asked gently. And then when Shona was silent, she added, 'Would you like me to talk to your father?'

A look of alarm sprang into the girl's eyes.

'No, don't do that, whatever you do. He'd kill me if he knew that I had been talking to you.'

And then, in a low voice, she added. 'I'm scared of him; that's the trouble. I dare not go against him. I have to do what I am told. He has threatened me. He'll tell everyone . . . tell everyone something about me . . . I'll be shamed in front of the world. I'll kill myself if he does that. I have to carry out his bidding.'

Mara smiled reassuringly. 'If you need protection against . . . against anyone that is threatening you, King Turlough will help. Just tell me and I'll talk to him.'

Shona shook her head violently. 'I can't,' she said. 'My own father; I can't betray him. I can't do it. He would be cut down and slaughtered. I've seen that done. But he would shame me first and then I would be fatherless and without an honour price and then I would kill myself,' she added with a brooding look.

Mara bit her lip. She was puzzled as to what to say next. The young are so intense, she thought and regretted that Shona, despite being in the foster care of a Brehon, had grown up with such a poor opinion of herself that her reliance was on her father, not herself.

'Enda,' she began tentatively and was rewarded by a quick blush that spread over Shona's face.

Don't worry,' she said. 'I can keep a secret. Tell me if you think I can help you in any way.'

But the moment, she sensed, had passed. The blush had faded. The huge dark eyes filled with tears. The girl had a brooding look on her face. She picked up Mara's wet clothes and deposited them in a wicker basket and then went around the room, straightening objects, emptying the water from the bowl into the garderobe beyond the bedroom. Mara said no more. Shona now seemed to be distressed and anxious to speed her visitor on her way and after renewed and very sincere thanks, Mara left her.

As she descended the stairs her mind turned over the possible reasons why Shona should have used the word '*betray*' and the even more revealing '*cut down and slaughtered*'. Why should she be guarding a secret, a secret which she held over her father's head, and which he held over her head – a secret which she feared would alienate Enda from her.

'*He told you about Shona then; he swore not to mention it to anyone, but I suppose he thought that he could trust your discretion . . .*' These had been Donogh O'Hickey's words.

What, she had wondered then, was Shona's secret? Now she knew that secret, but there was another one, also. Not the matter of the pregnancy and the birth – her father knew all about that, even if he didn't know the full truth. But what was on her mind now? What was her father forcing her to do or what was the matter that he wanted to keep secret?

Her anger grew again at the thought that a father would use that terrible event in his daughter's life in order to buy her silence and acquiescence through fear of disclosure.

And then as she mounted the stairs to the solar, an idea suddenly occurred to her and it was so outrageous that she stopped and almost returned to Shona's room. But then she decided to carry on up to the solar.

There was more than one source of information available to her.

Twelve

Cáin Íarraith and Cáin Machslechta
(Law of children)

A child under the age of fourteen has no legal responsibility for any misdeed.

Liability for a child's offence is borne by his father or by his foster-father if he is in fosterage.

A dependent child is classed as a 'táid aithgena' (thief of restitution) from the age of twelve to seventeen. If he steals something it has to be restored and no penalty need be paid.

'I'm sorry that I am so late seeing you all. I overslept and then had to see the captain of the guard,' she said apologetically to her scholars when she came into the solar to find them all chatting. No one seemed to know anything about her peril-filled morning. Domhnall politely made some reference to her anxieties. She hardly listened though. Her mind was busy. And if her surmise was correct, there was no time to be lost.

'Has anyone seen Cael and Cian this morning?' she asked.

'They're not allowed out of their tower,' said Cormac casually. 'There's an armed guard on the door. They came across to ask me to bring them food and drink before they starved to death.'

Mara raised her eyebrows. Though she had given orders that nobody was to be allowed to leave the castle grounds, she had no reason to suppose that there was a guard put on the whole of the south-eastern tower where the MacMahons slept. Shona had no difficulty in coming out, and she had not encountered any guards when she went up to the girl's bedroom. She guessed that the MacMahon twins loved to dramatize.

'So how did you see the twins if they are not allowed out of the south-eastern tower?' she asked.

'They came across the roof,' said Cormac with his mouth full and Mara smiled to think of the fun they were having, slipping and sliding among the slates and sheets of lead between the towers and pretending that their lives were in danger and that starvation threatened unless they could get hold of a friendly ally.

'Do you think that you could go back that way and get them for me, tell them that I have something belonging to them?' she asked, salving her conscience by reflecting that months ago, during holidays and the weekend in October, Cormac and the twins had been climbing all over that roof when she was far away in the Burren. If they hadn't fallen then, they would be unlikely to fall now. She looked around at the other boys when Cormac had disappeared and Domhnall, reading her mind, said hastily: 'We've just finished, Brehon. We'll leave you in peace.'

But not in peace, thought Mara, as they went off, debating whether to help Rosta in the kitchen or to go and try out the swing that one of the stable men had made in the barn. No, she thought, I am not at peace. I am uneasy. What secret does Shona MacMahon hide and is Enda aware of it? And why did Maccon send for his daughter? Why was he so anxious to leave two days after Christmas? A suspicion had come into her mind and she would have no peace until she had found the truth. She left the solar and went to stand at the bottom of the staircase, looking up anxiously.

It seemed forever before there was a movement from above. She stood and listened. There was none of the usual jokes and laughter and play-fighting that normally went on when the twins were present. The footsteps came down quite slowly and when they arrived beneath the candle on the landing outside the solar, Mara could see that her son's face looked puzzled.

'Thank you, Cormac,' she said and he took her words for the dismissal that she intended and made his way towards the kitchen where his fellow scholars were holding a shouted conversation with Rosta about the dinner menu.

'Come into my solar,' said Mara to the two silent MacMahon children. They followed her in and, as she had intended, their eyes went instantly to the small pile of silver that she had left conspicuously on the table.

She saw them exchange a look and had an impression that a question had been asked by Cian and answered by Cael. She hoped that it meant they were willing to give her information. They had hesitated near to the door, but then came further into the solar and perched on the edge of the hearth. She offered them a cushion each and they took them in silence, seating themselves without moving their eyes from her face. They had a cautiously, elderly expression and Mara felt sorry for them. However, if her idea proved to be true then the lives of all in the castle might depend on her ability to extract information from the pair. She seated herself at the table and turned to face them.

'Have you had any breakfast?' she asked and they both nodded silently. She had never known them to be so quiet and she thought that there was an air of apprehension about both of them. I'm right, she thought. Her sudden fear had been confirmed. Her heart started to beat uncomfortably. It was imperative to be careful, to proceed cautiously and cleverly; the consequences could be terrible if the information could not be obtained quickly.

'Do you know why your father is so anxious to leave the castle?' she asked bluntly. 'I imagine that not much escapes you two,' she added. Flattery was, she thought, a very valuable weapon when used judiciously with the young.

Again there was that glance between them.

'Guess,' said Cael after a minute.

'Hm,' said Mara, 'now that's a challenge that I never refuse. Let me see . . .' She pretended to consider, went across and put some light, very well-dried birch logs on the fire. They flared up instantly and illuminated the two young faces.

'Of course it is nonsense to imagine he just wants to do some business. I don't believe that. At Christmastime pleasure comes before business. Why should he make an arrangement to leave a week before all of the other guests?'

There was a slight smile on Cael's face and Cian almost nodded. Mara thought that she could proceed more quickly.

'It was not so much because he wanted to go home, was it,' she said trying to make her words sound impulsive, almost careless. 'It was because he didn't want to be here today, that's right, isn't it?'

There was no need for the extra light from the fire – both faces had swung around to look at her and there was a tautness and a tension about the two thin figures which told her that her guess had hit the mark.

'And why didn't he want to be here today?' she said thoughtfully. 'It couldn't be anything to do with the murder of Brehon MacClancy, could it? Did he want to escape my investigation? But that would have been stupid,' she said in a friendly, chatty manner and was pleased to see grins on their faces. 'Your father would have been very brainless to have virtually declared his guilt by a hasty flight,' she declared. 'After all, he is one of the King's tenants, someone sworn to loyalty. If anything was discovered which pinned the guilt on him the King would send an armed guard for him. Unless, of course, that he had changed his alliance and found another, just as powerful as the King . . . another protector . . .'

They looked at each other again, but did not contradict her. There was a flash of interest in Cael's eyes and Cian just gazed straight ahead of him. Neither showed much affection for their father, Mara thought, but then, perhaps he had never given them much affection. They may have been fostered from babyhood, may, in fact, as often was the custom, have had two or three foster homes.

'He knew something was going to happen and he didn't want it to happen while he was here, something that would be unpleasant to him, something dangerous, perhaps,' she said gazing into the fire. And then, quite suddenly, she swung around to face them. 'There's going to be an attack on the castle today, isn't there? Isn't that why he wanted to be out of the way, and wanted his children to be out of the way?'

Again there was a look between them. She waited, concealing her tension under a show of cheerful enquiry. They communicated almost like animals, she thought. A gleam of eye and slight movement of the head, a sudden restless crossing of a pair of skinny legs, a glance at her from Cael, the leader of the two, and then the girl nodded at her brother. Suddenly the tension had gone from the room and the twins were grinning widely at each other and then looking avariciously at the pile of silver.

'We've been helping him,' said Cian.

'But we've decided to change allegiance,' declared Cael. 'We wanted to stay and open the gates to the intruder, but he wouldn't let us – and he hit me, a foul blow.' She rubbed her ear cautiously. Mara could see that the cheek was swollen and a purple bruise showed under the eye. 'So now we're on the side of the King and against him,' she finished.

'Strange he wouldn't trust you to do a simple thing like that when you were already in his plans and when you had already undertaken a task for him,' said Mara sympathetically. Under the shelter of the table she clenched her fists with impatience at the slow pace. It was important, though, to get all the information. Another couple of minutes would change little. 'Though I suppose that was just an easy task that he gave you originally, wasn't it?' she added, trying to make her voice sound dismissive.

'What! Disabling King Turlough's cannon!' exclaimed Cian angrily. 'I can tell you that was no easy matter.'

'No, I don't suppose that it was,' said Mara soothingly. 'In fact, I wouldn't have the slightest idea about how to do a thing like that.' She clenched the seat of the chair to stop herself jumping up and summoning Turlough.

'Though it was his idea, originally,' admitted Cian. 'He thought nobody would notice a couple of kids. We just had to get up very early so that Cormac and the others didn't see what we were doing. We pretended that they were the enemy.' He grinned. 'We got filthy.'

'We stuffed the barrel and the thing that you put the gun powder into, the touch hole, we stuffed both of them with soaking wet clay from the marshes and then we poured a bucket of water down into the touch hole as well.'

'Clever,' said Mara admiringly. And then in an offhand way, she said thoughtfully, 'I don't suppose he trusted you with

the name of the people who are supposed to attack the castle.'
She took some sweetmeats from the table by the window
that Rosta had mended and offered them to the twins.

'We got it out of Shona,' said Cael with her mouth full. 'At
least we think that it is something to do with her, and with
him, of course. *Him*,' she repeated with emphasis,

'She hasn't even seen him, but he's handsome, so she's heard,'
said Cian.

'And she's not too bad herself,' conceded Shona's younger
sister.

'It's the Black Knight's son,' said Cian.

'So what we reckon is that it's going to be a marriage
contract. If he gets to attack Bunratty Castle and seize it, or
to demolish it, then the marriage will go ahead.'

'I see,' said Mara doing her best to make her voice sound
light and unconcerned. She did see now. The Black Knight
was the Knight of Glin, who lived on the Cork and Limerick
side of the River Shannon. He was first cousin to Turlough's
deadly enemy, the Earl of Desmond. She got to her feet and
pushed the pile of silver towards the twins.

'That's for you,' she said.

'Six pieces,' said Cian.

'Only six,' said Cael with disgust. 'We should have had thirty
pieces of silver at least for betraying our own father.'

'Stay here,' said Mara, but as she went rapidly down the stairs
towards the great hall, she heard them follow her.

The hall was full when she pushed open the door. Even
Conor and his wife had joined the crowd and they were all
listening to Raour, who was graphically describing how, single-
handed, he had killed a wolf who had just brought down a
deer.

'My lord,' said Mara imperatively and Turlough, looking
startled, broke away from the crowd and came towards her.

'Maccon MacMahon's twins have told me the true reason
why he wanted to leave here by today,' she said rapidly in a
low voice. 'He has betrayed you to the Black Knight, the
Knight of Glin.'

Turlough's eyes went cold. Immediately he beckoned his
captain of the guard. He looked past her to the twins and they

stared back at him with set white faces and fear-filled eyes. His face softened.

'Rosta!' he yelled. And then when the cook popped his head out from the kitchen, he said: 'Take these two into the kitchen and give them one hour's work.' As the two turned, Turlough winked at Rosta and then put his head back into the hall and jerked it at the captain of the guard. The man came instantly, closing the door behind them and allowing Raour to continue with his story about the wolf.

'Yes, my lord,' he said as soon as the three of them stood alone on the landing.

Turlough took in a deep breath. 'The Knight of Glin is proposing to pay us a visit,' he said. 'You can guess who's behind it, Desmond himself, I'd say.'

'That would be it, my lord; I'd say that you are right,' said the man unemotionally. He gazed out of the small loophole at the fog that surrounded the castle. 'They'll attack by river, my lord, I'd say.'

'They'll get an unpleasant surprise, then,' said Turlough with a grin. 'Get some men out to the cannon as quickly as possible.'

'The cannon has been disabled,' said Mara quickly. 'I've just got information about that. Wet mud has been stuffed down the barrel and into the touch hole. It will take you hours to get it clean and dry.'

'What!' roared Turlough. 'If I get my hands on the traitor who did that, I'll kill him. Who did it?'

'I believe that it was one of your guests who ordered it to be done, my lord,' said Mara, adding hastily, 'but the first thing of importance, surely, will be to secure the castle and the safety of the inhabitants.'

Turlough stared at her. 'One of my guests; I don't believe it,' he said slowly. 'It couldn't be. Him of all people . . . Across the river, of course . . .' His eyes sought those of the captain and they stared at each other. Eventually the captain nodded.

'I thought he was very anxious to get out of this place when the Brehon had said that no one should leave. The man seemed nearly demented when we brought him back. "*That man is*

afraid of something,'" that's what Peader said to me. But who
would have thought it.'

'And how did he meddle with the cannon? He's been with
me all the time.'

'He had some young helpers,' said Mara.

'Don't tell me,' said Turlough resignedly. 'It wasn't Cormac,
was it?'

'No, no, he was deliberately kept away from the scene,' said
Mara. She knew that he had guessed who the perpetrators
were, but Turlough was not a man to vent his anger on children. Already he was beginning to lose his angry flush.

'They might not get as far as us,' said the captain. 'But, of
course, we've always relied on MacMahon's men to guard the—'

Suddenly he stopped.

'The Knight of Glin!' Turlough exclaimed.

His eyes went to Mara and she nodded reluctantly. Of course,
she thought, Maccon MacMahon's property spanned the whole
northern sweep of the Shannon estuary. In the normal way of
things it would be very difficult for the Knight of Glin to get
ships to go upriver without being intercepted by him. Turlough
had always relied on MacMahon to keep his riverward boundary
safe.

'Do you know why? Maccon is the last man that I would
have expected to betray me like this,' suddenly asked Turlough,
looking from his wife to his captain. He didn't wait for an
answer, but turned and began directing operations.

'Put a chain across the river, my lord.' Rosta had appeared,
pan in hand, drawn by the shouts down the staircase for men
to arm themselves. 'Just by my salmon weir – that will be the
place for it, my lord. Let me go in the boat with the men. I
know just the place to fasten it.' He thrust the pan into the
hand of one of his assistants and limped rapidly down the stairs
behind Turlough. Mara followed more slowly.

The main guard hall was full of activity. Men were every-
where, taking down swords, shields and knives from their
places on the wall – Turlough had never believed in bowmen,
preferring to rely on the old Celtic weapon, the throwing
knife. In a minute, every man had a set of these inserted
into belts and others strung in bags from their belts. Several

were donning the heavy quilted jackets of boiled bull-leather
and she looked for one of her scholars to send up to the
bedroom to fetch Turlough's, as he was still casually dressed
in *léine* and tunic. But when she started to make her way
through the crowd that parted for her she could no longer
see any of them. She had definitely seen the five of them
at the top of the room and she had noticed that the twins
had joined them, but a minute later they had disappeared.
She continued to make her way around the main guard hall
and through the men, but there seemed to be no sign of
them. The group who had been arming themselves moved
away and she saw behind them an iron grille. She had
noticed that before and had assumed that it guarded a shaft
leading down to the moat – a place where waste food could
be thrown down to feed the carp that swam there. But now
the grille had been opened like a gate and she noticed that
a rope was tied to it.

And her five scholars, as well as the MacMahon twins, had
disappeared. Mara bent down and peered into the dark hole.
She could see very dimly that there was a dark passage. A raw
stench of mud met her nostrils. Could they possibly have gone
down there?

'Where does that lead?' she asked sharply of one of the men.

He glanced back, looked surprised and then bolted the grille.

'Shouldn't be open,' he said. 'What goes out can come in.'

Before she could say anything he had hastened out of the
room, joining up with the others. She opened the grille again,
peered down and called Domhnall's name a few times but there
was no reply. She beckoned to a man who had just unhooked
his shield from the wall.

'Have those boys gone down there?' she asked and he shook
his head.

'They've gone up to the roof, Brehon,' he said readily and
she hoped that he was right. She had decided that they should
be confined to somewhere safe if there was any chance of
fighting and the roof was probably not a particularly safe place,
she thought, and hastened back up the steps.

There were no voices from the roof, though she met the
captain of the guard coming down. He looked so preoccupied

that she hesitated to bother him. However, he passed her with a muttered, 'No sign yet,' and this cheered her.

Mara climbed the five flights of stairs right up to the roof of the castle but there was no one there. She looked across at the spaces between the battlements of the other three towers. These also were empty. She looked down at the river and found that she was less encouraged by the captain's words than she had been when she met him on the stairs. The fog was even thicker than on the day before and there would be little possibility of seeing or hearing any enemy on the river. She was just about to go down when she heard a low murmur of voices and some figures emerged on the south-eastern tower – the first out was Turlough. He did not look across at her, but went straight to the edge of the tower. She was about to call across but noted how low his voice had been so she went back down the stairs, crossed the great hall, and then went up the staircase leading to the south-western tower. She stood to regain her breath just beside the door which led out onto the battlements. She hoped that it might be her scholars and their friends with her husband, but it didn't sound like them so she was not surprised to see Turlough, his captain of the guard and young Raour standing above there looking down, and talking quietly. She joined them, but did not speak. This bore the marks of a war conference and was no moment to ask about missing scholars. Raour, she noticed, was giving his opinion eagerly – very keen to make an armed sortie from the castle and be ready with a rough greeting for the intruders. Turlough was amused and inclined to acquiesce, while the captain of the guard was sceptical, but cautiously careful about not offending his King's grandson and possible heir. Mara decided to say nothing, but just stood there, looking down for moment and trying to orientate herself.

'The fog is lifting,' said the captain and she could see that it was true. She looked all around her. She still could not see the grounds of the castle, but in the distance to the north was the wooded slope of Bunratty Hill, to the north-east were the meandering curves of the Raite with the long hogback of the heavily forested Cratloe Hills behind it. Mara's eyes had just gone to the south when there was an exclamation from Raour.

'Look! Down there! They're out there on the Shannon. They have to row against the tide, though; it's an ebb tide.'

Turlough and the captain crowded against him, leaning over the parapet, trying vainly to see something through the white mist of the fog. There was a strained silence and then the unmistakable clash of wood against water as one oar missed its stroke.

'That's them,' said the captain.

'Let's go,' said Turlough. There was all the confidence of a successful war leader in his voice. After all, nine years ago he had met the whole might of the troops belonging to the Earl of Kildare, supplemented by those of Desmond and vastly swelled by men sent over from England. Turlough, his men and his allies had defeated them at what was known at O'Brien's Bridge, spanning the Shannon on its exit from Lough Derg, on its journey towards the city of Limerick and then to the sea. Turlough had even captured a cannon on that occasion, the very cannon that had been disabled by the twins on orders from Maccon MacMahon.

'I'll just go and let my father know what's happening,' said Raour and Turlough uttered an absentminded 'good lad' before proceeding on down the stairs. If only they had a cannon these intruding boats could be given a rough welcome and would immediately turn and get out of range as soon as they could. Turlough, however, was not a man to bewail the impossible and his voice was hearty and even slightly amused as he gave orders for a chain to be put across the river. Mara hoped that it would work, but could not help thinking how ineffective it would be compared to a blast of ammunition.

At the thought of the cannon, Mara left her post on the roof and went downstairs.

The door to Shona's room was firmly closed and that of Maccon was now guarded by a hefty-looking man with several knives stuck through his belt. He greeted Mara effusively and was keen to hear the news of the sighting of the enemy. Bored, thought Mara.

'Any trouble from your prisoner?' she asked.

'Just keeps pestering to speak to the King himself,' said the guard. 'Thinks he'll be a soft touch. Thinks he'll talk him round.'

I'm not sure about that, thought Mara. Turlough could be easy-going, but this castle, this pride and joy of the O'Brien clan, a site that they had wrested from the Englishman, de Clare; this castle, built by his uncle, was of huge strategic importance to the whole kingdom of Thomond. It commanded the River Shannon and made sure that enemies could not get into the heartland of the kingdom.

And then there was the precious land beneath the castle; that was almost of more importance, having belonged to his clan from time immemorial. Turlough would fight to the end to retain both castle and land. The traitor MacMahon had better keep out of his way, she thought as she nodded to the guard and told him to keep the prisoner in close confinement and then went on down towards the lower part of the castle.

Enda had a room on the floor of the main guard hall. She stood for a moment in front of the door and then tapped on it. Yes, he might be a suspect, perhaps a prime suspect in the case of the murder of Brehon MacClancy, but just now she badly needed help, and after all, a man was innocent until found guilty.

'Enda,' she said impetuously when he opened the door to her, 'Enda, could you please help me. I'm very worried about my scholars.

His face had been closed up, the eyes shuttered by half-dropped lids, but at her words they opened up. A look of pleasure appeared on his face and he reached for his cloak which hung on a nail behind the door and in a moment he was by her side.

'Don't worry, Brehon; they can't have gone far,' he said in such a soothing manner, that, despite her anxieties, it brought a half-smile to her face.

'Would you go up and collect Shona?' she asked. 'I'd like her help, also.' There was no reason why the sixteen-year-old should stay in her room. Mara had intended questioning her further, but the whole truth had been obtained from the twins and Shona was not responsible in any way for the treachery of her father.

Ireland is a country divided against itself, she thought as she watched Enda bound up the stairs and listened to the clatter of his boots as he spiralled up without stopping. She had been accustomed to blame the English for their predatory attitude to Ireland. Their immense scorn for Brehon law had made her hate them. She recalled the description of the law of the native Irish as being 'repugnant quite both to God's law and man's'. But it was Ireland's disunity which provided England with its best opportunities. If Turlough Donn O'Brien, king of three western kingdoms, was to be defeated and taken prisoner by this treacherous act of a person who had been a friend, then that might prove a turning point in Ireland's resistance.

She waited, feeling a cold dread come over her as she wondered what was happening. Would Turlough and his men-at-arms be able to stop the onslaught? If the Earl of Desmond was involved in helping his cousin, the Knight of Glin, then there might be vast numbers of men approaching up from the River Shannon.

Shona looked apprehensive and guilty when she followed Enda down the stairs, but Mara smiled at her reassuringly. 'I'd like to get those youngsters back indoors, Shona, and I wonder could I rely on you to keep an eye on them once we get them there,' she confided and saw the girl look a little more relaxed. She cast a quick glance back up at the landing where the man guarding her father paced up and down impatiently and then looked at Enda.

'Let's go,' he said in a confident way and took the girl's hand.

The drawbridge was still down and the three of them crossed over it, Enda leading the way through the village street and down towards the marshland, close to the riverbank.

'They could be anywhere, but it's most likely that they went to the cannon so we'll try this first,' she told him, taking pleasure in the feeling that she could rely on one of her senior scholars once again. Domhnall was very promising, very well behaved and she could see a good future in front of him, but he lacked the sparkle and the sheer brain power of Enda, and the maturity – he was after all only thirteen years old – of Fachtnan who had been at her law school for so long. Mara missed Fachtnan, but it was good to have Enda at her side.

'The cannon is over here, just beyond the moat,' said Enda as they approached the bridge.

'How did they get past the guard on the gate?' Mara felt annoyed. How could any man have permitted these – these children – to leave the castle grounds when a state of high alert had swung into place? There were no guards there now – all of the men seemed to be down by the river's edge.

'Perhaps they got out by the passage way from the main guard hall – it goes under the moat and out by a bank,' said Enda. 'There's a big willow bush beside it and no intruder could ever guess what is hidden.'

'That will be it.' Mara's annoyance turned on herself. She had seen the rope and had seen the exit. She should have followed it through. But at that stage the possibility of an invasion had seemed to be more unlikely. Now, she knew that the enemy had already arrived. She quickened her step to keep up with Enda's long legs, thoughts running through her head. There had been talk of erecting a chain across the river, she remembered. Cormac was very attached to Rosta and she hoped that he had not joined the cook on this probably fruit-less effort. The enemy had arrived too quickly and there could be grave danger involved for those struggling to put a chain across the width of the river.

The children by the barrel were filthy, their clothes and skin were covered in wet mud, their skin was smirched with it, their fingernails were filled with it and their faces bore a look of desperation. They flicked glances at Mara, Shona and Enda without saying anything, but kept working steadily, trying desperately to scoop the wet mud from out of the touch hole and from out of the barrel of the slender cannon.

'It's no good,' said Enda, looking down into the muzzle of the cannon. 'It will never be dry enough to fire. Don't worry,' he added as the twins looked up at him with mute despair.

But the MacMahon twins did worry, thought Mara, feeling intensely sorry for the two. Cian's eyes had filled with tears and Cael swallowed hard. Shona's attempt at an embrace was elbowed away as the twins returned to their work. Perhaps it wasn't a bad thing to take the consequences for your actions. However, the place was too dangerous. Afterwards, if there was an afterwards, if there was a good ending to this tense day, then Mara decided that she would encourage them to try to undo what havoc they had wreaked. She watched them for a moment, admiring their tenacity. And then she realized that two of her scholars were missing.

'Where are Domhnall and Slevin?' she asked sharply.

'They've gone to tell the King that we can't get it clean,' said Art while Cormac muttered furiously and went on scooping at the wet mud.

'Leave it, Cormac,' commanded Mara. 'Don't worry; the King will manage without the cannon.' She endeavoured to make her voice sound resolute.

'You're just so stupid, you two,' muttered Cormac, taking no notice of his mother. 'What did you do a brainless thing like this for?'

'And you're brainless,' retorted Cian. 'We keep telling you. We were forced on pain of death to do the deed.'

'Pain of death,' snorted Cormac. 'You were afraid that you would get a slap; that's what scared you.'

'We were fighting on the opposite side, then, birdbrain,' said Cael, disdaining the refuge of coercion.

'Well, you shouldn't have been,' retorted Cormac. 'You deserve to be hanged from the battlements for your treachery.'

'So what!' sneered Cael with a shrug. 'Who cares about hanging?' She deliberately wiped her muddy hands on Cormac's cloak, which had been discarded on one of the bushes and then turned back to him with insolent grin pinned to her muddy face. 'So, what are you doing, hanging around here? Shouldn't you be fighting shoulder to shoulder with your marvellous father, the King?'

'Stop it,' said Mara firmly with one hand gripping Cormac's shoulder. 'None of you is to speak to each other for the next five minutes.' She looked sternly at the twins and dared them to say anything. 'Now go back immediately to the castle and stay with Shona until I come.' Then she had an inspiration and said: 'As soon as you are clean then go into the kitchen and make a cold meal for the King and his men when they come back from the river. Spread the food out on the table in the great hall and make sure that it is something that they can eat quickly and easily. Nothing hot – just bread rolls filled with meat – anything like that.'

They went off sulkily, but without further complaint. Enda walked with Cormac and she could see Cormac's face turned up towards him. Mara guessed that Cormac rather liked the prospect of providing food for the soldiers and hoped that he would forget the jeer. She made her way towards the edge of the river. From time to time, she glanced hastily over her shoulder wondering whether she was being followed. She was half-sorry that she had sent Enda back to the castle. She would have welcomed his presence and try as she would to shrug the memory aside, there was no doubt that someone had tried to kill her this morning. Her head still ached from the blow and her legs and arms felt heavy and weary.

It was not, she thought, an easy thing to feel that someone wanted to kill you. If she could put a face to the hand that had struck her down and locked her out to drown in the river, then she could have faced up to the person boldly.

But it was a hard thing to look at the faces around her and to try to distinguish the murderer from amongst the friends and relations of Turlough.

Thirteen

Brehon law treats all crimes as wrongs for which the law will prescribe compensation in the form of damages. The law is not primarily used to deter would-be wrongdoers or to reform such wrongdoers. The victim of the crime is the first consideration for each Brehon.

A Brehon has no role to play in crimes against society as such; only injuries done by individuals to other individuals.

Mara had to force herself to approach the riverbank. The fog was so thick that she did not even see the boathouse and it was only when she was within yards of the Shannon that she could see the entire garrison were collected here. It was a strange scene. The fog hung in wisps around the figures and no one spoke. The hush was eerie – so much activity and all of it carried out in almost complete silence. Some men were pacing up and down, some were standing knee-deep in the water holding a length of chain in their hands, others had climbed the sparse willows that grew on the bank and perched there like birds looking out towards the river and the incoming tide. The men in the water moved with such care that the slushing sound they made could almost be that of the incoming tide. Turlough was surrounded by a group with swords in their hands. She was thankful to see that he was dressed in his leather tunic now and that it had a piece of metal sewn over the vulnerable area in front of the heart.

Mara did not approach him. Now was not the time to trouble him. The reliance of his men on his whispered orders and nods was complete and she did not want to disturb his concentration in any way. He would immediately want her to return to the safety of the castle and that she thought was probably the sensible thing to do. There was nothing that she could contribute. She had never been involved in any warlike proceedings before.

And yet she felt that she wanted to stay. Turlough and she

led lives that were so apart for large portions of the year that they had got into the habit of being very involved with each other once they were together. And this was the first time that she had shared this warlike, dangerous part of his existence as a king of imperilled territories. She watched him as he moved about. Such a big, noisy man – she had never seen him move so quietly and speak so low. Her heart went out in love towards him and she wished that she could help but had the sense to know that, just now, she could only hinder.

Everything, she gathered, was centred on the manoeuvre with the chain. It must be immensely long because the men carrying it were already three-quarters of the way right across the inlet and there appeared to be almost the same length again being unwound by the men on the bank. They had talked of a boat when Rosta brought up the idea, but no boat could have been as noiseless as these men.

Rosta himself was standing on the side of the bank, propping himself up with the aid of a severely pollarded willow stump. Mara spared a moment of compassion for him. He had been, according to Turlough, one of the best and bravest of his fighters. Was he content now with his frying pans and his fish kettles, or did he yearn for the old days of the sword and the throwing spears? The latter, she thought watching the tautness of his figure and the way he turned towards the fighting men.

Still that was none of her business; her responsibility was towards her young scholars and she was glad to see Enda approach and nod in a reassuring way as soon as he glimpsed her.

'I've left them with Shona – she's promised to teach them how to bind up wounds,' said Enda in her ear. 'Don't worry. They've all promised not to leave the castle without permission.'

'Have you seen any sign of the other two, Enda?' Mara whispered back and then, almost as soon as the words left her mouth, she saw them. Domhnall had approached Turlough, and Slevin was just behind him. Mara moved nearer, treading cautiously and finding a safe resting place for each foot before she moved the other forward to join it. The ground was uneven marsh land pockmarked with the tracks of cattle hoofs. She marvelled how the men could move so silently and then through the fog she heard the noise of oars once again. The sound seeped out through the fog and instantly ceased. She could almost sense how breaths were held. Turlough's men froze into immobility. They had heard the sound as well as she. The men carrying the chain stopped abruptly. There was no doubt that this time the sound of an oar seemed to be very near. Did the enemy know how close they were? The question in Mara's mind was suddenly answered. A slight but unmistakable series of clicks was heard.

And then no more!

Mara looked over her shoulder at the six-storey-high castle behind her. Surely the men would be safer behind its immensely thick stone walls. She crept a little closer to Turlough. He knows what he is doing, she told herself, but habit, the habit of being in charge, being the one who knew the best thing to do, was too strong within her. *I'll just suggest it to him*, she thought, though she knew that he was a man who had been fighting battles for nearly half a century. In any case, she had to get Domhnall and Slevin away from this dangerous situation and sent them back to join the younger boys.

And then, just when she was within a few feet of him, Turlough raised his arm, sweeping it along in a left to right gesture as a signal to the men with the chain. Once again they began the tortuously slow business of inching their way through the water, avoiding stones underfoot and carrying the chain with such immense care that not a clink was heard. The men on the side banks and the men beside Turlough at the head of the inlet seemed to move silently and Mara saw how the ones near to her put their hands to their belts and withdrew a throwing knife.

That was the strategy and perhaps it would work, though Mara wondered why it was that Turlough's men could do it in complete silence while that series of clicks had sounded from the boats. She could not imagine what made that sound, unless it was some new sort of throwing knife. After all, the men from the Earl of Desmond, like those from his cousin, the Earl of Kildare, would be supplied from England with the latest weapons.

And then at the word weapon, her heart abruptly stopped its beat for a long second. She felt her hands suddenly wet as the sweat broke out all over her body. She had guessed what those clicks might be.

Guns were a rarity in this part of Ireland but Mara knew that they had been used in the famous battle that the kingdom of Thomond had fought against the Earl of Kildare at O'Brien's Bridge. It had been the time of Cormac's birth and Turlough had returned in great triumph. He had captured one of the English cannons – and it had been his pride and joy and had guaranteed the safety of Bunratty Castle until sabotaged by the treachery of one of his best friends. He had also captured many hand guns – had fired one off in her garden much to the alarm of all about – it had even caused a herd of cows in the field across the road to stampede. However, noisy and effective as the guns had been in that hot June, they had proved unreliable in the wet climate and they had rusted away, unused.

But they had made a click when loaded and ready for use.

'Turlough,' she said in a very low voice in his ear, 'Could these clicks have been guns?'

He showed no surprise at her presence. His whole attention was concentrated on the slow movement of the chain across the inlet. He just nodded acquiescence and then whispered back: 'Don't worry. In this fog, they'll never get those things to fire. The ones that I had were useless.'

It is nine years since Turlough captured these guns, thought Mara stepping back. In nine years something like a gun could have been improved. Perhaps it had been made more weather-proof. She was so tense that the sudden explosion of light and sound from beyond the bank of fog almost came as a relief. Yes, it must have been guns and they were firing. But could the shots reach to the men in the water?

This time, she reckoned, the boats had managed to get quite near. There was a sudden yell, startling through all the silence that had previously held everyone whispering and moving on tiptoes. Then a heavy splash came, another scream and then another and another. The men holding the chain were right in the line of fire. Screams of agony seemed to splinter the density of the fog. Mara winced. This was warfare, something that, until now, she had only known as a story told after victory. Now every nerve in her body strained to know the fate of these men who were loyal to her husband. Their enemy was better armed – would courage and audacity serve to balance the two.

A shower of throwing knives had answered the gunfire, but no responding cries were heard. These throwing knives, so deadly accurate when an experienced man could pin-point his enemy, were of little use thrown into the dense yellow fog.

'Get back, back to the castle,' shouted Turlough. 'Bring the wounded.'

Mara grabbed her two scholars by the arms. Enda had left her and was plunging recklessly in the water. The guns rang out again and she felt sickened by the answering screams from Turlough's men. There was nothing that she could do, though. Her duty was to her two scholars and to the others, including her son, who might be tempted out of the castle.

'Back!' she shrieked and with such emphasis that Domhnall started to run and he and Slevin now appeared to be dragging her from the place of danger. In a moment they were surrounded and overtaken by men running, swords clapping uselessly by their sides, but each with a throwing knife grasped in his hand.

'First forty men up on the roof – ten to each tower,' shouted the captain. 'Two men go to the drawbridge! The rest stay near the gate. Wounded men should be taken to the main guard hall.'

Mara was soaked in sweat and stumbling by the time they reached the castle. There was a stench of smoke in the air that she had not been conscious of before and still the guns cracked out, almost stunning the ears with their explosive sound. She looked up and saw faces peering down through the murder hole above. Oil, by now, would be being heated on the fire in the kitchen; she shuddered at the injuries that it would cause when poured on the heads of intruders.

The women and children from the small village were crowding the pathway and she was glad to see that the sturdy walls of the castle could give them refuge. They were white-faced and tense, the women drawing the children back so that they did not get in the way of the flying feet of the men-at-arms who thundered past without glancing from right to left, each determined to get a favoured place on the roof of one of the four towers.

Once inside the castle Mara went straight to the main guard hall. Pallets of straw were piled in orderly neatness against the wall and she sent Domhnall and Slevin to pull them out and arrange them in rows. In a minute they were joined by her other scholars and by the twins and they all worked, white-faced and silent.

'Fetch the physician!' Mara felt the words almost spit from her as she saw one of the castle servants appear around the door. Why was the man not here already? Donogh O'Hickey must have a store of medicines and bandages and these would be needed soon. The screams of the wounded still rang in her ears and there would have been more since she had left the riverbank. The guns had cracked again and again; firing blind, but finding their mark since less than a hundred men had been crowded into the small space, each believing that a sword and a quiver of throwing knives would be enough to protect him.

Only when the physician had arrived in the hall, accompanied by two servants carrying a small wooden chest, did Mara feel that she could leave the place. Donogh O'Hickey looked perfectly well, she was glad to see, and she welcomed him effusively before leaving. She did not care whether he had feigned illness previously, the important matter now was to see to the wounded men. A trestle table had been set up for him, and Shona, with the twins and the younger scholars, joined him, each of them bearing leather buckets of water and small baskets filled with strips of linen. Shona, thought Mara, had been well trained, perhaps by the Brehon's sister. She seemed to be competent and efficient, sending Art flying for linen sheets to place over the straw pallets, and Cian to fetch some lengths of kindling wood from the kitchen to act as splints for arms and legs.

The first patient was brought in by Enda and another man. Cormac exclaimed in horror when he saw that it was Rosta. The heavy body was dumped on one of the beds and the two went off to bring in more. Cormac was kneeling beside the cook, holding his hand, but Rosta had mercifully slid into complete unconsciousness.

'Just a flesh wound,' grunted the physician as he approached and knelt down beside him. 'Water, bandages,' he snapped at Cormac and the boy flew to do his bidding. 'Let's get this out of him quickly while he's out of this world,' he said as he slashed open the tunic, bared the bleeding chest and used the point to flick out a small lead ball. 'Quick,' he said and Cormac, white-faced, clapped a pad of linen to the bleeding wound.

'Let me bandage it,' said Shona coming over and winding the bandage around – making a very efficient job of it. By this stage there were more wounded coming in, but there were plenty of woman, all seeming skilled in this matter of attending to the wounded. Mara cast a swift glance around and decided that she could be spared.

As she came out onto the landing she heard a creak of chains and a few shouts, and then a sharp loud bang as the drawbridge was lifted and slotted into its position.

The climb to the roof was a difficult one. Each of the window slots beside the steeply spiralling staircase had at least one man standing beside it, knife in hand and straining his eyes to pierce the fog and pick out an enemy. They stood back and made way for Mara but she felt an intruder on their deep concentration.

'Any sign?' she asked anxiously from time to time and each time received a frustrated shake of the head.

'My lord is up there, Brehon,' said one of the men as she hesitated outside the great hall.

'Yes, of course, that tower is nearer the river, isn't it,' she said readily. 'Anything happening yet.' Her voice did not really hold a query – it was obvious from the stillness and lack of noise that nothing was happening – and he passed on down the stairs without answering, his brow creased in a puzzled frown. Mara continued on up the steps and slipped unobtrusively through the door that led out onto the roof leads. The ten men with their throwing knives still resting in their quivers were standing at the battlements gazing down. Turlough, his lips pursed, was very still, not striding up and down as usual, but standing, hands slightly clenched, green eyes straining through the mist.

'That's it again,' he said suddenly, his voice low. 'That's the same sound – wood on wood – I'd swear to it. What the hell are they doing?'

He did not acknowledge Mara's presence, though she saw his eyes go to her, but remained where he was, looking and listening. Mara listened also, but she could not make sense of the sounds – perhaps they were stacking the oars on the bank – but why?

The door opened again and she saw Enda come in quietly and go to stand beside the King. Turlough turned eagerly to him.

'How is he? How is Rosta?'

'Just a flesh wound in the chest near the shoulder,' said Enda reassuringly. He turned to go back and Mara followed him. He went down quickly, but was conscious of her presence because he waited for her halfway between the great hall and the main guard hall. His hand was on a door to one of the small rooms in the tower and she immediately said, 'Where are you going, Enda?'

From memory she thought that it led to the musicians' gallery, but could not see why Enda should go there. He was not a man trained to fight, of course. When other young men of his age were practising with swords and throwing knives, Enda was studying the law. And yet, he looked happier than she had seen him look for all of the time that she had been in Bunratty. His blue eyes were blazing and there was a small confident smile on his lips.

He hesitated at her question but then said, 'I'm going out, Brehon. It's one thing I can do. Don't worry: I won't be long.' He opened the door and she followed him in. Two men stood there, a selection of knives laid out on a table by them. Enda stood, and looked frustrated. Mara wasn't sure what he had intended, but the presence of the men was going to impede his plans and she was glad. The men looked at him suspiciously and in a hostile way and she didn't blame them. The word had gone around, she was sure, that there was a traitor within the castle walls, and Enda, a man who had not been trusted

by his own master, might well be in league with him, so far
as these men were concerned.

'Come, Enda,' she said and made sure that he went out of
the room before her. 'Let's go and see how the wounded men
are getting on,' she continued, but he had already gone down
the steps ahead of her and had turned in at the door of the
main guard hall by the time that she had finished speaking.
Slightly surprised, because Enda, even in the difficult years of
his adolescence, had always been well mannered, she followed
him into the long room. There were still a few groans, but
most of the wounded appeared comfortable, with white bandages cloaking the worst injuries. Her scholars were going from
man to man offering drinks, and she felt proud of them all.
Cormac was solicitously feeding Rosta some of his own cake
and the cook, who was now sitting up, seemed able to swallow
some. She would tell Turlough, that, she thought. The man
had a special place in her husband's affections.

And then she forgot Rosta. There was no sign of Enda
anywhere. This was the second time that she had mislaid
someone in this room and now she knew instantly where to
look. She wound her way through the straw pallets and came
up to the top of the room. Domhnall was there and he had
just fastened the latch of the grid. There was no sign of Enda,
but she surmised that, young and slim as he was, he had easily
slipped down through the tunnel and was now making his way
down through the passageway that led under the moat and
would shortly be near to the riverbank.

'Just . . . just shutting this as a precaution.' Domhnall met
her eyes with a guilty look and she guessed that he had been
told to keep his mouth closed about Enda's disappearance.

Mara sighed. It was hard, she thought, to remember that
scholars grow up. She had to stop thinking and worrying about
Enda as if he were still about the same age as Domhnall, and
the bright temperamental star of her law school, leading the
other boys into trouble, but always able to win her forgiveness
by his intrinsic honesty and sense of humour.

'I suppose you should stay there until he comes back,' she
told Domhnall who was now joined by Slevin. 'You can take
turns if he is a long time.'

I hope not, was her private thought. This was an extremely risky undertaking by Enda and she tried to keep her thoughts away from the young man creeping through the fog towards the riverbank in an area of ground that was now occupied by enemies. But what were they doing? Why were they not trying to gain access to the castle? What had been the point of this expedition? Why bribe Maccon to take away his surveillance of the River Shannon estuary just a few miles from its entrance into the Atlantic Ocean? And why bribe him to make sure that Turlough's precious cannon, the bulwark of his security at Bunratty, was disabled – what was the point of the whole elaborate manoeuvre? It would need an enormous army to storm Bunratty Castle, not just a few men in boats.

'He's coming back, Brehon.' Slevin was at her side and she moved swiftly to the top of the room. It had suddenly occurred to her that Enda might be followed back through this secret entrance to the heart of the castle. She wished that there was a man-at-arms there, but all had left the hall to the care of the physician and his women and children helpers. Domhnall, she was sure, had thought of this also, as he was a little pale and he fingered the knife at his belt as he waited and listened.

But it was only Enda himself and, though filthy, he was composed and with the help of the rope climbed in an agile way out from the hole and then watched while Domhnall latched and locked it carefully. Mara had opened her mouth to question him but seeing his expression she shut it again and went after him as he made his way neatly through the rows of wounded men and towards the door leading to the stairs. She followed him the whole way up, but could not keep the pace of his young legs. By the time she reached the roof where Turlough and his men waited the bad news had been given.

They had indeed heard the noise of wood being unladen and also the noise of joints being hammered together. The Knight of Glin, as well as his cousin's troops, had apparently brought with him something called a *trebuchet*. The word was echoed from man to man and she saw puzzlement on many of the faces around her.

'What's a trebuchet?' she asked and although it was Enda who explained about this machine, made from wood, which could lob from the sling a stone or stones of up to hundred-weight, it was the black despair on Turlough's face and his laconic: 'They'll have the castle down around our ears unless we manage to stop them,' that made her realize the full desperation of the situation.

Fourteen

Heptad Six

There are seven bloodlettings which carry no penalty:
Bloodshed inflicted by an insane person.
Bloodshed inflicted by a chief wife in jealousy of a concubine who
*   comes in spite of her.*
Bloodshed by a physician authorized by the family to care for a sick
*   person.*
Bloodshed inflicted in battle.
Bloodshed by a man who enforces suretyship.
Bloodshed by a man who takes part in a duel.
Bloodshed by a boy in playing a sport.

It was about an hour later that the castle felt the full onslaught. A couple of men had been sent down the passageway under the moat to see whether it was possible to attack, but came back to announce that there was a ring of protectors around the trebuchet, each one of them armed with a dreaded musket. It was, thought Mara, the flash of fire and the explosion of sound that made these guns so terrifying to men who were used to the silent cold steel of knives, swords or pikes. The garrison here at Bunratty Castle was a small one – already one fifth of it had been injured or killed and Turlough, she guessed, did not want any more heavy casualties.

Mara felt unable to stay down below in the main guard hall. She had no nursing skills – her girlhood had been spent in study of law texts and during her adulthood she always had her housekeeper, Brigid, who looked after any of the scholars or farm workers during illness. She gave a nod of approval to Shona who quietly, but competently, seemed to be directing all of the women and children in their work and then slipped out of the room and began, once again, to climb the steep steps to the roof.

Mara was about halfway up the stairway to the great hall when the first blow struck. The impact was so great that she gasped almost as though she had been struck in the midriff. Her ears had almost exploded with the thunderous sound. She stopped, put her hand against the twelve-foot-thick wall and felt a tremor go through it. This must be the action of the trebuchet. It was worse than she expected. When she went a few steps further she could see dust in the air ahead of her and then saw that one of the very small window loops, set on the outside of the castle wall, had its central mullion cracked in half and stones from above were dropping from the wall. There was a shout of exultation from outside and Mara, as she hastened up the steps, wondered for a moment how they could see what they had done and then remembered the report that the fog had lifted somewhat. A quick glance through the next small window on the tower staircase showed her the truth.

The last couple of men sent to reconnoitre reported that they dared not go more than a pace. The sky had cleared and a pale winter sun had lit up the marshy ground and the river beyond. Everything could be seen by the men with guns.

It must have just happened in that strange way that it often did in wintertime. Now she could see the river, the boats, the line of men on guard, and the muskets pointing towards the castle and beyond them another group of men clustered around a flat-bottomed boat.

But what took her attention was the trebuchet – that fearsome engine – the height and the size of it. As she watched she saw men unload some enormous rocks from a barge tied to the jetty. These were manhandled onto the machine, the great arm swung and once again, the mighty stones were lobbed through the air and with a deadly accuracy seemed to hit the same spot of Bunratty Castle because there was a great explosion, the ground trembled beneath her feet and she could see that one of the well-cut, squared-off stones from the outside of the castle – that castle which had been the pride and joy of O'Brien kings for the last seventy years or so – fell to the ground. Could any castle stand up to hours of bombardment like this; it almost seemed impossible, thought Mara. If the attacker concentrated on one tower, could they bring the whole castle down? The four towers were an integral part of the building, not an add-on. Mara grimaced – she felt that she probably knew the answer to her own question as she turned away from the window and went towards the stairway. Then at the sound of running feet pounding down the steps she drew back a little, but was immediately spotted by the young man racing downwards.

'All women, children and wounded men to the basement!' he exclaimed trying to sound authoritative.

'Good idea,' responded Mara, and bestowed a smile of approbation upon him.

The young man in his protective tunic of thick quilted leather cast a look at Mara but did not attempt to stop her as she proceeded upwards. The King's wife could not be questioned. I should go down, thought Mara guiltily, but the thought of that basement with the dead bodies – and then her thoughts seemed to skid to a halt. The dead had been taken in there, but among those bodies of the slaughtered men-at-arms there should have been one other body, of course, the body of Brehon MacClancy. But now that body of the man murdered two nights ago had disappeared, had been dragged to the end of the basement, through the grille, and then had toppled down into the river. But why? And who had done that deed? She thought guiltily that in the immediate danger of this attack from the Knight of Glin she had almost forgotten her quest for the truth of that earlier death. But now, despite all the peril, her mind ranged over the evidence. What was it that the old man had said the night before his murder? That someone the King loved had betrayed him. It almost seemed to be too much of a coincidence that two days later Maccon MacMahon had unleashed this terrible attack on a man who had been his friend for forty years – and all just to make a good match for his daughter. Deep in thought, Mara passed the entrance to the King's solar and went on up towards the roof. Why on earth didn't MacClancy tell Turlough immediately if it had been something so serious?

And then she thought of a solution. It was probable that the attack had been scheduled for the following week when Maccon would have returned to his own home – but perhaps the Brehon's words had prompted Maccon to send a message, perhaps to send his groom, to his ally with a message to attack more promptly. He would have surmised that he could get himself and his children to safety before the deadly trebuchet and the men armed with guns arrived. But if her surmise was true there would have been one thing that he had to do as soon as possible. It would have been imperative to stop the mouth of the man who threatened to tell the King about the treachery of one that he had considered a loyal friend.

So was MacMahon the murderer of Brehon MacClancy? It does seem very likely, Mara acknowledged to herself; although the evidence that her scholars had gathered did not seem to back this up – none had seen Maccon MacMahon approach Brehon MacClancy. And yet, could anyone have been sure of what happened on that festival night when all had been confused with loud music, flickering lights, continual movement? Deep in thought Mara pushed open the door and came out onto the roof.

She had just closed the door softly behind her when her eye was caught by something like a thunderbolt cutting through the air towards the castle. The trebuchet had flung its next missile, but this time it was not heavy rocks but a pot of fire that came hurtling through the air, not angled to hit low down on the tower, where the previous damage had been done, but aimed directly at the King himself.

'Turlough, get down!' screamed Mara, and trained to instant reaction by a lifetime of warfare, Turlough ducked down below the parapet. The pot of fire went straight over his bent back and struck a young man standing behind him. There was a stench of boiling tar, of searing heat and of burning flesh and almost instantly a scream which Mara thought that she would never forget. For a moment it looked as though the man wore a pot on his head. He snatched it off and instantly flung it over the parapet into the river. For a moment he stood there as everyone got to his feet and stared at him. Then came another terrible scream, almost immediately cut off. The man was a pillar of fire. Blazing tar dripped down over his head and ran down his face. As Mara watched the two eyes were gone, and then the nose shrivelled, the mouth was sealed.

Hands outstretched he moved instinctively towards the parapet. Turlough left her side and went hastily towards him, and then pulled back and watched, grim-faced, while the boy plummeted down the wall and into the river. Mara did not see him hit the water, but she heard the splash and then a shot. Unbelievably the terrible death was followed by a cheer from the troops below and a series of cat-calls and derisive whistles.

'Father wants to know what's happening, he heard a thudding noise.' Young Raour was at the door, his plump lips pursed and his eyes apprehensive.

'Get out of here, get down to the basement with the women and the children, you and your father, go on, get out of here,' yelled Turlough savagely. Mara knew what was in his mind. His grandson, Raour, was very much of the same age as that boy whom he had allowed, a few minutes ago, to go to his death. Raour, of course, could not know what had happened, and his face was white with shock to be spoken to so roughly by his easy-going grandfather who had so petted and indulged him. He backed out of the door without a word and Mara heard his footsteps going slowly down the steps. She brushed him from her mind and went forward and took Turlough's hand, pressing it for a second and then dropped it as he turned to face the captain.

'You did the right thing,' she said to her husband in a low voice before standing back and allowing the two men to confer.

And of course, she thought, he did do the right thing to allow the boy to go to his death. Not even the best physician in the world could have healed those terrible burns – and even if they could the young man-at-arms would have been blind and dumb for the remains of his life – the more likely possibility, though, would have been that he would have died a few hours later in screaming agony. It had taken courage to do what he had done, and it had taken courage and compassionate understanding for Turlough to stand back to allow him to go over that parapet. But now provision had to be made for the living and all eyes turned towards Turlough.

'We have no other choice; we can't just stand here and allow them to raze the castle to the ground; we must sally forth. Let

me get my hands on a few of those bastards and I'll die happy.'
Turlough's voice was harsh and almost unrecognizable.

'You'll die all right, my lord,' said the captain uncompromisingly. 'We haven't a chance. We would have to sacrifice fifty
men to their gunfire before we could get near enough to them
and even then we mightn't succeed. None of us knows enough
about those guns – or that trebuchet, either – and they have
boat-loads of stones; as for the guns, they'll have brought plenty
of ammunition. We haven't that number of able-bodied men
to sacrifice them to a chance of getting nearer – a spear once
thrown can't be recovered and you need to be at close quarters
for the throwing knives to work. You know that yourself, my
lord,' he added and then instantly ducked down. Mara did the
same; the captain had seen the swing of the giant sling on the
trebuchet, she thought, as she cowered into the wall and pulled
Turlough close to her, waiting apprehensively for another one
of those blazing cauldrons of fire to land amongst them.

But nothing hit the roof. This time the trebuchet lobbed
one of those huge rocks. The wall of the tower was hit again
and there was another tremendous crashing and the ominous
sound of falling stone came to all of their ears. They stayed
very still for a moment, feeling the castle tremble and Mara
wondered whether this might be the last day for her husband,
her son, herself and all of the men and women at Bunratty.

'There must be something we can do.' She said the words
aloud, but to herself only. Turlough was not listening. Then
the door behind her had opened and Enda was with them and
she turned towards him with hope that some solution might
have occurred to this clever young man.

'I was thinking,' he began and then was interrupted by a
roar from the men by the trebuchet. A white flag waved and
Mara held her breath for a moment. Was it possible that they
were going to surrender? One man had climbed up on top of
the trebuchet, his head flung back and his arms held out in a
gesture that seemed to demand attention.

'Turlough O'Brien,' he shouted in strangely accented Gaelic.
'I call on you to surrender your castle.' He did not wait for an
answer, but continued loudly: 'Before the day is ended all
of your men will be dead and your fine castle will be a heap

of stones if you don't. These are our terms.' He paused and then said even more loudly. 'Surrender the castle to us and we will be merciful. All women and children go free. Men will be taken to Limerick prison and you, Turlough O'Brien, so-called chief of your people, will be taken to London to meet the King of England.'

'No!' exclaimed Mara. 'Bargain with him, Turlough. You can't let yourself be taken to England.'

Turlough snorted. 'Do you think that I couldn't outwit that crowd? They wouldn't get far with me. I'd be a very troublesome prisoner for them to convey to London.' There was a strange smile on his face and for a big restless man of action, he stood very still, and his eyes wore a thoughtful look.

He's going to do it, she thought, her heart plummeting. She wished that she and Cormac had never come to this castle. Perhaps the thought of his wife and his youngest son being able to go free had influenced Turlough towards an uncharacteristic decision. She saw the captain look at him with an air of puzzlement.

'I've found a bucket of tar in the basement, my lord.' Enda interrupted the strange silence. 'I have it outside the door. Could your men dip their throwing spears in that – I've brought up some candles. I'll light the tar and your men can throw the spears.'

Isn't it too far for throwing spears, thought Mara and looked to see Turlough's reaction, but he only patted Enda on the shoulder, and said, 'Good lad, good lad, good thinking; that will keep them busy. Peader, you organize that.'

'Five minutes!' he shouted back to the men on the ground, holding up a hand with five fingers displayed and then grasping his captain by the arm he pulled him back to the other side of the roof. Mara wondered what was going on. It was a strange feeling for her to be relegated to the position of an onlooker whose opinion was of no account. She was used to being the one who decided what action to take at a time of unrest and peril.

Enda, his face glowing, had brought in the bucket-full of cold tar with some candles lying on it and a covered lantern. Quickly he struck a light from his flint and steel and ignited the candle in the lantern and then the stumps of candles stuck

into the tar. After a minute the heat from the candles caused
the tar to become liquid. The men dipped their spears into it
and then waited for the word. Several looked slightly puzzled.
Mara thought that they were doubtful of the use of throwing
those spears for such a distance. The captain and two other
men had left the tower top, but others came across the central
roof to join their King.

Turlough stood impassive at the parapet. One large hand
with fingers splayed widely apart was held up and his lips
moved – counting out the seconds, thought Mara. After what
seemed more than a minute he lowered one finger and the
bloodthirsty crowd below cheered and whistled.

'Carry on, lads,' said Turlough in a low voice, still maintaining
his stance at the parapet. The hand that he held aloft was steady
and he gazed out towards the river impassively, the prominent
O'Brien nose making his face look like a carved statue.

Enda worked like a demon. He had brought with him an
iron poker and he continually prodded the tar and relit the
candles until it flowed like honey and completely coated the
tips of the spears. The day was still and what breeze there
was hardly stirred the flame of the candles and behind the
half-closed steel shutter of the lantern the flame of the large
candle burned steadily. Mara hoped with every fibre within
her. If only they could damage the trebuchet. That was the
real problem. The castle had a well; it was richly provisioned
with food-stuffs; they could withstand a siege more easily
that the attackers could stay out in the wet and the cold of
mid-winter.

But wasn't it unlikely that the Knight of Glin would allow
his trebuchet to be set up within reach of throwing spears or
knives?

'Three,' said Turlough, folding down the third finger and
Mara realized that she had missed one of the minutes. Time
was going faster that she could cope with. There was a feeling
of unreality about the scene.

The declaration of 'four' came more quickly. All now was
in readiness, so Mara guessed that Turlough was counting more
quickly. Fifteen men stood with spears coated in liquid tar and
tiny flames were beginning to flicker from the iron bucket.

The captain had returned, though not the two men who had accompanied him.

And yet something was happening outside. There had been a few shouted commands and then many footsteps had thudded on the stairs, coming up, a sound as though something was being dragged around the spiral staircase. And there had been an angry exclamation. And then the men had reached the doorway, but had not come in. They were waiting outside the door, she thought and wondered why.

'Five!' shouted Turlough. 'And rot in hell the whole breed and seed of you all!' and then he stood back. From where she stood, Mara could see that the white flag lowered and the men begin to pile more stones in the sling of the trebuchet. The castle and its occupants might now be fated. She felt a sense of relief that Turlough had not surrendered to them, but puzzled at his sudden change of attitude.

'Go on, lads!' said the captain. Four men dashed to the embrasures between the four upright merlons and launched their flaming spears. Three fell short, but the fourth, thrown by a very tall, very powerful-looking man, reached the small crowd near the trebuchet and scattered them. There was a shout, and a yell of pain which brought a grim smile to the men's lips, but no great injury, thought Mara, as she noticed one man leave his post and dip his arm into the river.

'And again!' shouted the captain, while the first four went back and picked up new spears. By now the routine of setting them afire had been established, but Mara's eyes went to the pile of spears in the corner and she wondered how much time this could gain them. She had little hope that the trebuchet could be injured. Some of the Knight of Glin's men had run forward and held up shields, English shields; long, heavy shields, unlike the small round shields of the Irish; each one of these shields was about the size of a man. They held them up in front of the trebuchet, the deadly besieging weapon. Just two of the third lot of flaming spears pierced the wood shields, but they were easily plucked out and thrown into the river to quench the flame. The other two fell short and blazed uselessly on the marshy ground.

The attackers began a scornful chant in English and Turlough stood very still in grim silence.

When there were no more spare spears left, he made a signal to the captain, who brought forth a piece of torn white material – rather like what Shona had been using down in the great hall for bandaging wounds. He handed it to Turlough, who waved it aloft. Instantly there was a wild cheer and faces appeared from behind the huge shield; even a few wounded men, lying on the bank, raised their heads and supported themselves on an elbow.

'Knight of Glin,' roared Turlough. The cheers and catcalls were cut off at a signal and a squarely built, short man stepped forward.

'I am the Knight of Glin; what do you wish to say to me,' he said in English.

Mara quickly translated.

'Lived in this country for the whole of his miserable life and doesn't speak a word of the language,' said Turlough with disgust. Once again he spoke but this time to Mara's astonishment he quoted in Latin from the Bible.

'*But thou, O God, shalt bring them down into the pit of destruction: bloody and traitorous men shall not live out half their days.*'

There was a puzzled silence from the attackers. Heads turned. The Knight of Glin conferred with his captain. Turlough stood very still and said no more, just gazed straight ahead and down at the River Shannon which had kept the castle at Bunratty safe for over seventy years.

And then the door behind Mara opened and a cluster of men came in, dragging something amongst them.

For a moment Mara thought that they had captured one of the attackers – a medium-sized man, his face bleeding, his lips drawn back over his teeth – and then she realized that this was Maccon MacMahon. One of the men held a rope coiled in his hand – and the other end of the rope was around the neck of the prisoner. Mara stared in horror. Turlough's face was a grim mask. He watched as MacMahon, chains on both hands and feet, noose around his neck was dragged roughly forward. The captain made a neat loop on the free end of the rope and slung it over one of the merlons and forced the man to stand beside the embrasure. The sun struck that spot, illuminated the bowed figure, the noose and bore down on the bald patch in the middle of the man's head. Somehow there was something about that bald spot, almost a tonsure in shape and size, which seemed to make the situation almost unbearably pathetic.

Mara took an impulsive step forward. 'Turlough,' she said softly, 'you can't do this. The man has committed a crime, but he must be tried for that crime and the verdict of the court must be accepted – if guilty he will be punished. You cannot do this deed. It goes against every tenet of the law that we both believe in.'

But Turlough did not even look towards her. He stood, immoveable, at the battlements and gazed down. Rosta, the cook, white-faced but seeming unaware of his injury, looked from Mara to his master. Then he looked back at Mara and slightly shook his head. *Leave him alone* the gesture seemed to say and Mara closed her mouth on the legal argument that she was about to utter. Somehow, here in the middle of the bloody battle scene, there was, she knew, a feeling that what had this man had done, in betraying his King and in betraying all the clans who owed allegiance to this King of the three kingdoms, what this man had done was beyond forgiveness; that there was only one possible penalty and that was the biblical one – a life for a life.

But the Bible was full of savagery and Brehon law respected life and sought to avoid bloodshed.

And every fibre within Mara cried out against this deliberate killing of a man of the kingdom. She had spent almost her entire life – ever since the age of five – in the study of a law which had been drawn up in order to keep peace between neighbours and members of the same kingdom by providing a bloodless penalty for every possible crime. What this man had done was wrong, evil, and he and his clan should pay for that. There should be a heavy fine, but not a death. She could not countenance that; but could she help it? And she felt suddenly quite sick and powerless. There was a tense silence now from the attackers, no whistles, no cheering. The Knight of Glin gazed upwards and although Turlough spoke in Gaelic now, his gaze and his words were directed at that stocky figure of the Knight of Glin. And it seemed as though their meaning was instantly understood. The Knight looked upwards, and his very stillness and the angle of his gaze seemed to ask for more information.

'The man, your agent, this renegade MacMahon, will be hanged – his troubles will be over quickly,' continued Turlough, 'but yours are only beginning. What do you think will happen to you? Will any other clan leader be willing to join with such a treacherous race as the English and their bastard half-castes?'

There was an angry murmur of talk after that. The man who had spoken first was at the Knight of Glin's ear. He must be translating Turlough's words into English. Mara strained her ears but could not hear much that made sense to her. They were perhaps wondering whether Turlough was bluffing, whether he would, in fact, carry out his threat to hang a friend, a tenant, a man whose family and clan were related to the O'Briens, bound to them by ties of blood and of marriage. The MacMahons had given their allegiance to the O'Brien kingship from time immemorial. They were descended from the brother of their great ancestor, Brian Boru. And through the five centuries that had elapsed since then, the bond between the MacMahons and the O'Briens had remained, had grown stronger and firmer.

Mara looked down on the attackers. The buzz of words rose louder and she prayed for the words to continue. While they were talking, no action would be taken. She had a great belief in words.

Let's hope it all spends itself in talk, she thought. She hoped that Turlough had not given offence by his reference to bastard half-castes. The Knights of Glin, under English law, were descended from an illegitimate line of a previous Earl of Desmond. Brehon law, of course, took no notice of such things – a son, no matter who was the mother, once acknowledged by his father, according to the law, had equal inheritance rights with all other sons. The English, however, had different views and Turlough's sneer was probably deeply insulting to the

Knight of Glin. There had been a tense silence after those words. Mara moved a little closer and gazed down. The group of men seemed to be talking together, seemed to be arguing. From time to time their glances went up to the tower roof – they did not appear to be looking at Turlough, but at the rigid and immobile figure of the man who had betrayed him to the English foe. Maccon MacMahon was a traitor and a money-hungry blackguard, but he was no coward and he stood, very straight, looking down at the River Shannon, thinking, no doubt, how that river flowed in front of his own castle in west Thomond. Did he think about his motherless children, she wondered – about Shona, who had been neglected and abused by a man who should have cared for her, about the intelligent, angry Cael and Cian, who hung around stables and got little attention from his father? Did he ever regret that he had betrayed the man who had been his friend for almost forty years – and his King for twenty of these years? Nothing could be told from that immobile figure.

Mara moved restlessly. The tension had broken in the group behind her. Some sort of decision had been taken. The movements and gestures of those on the ground had been read and a verdict was anticipated.

From the corner of her eye Mara saw the captain speak softly to the group of men. One by one they slid out of the door; even Enda went with them, leaving on the tower roof only Turlough, the captain, and herself – and the man with the noose around his neck.

There had been no dramatic counting of the minutes this time. And yet it seemed as though both parties were working to an invisible clock, because suddenly everything began to happen. The attackers loaded rocks onto the trebuchet and Turlough's men burst from the tower, running at full tilt and launching knives flaming with pitch at the enemy. It was a brave try, thought Mara, watching with clenched hands. They hoped to surprise the enemy, but the guns were aimed at them almost instantly. The shots rang out and Mara saw two men fall.

And then her eyes went to her husband. He was not looking

downward. As soon as his men burst out from the gate and had begun to run towards the river, Turlough had lifted his hand in a signal. Mara looked towards him, horrified.

'Turlough, no!' she exclaimed.

Fifteen

Míadshlechta

(sections on rank)

The King's justice is the most important thing in each kingdom. If the King is just, his reign will be peaceful and prosperous, whereas if he is guilty of injustice, the soil and the elements will rebel against him. There will be infertility of women and cattle, crop-failures, dearth of fish, defeat in battle, plagues and lightning storms throughout the land.

And then, suddenly, it appeared as though something cracked within the immobile figure standing by the rampart, his hands bound and the rope slung around his neck. He turned his head and looked into the eyes of his King.

'Spare me, Turlough,' he pleaded. 'I will never do such a thing again. It was just concern for my daughter. She wished so much for this match with the son of the Knight of Glin. I could not bear to deny her, to ignore her pleadings, her tears. If you pardon me this one time, then I will be your most fervent follower and most faithful servant for the rest of my life.'

He paused and began to sob brokenly. Mara looked around at the faces on the castle roof. Not one of them showed any sign of being moved by the appeal. Most looked contemptuous. Turlough's face looked like an effigy from the tomb of one of his ancestors – colourless, carved from limestone. There was a dead silence. Mara could hear the pulse of blood in her ears, her hands clenched and unclenched. She moved a little closer to her husband and murmured his name.

'Turlough,' she said and then when he made no response she touched his hand. 'Turlough, you cannot do this,' she said quietly. 'The law does not permit the taking of the life of a clan member for any reason. The final judgement is God's, but the law . . .'

And then Turlough moved. He walked away from her and towards the edge of the rampart so that he took his place beside the condemned man.

'No!' he said loudly and vehemently, and she did not know whether he spoke to her or to Maccon MacMahon. The man turned his face away from his King in a gesture of despair and Mara could see that tears now coursed down his cheeks. She followed her husband to the rampart.

'Turlough, I beg you,' she said, but she had the feeling that her words were wasted.

'Let me at least have a priest.' Maccon's voice was high and almost unrecognizable – its pitch shrill as that of a child in pain.

'I've no priest for you,' growled Turlough. 'I've a basement filled with bodies of the dead and a hall of wounded men where many may still die. If there was a priest available I would not want a single word to be omitted, a single prayer from the sacred anointing to be hurried through for these loyal friends of mine, just because there is a traitor on the roof here who is afraid to face the death that his sins merit. Say a paternoster if you wish to make your peace with God. You can say nothing to me that will influence me one jot.'

No word came from the condemned man, just a torrent of helpless sobs, so Mara stepped forward and in a steady voice recited the prayer. She was not particularly religious herself – at the one time of her life when she had thought her life was in danger, as she gave birth to Cormac, she had not even thought about a priest, or even a prayer, but now she felt that she would do anything to delay matters. Perhaps in the course of the paternoster Turlough would relent. He and the rest of the men were stony faced and pitiless in appearance, but she had noticed that Rosta the cook had suddenly left the rooftop, as though he could not bear to watch the scene.

'Knight of Glin,' shouted Turlough, his loud voice causing a flock of rooks to rise up suddenly in alarm and fly over the heads of the enemy. There was a small, brave cheer from Turlough's men. Rooks were considered to be birds of evil omen and it boded death for those whom they overflew.

'I am here,' said the Knight of Glin, still resolutely speaking in English. He gave some order in a lower voice to the man at his elbow. There was a hurried movement towards the trebuchet and Mara saw how they bent back the sling and piled on the rocks, getting ready for the next deadly assault on the castle.

'You will not murder your own countryman!' The Knight of Glin inserted an ironical, mocking note into the English words, but the man translating rendered his words in an assertive and challenging fashion.

'Turlough, you cannot do this,' said Mara in despair.

'On my head be it,' roared Turlough

'Surrender or die, Turlough O'Brien!' called the Knight of Glin without waiting for a translation.

'Knight of Glin, you and your men must start to withdraw before a minute is up or this man dies, and then you'll see whether I am in earnest,' shouted Turlough and without waiting for an answer he began to count slowly and loudly, his voice completely steady.

Mara drew closer until she was standing against the stone of the merlon. There was no more that she could say to persuade Turlough; she knew that his mind was made up, but she had a feeling that this man should not die without a touch on the hand from someone who, though she hated his sin, sympathized with his plight. She reached out and squeezed Maccon's bound hand and then noticed something down on the ground to the front of the castle, a man moving cautiously, bent double over something, something that he was carrying hugged tightly to his chest.

With a shock she looked towards the Knight of Glin wondering whether he had seen the figure. But just now there was no indication that he had. He, and the men who stood beside him, were all looking upwards at the miserable figure with the noose around his neck. Even the men beside the trebuchet were looking in that direction as the numbers, intoned by Turlough, went on inexorably. The thirties had now all been enumerated and the forties seemed to flash past, though Turlough's voice was measured and unhurried.

'Fifty-one . . . fifty-two . . . fifty-three,' said Turlough and Mara caught her breath.

She wondered whether Turlough had seen that there was

someone down there stealing through the marshy land – just
one man, but she guessed that he carried death and destruction
in his hands. There was only one reason to carry a cauldron
out to a battlefield. Perhaps, after all, Turlough might be
bluffing, might have sent a man on a mission and was keeping
all eyes averted from him.

For a moment Mara feared that it might be Enda, but it
was too small, too square a figure. And then something about
the way that he moved struck her with its familiarity. The
man limped slightly, she noticed, and she realized that it was
Rosta, the cook.

For a couple of seconds Mara had lost sight of Rosta, but
now she saw him again and he had broken into a trot, still
carrying his dangerous burden. Both hands were needed to
carry the enormous iron cauldron, filled to the brim with
something liquid, something black – tar, as she had guessed.
He had no throwing spear with him, though, and she could
not see a glint of knives at his waist.

Turlough, also, Mara guessed, was watching Rosta, watching
him intently. The last five numbers came out slowly and singly.
No one on the ground had seen him, not one of the Knight
of Glin's men had spotted him, no one realized what he was
doing. But what was he doing? He could not get near enough
to harm the boats, they were all moored out on the river,
beyond the useless chain – the men had just climbed over it
and waded into the bank.

And then Mara realized where Rosta was going. He was
headed straight for the fearsome trebuchet. He limped along
resolutely, carrying a weight that few men could have managed
without help. A moment earlier he had seemed to stumble over
one of those uneven patches of marsh, and then she had lost
sight of him. When she saw him again he was going faster. He
had diverted to the horse track along which Mara and her
scholars had come on the day before Christmas. The ground
here was solid and smooth and was enclosed by hedges. He did
not look back but Mara had an impression that he was listening
to the King's words, to that measured counting away the seconds
of a man's life. Now he was within a few yards of the trebuchet,
but the hedge was still between him and the attackers.

And then he came to his destination. How he managed it, she did not know, but he had hoisted the cauldron up and then clambered onto the top of a large block made from an immense slab of limestone, probably placed there as convenience for the hunters of the marsh birds. He crouched, hidden from the attackers by the hedge, bending over the cauldron of tar, doing something. There was a long moment and then flames rose up from the cauldron – the black, sticky, liquid tar had been ignited and was now blazing up, shooting out orange tongues of fire.

'Fifty-seven, fifty-eight, fifty-nine . . .' Still the words were measured evenly, but the pace had quickened. The men on the ground had reacted to the increased urgency of Turlough's voice. Even those loading the stones onto the trebuchet ceased their labours, turned their backs on the instrument and with heads tilted back watched the drama being enacted on the roof of the castle. This was the second time this morning that time had been counted out and Mara prayed that this was just a subterfuge and that Turlough might spare the life of Maccon MacMahon.

'Sixty,' said Turlough and he roared out the word with huge emphasis. He lifted his right arm, stared down, not looking towards Rosta, this time, but turning his head towards the Knight of Glin. He waited a long moment and then with a swift and decisive action, lowered the arm.

And then everything happened all at once. Without a moment's hesitation the men standing at the parapet pushed Maccon MacMahon off from the precarious perch where they had held him during all of the negotiations. The rope had been coiled, but now all of the loops unravelled quickly and Mara could see that it was an immensely long rope.

And it was a long moment before they heard the sickening crack. Mara hoped that meant the neck of the man had been broken . . . Or perhaps it was the sound of his feet striking the castle wall. That noise came again and again until she felt that she could hardly bear it. She hoped fervently that he was dead, but her imagination clearly pictured MacMahon dangling there from the castle rampart, frantically kicking with his feet and slowly strangling to death.

Everything was confused and jumbled. So much is happening! she thought. Just as the bound man with the noose around his neck had been pushed from the parapet, down below, on the small narrow road, there was another man who was lifting his mighty arms with the flaming cauldron held aloft within them. The orange light was on his face, or perhaps it was not his face, perhaps it was the hair that burst into bright flames; then the clothes were on fire, the arms still holding the burning mass. Then the man was finding that last ounce of strength to hurl the cauldron down from his height, and down from where he stood. For a moment it looked as if it would be an impossibility for any man, no matter how powerful, to bridge that gap with the weight of a blazing cauldron of tar.

But over it went, the cauldron curving through the space in a slight arc. The men standing by the trebuchet, looking up, were frozen for an instant, then began to move, trying to run, but too late. The deadly contents, the flaming pitch, spilled out looking like scarlet syrup: syrup that was coating and burning all that it touched; burning wood and flesh and even stone.

It took a moment to realize that there were terrible sounds as well as terrible sights. Dreadful screams, awful, ear-splitting screams. A nauseating smell of burning flesh came upwards to them on the mist-laden air. Where the trebuchet had stood, there was now a huge fire blazing up in its place. The flaming tar had coated it and the wood was burning like tinder.

But not just the wood was burning. The liquid burning mass had splashed over the men also. Mara was tempted to stick her fingers in her ears, but stood there stoically feeling that to do so was the act of a coward, was to deny and to denigrate human suffering. The screams seemed to go on for ever. She narrowed her eyes to try to pierce the smoke, to endeavour to see if there were any humans left alive near to that terrible fire. The flames crackled and now there were no more screams. A couple of the men who had stood at a distance from the trebuchet had dived into the river to soothe their hurts, but the majority must have burned to death. The stench was terrible. The fire roared. Not just human flesh, now, but a strong smell of timber burning. Some of the limestone rocks already loaded onto the sling exploded with a noise that sounded like cannon fire.

The party on the roof waited in dead silence. A slight ripple of a breeze was coming from the river and the smoke wavered in the current of air and then began to dissipate. Mara found herself desperately holding on to the parapet as her legs trembled beneath her. Turlough, she saw with amazement, looked quite unmoved. His head was slightly angled and she could not tell whether he was looking at the Knight of Glin or at the trebuchet and then she realized that his eyes were further over, fixed on the spot behind the hedge of the roadway. The pyre of flames had ignited the thickly interwoven twigs of blackthorn and ivy and the fire burned intensely. No man could be alive within it.

There was now a movement from the survivors. The man standing beside the Knight of Glin had blown a shrill whistle. The unharmed men and those slightly burned scrambled for the boats, leaving behind the dead and the dying

Poor Rosta was now undoubtedly dead, thought Mara, burning inside his pyre like a Viking in one of the old tales that she had read from the books that her father had collected.

The boats were not allowed to depart unscathed. Throwing knives were hurled after the attackers from the small loophole windows low down in the castle and a few from the roof of the building. There were a few screams and cries of pain but the boats were now well afloat and the men of Glin seized the oars to take them away as quickly as possible from an expedition which had turned out so badly for them.

'Let them take their carrion with them,' yelled Turlough. Mara had never heard him sound so savage. For a moment she thought he meant that they should take their own dead, but after a gesture from his king, the captain of the guard had seized the rope that still dangled over the rampart. Another man sliced through it and with all his strength the captain endeavoured to hurl it towards the boat where the Knight of Glin was being pushed out into deeper water.

The corpse fell short, of course. It fell into the river. The outgoing tide would probably take it downstream, down past the lands of Corcabascin that Maccon MacMahon had ruled over as *taoiseach* of his clan, past the castle of Clonderaw, his birthplace and the birthplace of his children, and then on and into the Atlantic. A Christian burial had been denied to him, but on the whole, Mara felt that, for the sake of the twins, it might be best to allow the river to take the body and its noose. It gave the possibility to allow his death to be categorized as 'killed in action'. Shona, of course, would have to know the truth.

'Come on,' said Turlough abruptly to his captain. 'Let's find something to put the remains of poor Rosta in. We'll let him burn cleanly and then bury his bones when the fire cools.' He stopped at the door leading from the roof to the steps and then said in a broken voice: 'Poor brave fellow. He gave his life to save us all.'

Sixteen

Ɑn Seɑnchɑs ɱór

(The Great Ancient Tradition)

The King is bound by law to do justice to his meanest subject.

A king carrying building material to his castle has only the same claim for right of way as the miller carrying material to build his mill.

The poorest man in the land can compel payment of a debt from the King himself;

On the Eve of the Epiphany, January 1520, Mara took her place as judge in the great hall of Bunratty Castle. She sat in the chair of state placed behind the middle point of the long table on the dais and looked around. Her husband, King Turlough Donn O'Brien, sat at the end of the table with Enda, as lawyer, sitting beside him. There were a number of people present to hear her give judgement, members of the garrison, people from the village and some of the guests that had been staying in the castle for the celebration of Turlough Donn's twentieth anniversary of his accession to the leadership of the O'Brien clan and to the kingship of Thomond, Corcomroe and Burren.

Mara looked around and felt wrong and out of place. She was accustomed to giving judgement in the open air and beside the ancient dolmen of Poulnabrone. Hundreds of people usually thronged into the field to hear her judgements. She was used to a crowd, used to pitching her voice to dominate wind and rain, and to reach to the furthermost corner and above all she was used to the large mass of her own people. This small audience and the indoor location in the warmth and luxury of the great hall of the castle seemed an alien environment to her at this moment. The chair, also, did not suit her. It had been the custom of Brehon MacClancy to sit there and she felt that she should follow custom for this first occasion on which she would have to give judgement at Bunratty. And yet it felt wrong, made her feel as though she were not in command but was a part of the onlookers.

And she did not like to have a table between herself and them.

Resolutely she rose to her feet, stepped to one side of the long table and looked down at the sparse number of people scattered throughout the hall, and greeted them in a voice which she strove to make sound normal and unaffected by any doubts.

'There have been many deaths here at Bunratty during the last week,' she said, pitching her voice to the end of the hall, but making sure that it did not ring out in its usual carrying tones. Shona had undertaken to keep the twins out of the way, but Mara was conscious of the various entrances and exits of this hall and did not wish her voice to carry beyond it. 'Most,' she continued, 'were by the act of war and could not be helped. The community here at Bunratty was attacked and it had to defend itself. The law permits this; warfare between clans and divisions has, unfortunately, always been a part of our history. And, on this occasion, I can verify that the amount of violence used was in accordance with necessity.'

Mara paused and looked around. There was a slight stir of interest at her words. They were unexpected and not according to the usual protocol of judgement days at Bunratty.

'However, a murder of a member of the clan or the kingdom is a different matter,' she continued. 'The first case that I have to deal with is the secret and unlawful killing of the Brehon of Thomond, Brehon Tomás MacClancy. Brehon MacClancy was killed soon after midnight while sitting at a table at the end of this hall during the festivities of Christmas Night. He was not taking part in the dancing, but was drinking fairly heavily and was possibly fast asleep – certainly he was lying sprawled across the table when the blow was struck. He was killed by means of a knife which lodged in his back, just below the shoulder blade.'

Mara paused and looked around. She missed the

atmosphere of tension that usually occurred as she detailed the progress of her investigation at the Burren. The people sitting in front of her belonged to a small, tight-knit community and most had been present in the castle on the night of the murder. She had told them nothing that they did not know already.

Nevertheless, she had to go step by step through the whole matter and explain her thought process and the conclusion to which she had come. She looked down at the strained faces of Turlough's friends and relations and proceeded smoothly.

'There were many puzzling features to this murder. About half an hour before the murder Brehon MacClancy was definitely alive according to the testimony of various witnesses.' Here she thought of the twins and their report of the man passing wind and apologizing to a flagon and she bit back a smile.

'During that half-hour, a very fast jig was played and most people were dancing or else standing beside the table here.' She touched the wood with her fingers and wished that it was the rough, cold capstone at her usual judgement place, at the Poulnabrone dolmen. A few faces looked curious now and she proceeded carefully, making sure that her thoughts were in order and were expressed as clearly as she could.

'And,' she added, 'the doors leading out of the hall, as testified by most of those who were present, were not opened during that time. The serving of the food had finished; the cook and his assistants had retired to the kitchen. This then appeared to mean that the murder was committed by one of those guests of the King – one of the twenty people, including seven children, who had remained in the hall when others went down to dance to the music from the players in the main guard hall.'

Now every eye was on her and Mara proceeded with her story.

'One of the puzzling features was the fact that the murder was committed within the sight and sound of these twenty people, including the very sharp-eyed children. And another was that it appeared as though the murder weapon, the knife, was driven in with the left hand. The third, and perhaps the most puzzling one of all, was that the knife was driven in such a small distance that it actually fell out of the shallow wound shortly after the man's death.'

Mara allowed them all to think about that and to whisper to each other for a moment and then held up her hand for silence.

'One person, a left-handed person, was seen to bend over Brehon MacClancy and to whisper in his ear and some of my suspicions did focus on that person . . .' She did not look towards Enda as she said this, but went on quickly, 'But then I began to think about it and to wonder why the knife fell so quickly from the wound. One would expect that a knife, plunged into the back of the victim, by any adult, a knife driven in hard enough to kill, would remain until extracted, but this knife had made such a shallow wound that it fell out as the flesh relaxed.'

There had been a time when Mara had considered the girl twin, Cael. She was the owner of the knife and she was only a young and a very thin child. A blow from her, without adult muscle or weight, might well have only penetrated a small distance. And Cael had hated Brehon MacClancy, whether because of what had happened to her sister, or anything that had happened to herself. The boys' clothes and boys' attitude may have been Cael's defence. Brehon MacClancy, thought Mara viciously, had been a nasty man with a liking for dominance over children and a desire to hurt and to torture his victims. He was a blackmailer, not for any gain, but for the pleasure of seeing his victims squirm. Still, *to no man is justice denied* and his murder had to be solved, just as if he had been the most worthy man in the kingdom.

'It was then that I began to think that there might be some cause of death other than a knife wound,' she said, looking around at the assembled people and tacitly inviting them to join with her on the journey towards the truth. '"*After all*," I said to myself, "*there was very little blood. The man had not bled to death; the knife could not have touched a vital organ, so why did he die?*"'

Now everyone was leaning towards her and some part of her, of which she was always slightly ashamed, revelled in her ability to tell a story. She nodded her head at her audience.

'Of course, the next step was to inspect the body properly and to find out the real cause of death. It didn't seem as though it was a failure of the heart – I've observed that when that happens there is a purple colour in the face and a congested appearance of the eyes and this was not present. Unfortunately, the physician fell ill and by the time that he had recovered . . .' Her eyes rested politely for a moment on Donogh O'Hickey and she was pleased to see that he looked uncomfortable.

'By the time that the physician had recovered,' she repeated, 'the body, in its box, had been slid from its position in the middle of the basement, right down, past the iron gate at the end of the room and had disappeared into the river. I would presume that this action was taken by the murderer in order to avoid any medical inspection. No doubt my request had been overheard.'

She would leave it at that, she decided. What had happened to her, that attempt to drown her, was her own business and she did not wish to distress Turlough by detailing the effort made to get rid of the investigating Brehon by murdering her. She continued in a matter-of-fact tone.

'On the night when the murder occurred one of the many dishes cooked for us by Rosta was a pie of lampreys. Now these eels have a very poisonous sac within them. A young physician in the Burren, someone who has learned from your own physician here and has spent many years studying in other countries, told me some time ago that this poison is so very potent that once it enters the bloodstream then a person can die within minutes. And when I picked up the knife after it had fallen from the wound I was surprised to find a strong fishy smell from it. It did not occur to me then, but later on the fact struck me and I wondered whether that could be the solution to the man's death.' Mara thought back to her conversation with the physician about Nuala and her theories relating to the death of that early King of England from a 'surfeit' of lampreys. Now she declared boldly:

'I do believe that the tip of the knife which entered the blood of Brehon MacClancy had been soaked in the deadly poisonous sac of one of the lampreys and it was poison entering the blood, not a wound, which caused the man's death.'

The silence was now intense. Mara looked around the room at the waiting faces and said quickly: 'You may ask me how the murderer managed to get hold of the poisonous sac from one of the lampreys and my answer to you is that was easily done as the murderer was the man who cooked and cleaned out the fish.'

From the corner of her eye Mara saw Turlough stand up abruptly and then sit down again. She did not look towards him, but continued slowly and carefully.

'Rosta, the cook, was a good man, a kind man, a man whose whole life was dedicated to serving and pleasing the King whom he had served in battle for as long as he was able, and who, after the injury to his leg, went on serving him by cooking the wonderful meals that were so enjoyed. We all know now that he has given his life to save the King that he served. But men are fallible and Rosta yielded to temptation to sell off some of the King's salmon and Brehon MacClancy found evidence against him and was about to shame him in front of the King and the people of Bunratty on this day by accusing him of theft. The evidence was there, locked in the cupboard in the Brehon's room.'

And in the large cage full of salmon below the nets at the entrance from the basement to the river, she thought. This made an ideal place, perhaps, for these illicit salmon to be reserved. All salmon from the river belonged to the King and Rosta had no right to sell any of it – a venial sin and one that would have been readily forgiven by his easygoing master, but Rosta could not bear the shame of public disgrace if his thievery had been unveiled at the Epiphany judgement day.

Brehon MacClancy had died of poison from a lamprey, but he had also died from the poison of his own malice.

Turlough was whispering loudly into Enda's ear and Enda rose from his seat.

'May I put the case, Brehon, that Rosta, the cook, was not, at any stage, in the great hall during the time when Brehon MacClancy met his death,' he said with dignity.

'No, he wasn't,' admitted Mara and saw the heads, which had turned towards Enda, turn back to her again. She waited for a second and then pointed dramatically to the end of the hall. Every head swivelled and then turned back again. A few had understood, but the rest looked puzzled.

'I had forgotten the "squint" of course!' Mara allowed a note of exasperation to enter her voice and, indeed, every time that she thought of the obviousness of it, she felt embarrassed at her own stupidity.

'The squint, as those who are acquainted with this castle know well, gives an extremely good view from the King's solar, although from here, in the great hall, it's almost impossible to see a figure who stands there in the angle. I have often stood there and looked down and noticed that no one ever looked up at me, or seemed aware that there was a watcher. It was very easy for the cook to go up to the King's solar,' she continued. 'If found there he could have the excuse that he was placing refreshments on the table – as, indeed, was his habit at various times of the day. He went up to the solar – no doubt the knife, anointed with the deadly poison, was in some sort of container, hidden below a basket of rolls or something like that. He launched it from the squint at a moment when nobody was looking. No one saw him stand there, no one saw the knife come down. It is, in fact, as I have just said, quite difficult from the hall to see anyone standing up there because of the angle in which it is set. He waited for his opportunity, launched the knife – remember this cook, Rosta, was a great knife thrower, when a member of the King's guard, before his leg wound made it impossible to continue in that service. He flung the knife and it entered into the man's back just below the shoulder blade and the poison went straight into the bloodstream and killed him – in his sleep. There is one other matter,' Mara went on, 'because Brehon MacClancy was sitting opposite to the squint, sleeping at the table – as Rosta would have observed before he left the room – he was actually facing the squint, therefore the knife entered the flesh from the left-hand side, though, in fact, Rosta was right-handed.'

Mara did not give them time to debate this matter. It was time for the case to be wound up.

'I tell you all of this because the deliberate killing of a fellow person must never go unmarked,' she said in a loud, clear voice. 'However, there is a tenet in our law, the law that has served this country since before the time of St Patrick, and will, I hope, serve it in the centuries to come, and the law says: "*Marabh cach marbh a chínta*" ("*every dead man kills his offences*"). Rosta the cook has given up his life to save the life of all here at Bunratty; his offence is dead and his name will be honoured in the kingdom of Thomond for as long as memory lasts.'

There was a great stir among everyone. People sat back and spoke to neighbours, smiles wreathed faces and heads nodded. The offence was as nothing when put in the balance of the heroism of the deed that followed it. There would be no mourners of that unjust man, the Brehon of Thomond, and many who would mourn the cook who had died so heroically in the service of the King whom he had loved and venerated. Mara saw Turlough sit back. The flush of anger had disappeared from his face and he spoke eagerly with Enda. He was probably, she thought affectionately, planning some sort of memorial to Rosta, the cook who had given his life for the beleaguered garrison.

Mara wished that she, too, could relax; that she could sit back and chat and answer questions and revel in the thought of a mystery worked out and solved, but she could not do it. From the time that she was three years old a great reverence and respect for the law, taught to her by her father, had filled her and she knew that the law had no compromises. She had to carry through what she had set out to do. She sat in silence for a couple of minutes and then once again rose to her feet and held up her hand.

'There was another unlawful killing which occurred this Christmastide,' she said and saw the puzzled faces swivel around towards her. 'This death was not a secret killing; responsibility was immediately acknowledged for it. Nevertheless, the law demands not just full confession but also restitution.'

Mara waited until the murmurs died down. She did not glance towards Turlough, but looked stiffly ahead of her.

'I speak,' she said, 'of the unlawful killing by strangulation of Maccon MacMahon. The man responsible for ordering the deed was the King but the law expects that the King, like other members of the clan and kingdom, must observe the law and must, if he breaks it, pay the penalty, or else lose his honour price.

'The man who died, Maccon MacMahon,' she continued 'was a man who had betrayed his King and the people of the kingdom. He brought death and destruction to Bunratty by arranging for enemies to attack the castle and the village and by disabling the cannon which was positioned ready to defend against an assault from the river. For these crimes he deserved punishment.' She stopped for a moment, scanning the faces and feeling within her an urge to share her view of the law, to make them and their children and their children's children understand the importance of keeping the letter of a law which in this part of Ireland had resisted three centuries of English endeavour to denigrate and to destroy it.

'Brehon law,' she went on, 'has a penalty for almost every crime or misdemeanour known to man. Maccon MacMahon committed a crime and should have been judged, in front of the people of the kingdom, by the law, and retribution exacted. But Maccon MacMahon was not so judged, but was unlawfully killed and so the man who gave the order for this killing, the man who said, "*on my head be it*", this man is guilty of an unlawful killing.'

Mara took a deep breath and then said in a calm, clear voice: 'I judge you, King Turlough Donn O'Brien, to be guilty of the unlawful killing of Maccon MacMahon, and I call on you to pay the fine of forty-two *sét*s, or twenty-one ounces of silver, or twenty-one milch cows for this homicide and in addition to that the honour price of the dead man which I reckon, since his status was that of an *aire déso*, to be ten *sét*s, or five ounces of silver, or five milch cows. So, therefore, a total fine of fifty-two *sét*s, or twenty-six ounces of silver, or twenty-six milch cows must be paid by King Turlough Donn O'Brien to the children and heirs of Maccon MacMahon.'

There was a long pause. Everyone in the hall sat very rigid, very quiet, though eyes were all on the figure at the end of the table. And then Turlough said curtly: 'So be it.'

'Then the business of this court is over,' said Mara. 'Go in peace with each other and with your neighbours.'

And then she sat down and wondered whether her ten years of marriage had come to an end.

Seventeen

Cáin Lanama
(The Law of Marriage)

Exempt from legal suit for each, is what each may have used or have consumed as against the other, except what lien, obligation or loan may have imposed, or what one of them may have misappropriated from the other.

Exempt from legal suit is:
Everything useful to the partnership
Everything done in good faith.
Liable to legal claim is everything done in bad faith in the law of the couple.

Mara and her five scholars arrived back in the Burren before the light faded on seventh January. The boys were tired, subdued after the tragedy of so many deaths, puzzled by the verdicts of yesterday and they rode in silence for much of the time, leaving Mara free to think her thoughts. Her mind was bleak. She and Turlough had been very happy together during the last ten years. Custom had not made stale their feelings for each other – he had been a husband, a lover, a friend and the only one in her life whom she trusted with her innermost thoughts, doubts and fears. She had worried about this marriage before she had finally agreed to it; had been concerned that it might interfere with her professional life as a Brehon, but Turlough had always accepted her work, her obligations to the kingdom and to her law school and had never sought to change her in any way. Until now the marriage had been a success. But now?

Her mind went around and around, ceaselessly going over the events of the last few days. Could she have omitted that verdict? Could she have classified the hanging of Maccon MacMahon as an act of war? But she knew that had not been possible. Brehon law made a sharp difference between any action taken against an enemy clan or a person from a foreign land and an act of violence against a member of the clan or kingdom. Maccon MacMahon should not have been hanged, but should have stood trial and paid the fine due for his treachery, his betrayal of his King and over-lord.

How had Turlough reacted to her judgement? Other than that brief and abrupt '*so be it*' he had not spoken to her. She had been busy with her papers and he had his relations and his friends to talk with. From time to time she had looked across at him, but could read nothing from his face, courteous, friendly, interested, as he had exchanged ideas and plans with his guests. They had all eaten a brief meal, served with food as good as they could make it, by Rosta's assistants and the party which had arrived for the festivities had begun to break up.

Turlough had left Bunratty almost straight after the meal. He had decided to escort Conor and Ellice by easy stages to the abbey near the sea where a skilled monk would once again try to bring his delicate son back to some measure of health. Mara had refused the midday meal and had slept for most of the afternoon and then spent a wakeful night, lying wide awake and alone in the large bed of the sumptuous King's apartment. If it had not been for the scholars she would have set out for home on the day before, but she dared not allow them to run the risk of doing the last stage of the journey in darkness and mist.

The mist was still there on the morning as they rode along the high path above the marsh, but their way was straight and narrow and the roadway enclosed with stout blackthorn hedges. They skirted the flooded plain around the Franciscan abbey at Innis, burial place of a former O'Brien king, an ancestor of Turlough's, one of the many King Turlough O'Briens that had reigned over the people of this portion of Ireland.

And then they had turned towards the west.

It was only when they reached the Burren that the land opened out and the sight of the vast tracts of stone-paved fields made Mara's spirits begin to rise. A brisk west wind had risen and the fog was being blown away in tatters of cloudy white. The limestone clints, each as much as ten yards in length and breadth, ever-changing in colour according to the sky and the sun and the rain, now gleamed black as wet tar. Cows strolled across them, plucking the succulent grass that grew, winter and summer, in the grykes between the clints, where the limestone retained the summer heat right through the winter months. The red and white cattle raised their heads to look from mild eyes with astonishment at the party that rode past them and the boys called out jocose greetings to them. Cormac tossed an apple from the storeroom at Bunratty Castle, but they ignored it and his own pony neighed a reproach.

It had not been a hard winter, thought Mara looking around at her native territory with a sort of hunger for its familiarity. The bare twigs of the hawthorn still bore the dark red berries and a flock of goldfinches fed noisily from the dangling cones of alder trees in the hedgerows. Some fruits of the guelder rose still remained, shining as pink as the sugared cherries in a fruit cake, and these were attacked greedily by a flock of redwings. A plump fox, its coat gleaming gold in a sudden ray of sunshine, emerged from the undergrowth with a large rat dangling from its mouth and then disappeared under the splayed stones of an ancient tomb. In this part of the west of Ireland spring came early and there were signs of birds flying in pairs and even a beginning of nest-building. As Mara watched, she saw a tiny wren with a clump of moss in its mouth investigate a possible site on a field boundary. The walls in this part of the Burren were traditionally made by vertically stacking inch-thick long slabs of stone, each of the slabs angled so that it rested against its neighbours. The resulting wall allowed the wind to be filtered safely through the cracks, but also provided wonderfully inviting spaces for small birds to build their intricate nests. Mara heaved a sigh of relief. I'm home, she thought.

'Domhnall,' she said impulsively, 'would you and the other boys like to ride on ahead. I think my horse is tired and so am I. I will only hold you up. You go on. You can tell Brigid all the news. She'll want to know everything.'

And that might be a neat way of getting out of having to relate whole story and avoiding too many penetrating questions from the woman who had been her nurse, her mother after the death of Mara's mother, and who had run her household and looked after her scholars with unceasing devotion. Sooner or later, of course, she would have to discuss the matter with her if there was going to be any parting between herself and her husband. Brigid was devoted to Turlough, who charmed her by his enthusiastic reception of every meal put in front of him and by his deep interest in anything to do with her or her husband Cumhal.

At the thought of Turlough, Mara felt the tears come to her eyes. Now that the boys were ahead of her, galloping enthusiastically across the fields towards Lissylisheen, she was able to indulge in a few regrets – perhaps she had mishandled the business, perhaps she should have warned Turlough of what she was going to say.

But it would have been difficult. There had been no opportunity when she and Turlough could have talked together, an opportunity where she could have explained to him why she had been driven by her respect for the law to have given that verdict at the court of Bunratty. Turlough had just been too busy, too preoccupied. There had been no time where husband and wife could have communicated.

In fact, instantly after the retreat of the Knight of Glin, once the dead were buried and the castle wall shored up and repaired, Turlough had mustered his men, and galloped across the western parts of his territory in order to make sure that there was no attempt to seize the lands and the castle belonging to the MacMahon. He had only returned very late on the night before judgement day. She had already been in bed and in the face of his exuberance, his ardour and his desire for her; she had shirked telling him of her decision.

It had been wrong to have taken him by surprise; she knew that and she admired the dignity of his response.

And wished desperately that things could have been different.

She stopped under an old yew tree beside the tiny church of Noughaval and remained so still that a pine marten, with a splendidly bushy tail, ran cat-like down the trunk of the tree and then disappeared in a streak of dark gold and brown beneath the elaborate stone tomb of the O'Lochlainn family. Her own father was also buried in this graveyard and she dismounted from her horse and walked across to his tomb. She should say a prayer for his soul, she thought, but the words would not come. Instead she just stood there and allowed her mind to calm.

This is the law, she quoted to herself sadly, remembering what she had memorized as a child within her father's law school. *'No Brehon of the Gaedhil is able to abrogate any law that is found within the Seánchas Mór. In it were established laws for king and vassal, for queen and subject, chief and dependant, wealthy and poor.'*

These were the words. She was a servant of the law and she could not change it to fit her individual circumstances. She had done the right thing so far as the law was concerned, but her marriage, her relationship with Turlough – had she served that well?

By the time that she reached sight of her law school, the faithful Brigid was standing at the gate looking anxiously down the road. By her worried looks, Mara guessed that she had heard the whole story of the judgement day at Bunratty and the verdicts that had been declared.

Cormac and Art, sticks in hands, were walking in the opposite direction down the road in the company of Cumhal. The sound of their high excited voices came to her and she knew that they were glad to be home. She guessed that they would be fetching the cows home for the night from their grazing on the High Burren, a mountainous plateau of flat rock which stretched from Cahermacnaghten right across to beyond the judgement place at Poulnabrone. Mara was glad to see them go. Cormac, adoring of his kingly father, had not spoken a word to his mother ever since the judgement at Bunratty on the morning before. Art, Cormac's foster-brother and loyal friend, had also been uneasy with her, Finbar and Slevin, too, had been embarrassed and unsure. Only Domhnall had been approving, she sensed; and admired his thorough understanding of the laws in which she had instructed him for the past five years.

But now Brigid had to be faced and Mara kept her head down until she could no longer have any excuse not to raise it in greeting. Brigid would know the whole story by now – she would have demanded all details from the boys. But Brigid's first concern was for her mistress, her nursling, the Brehon whom she and her husband venerated and served.

'You're dead tired, *alanah*, I can see by your eyes; now for once in your life do as I tell you,' scolded Brigid. 'Cumhal has lit the fire and filled the bath and your bed is all ready for you. Don't you worry about the boys today – there's plenty for them to do; Cumhal will occupy them. "*That will bring you all down to earth and away from all your talk of castles and battles and feastings,*" that's what I said to them. And do you know what young Domhnall said, Brehon?' Brigid stopped to draw a breath, 'He said to me, and not a word of lie, "*It's great to be home again, Brigid; I've missed your cooking!*" Would you believe that? After all the excitement, all the banquets, that's what he said. Now, just you leave that horse,' she went on, looking anxiously up at Mara, 'don't you know that young Dathi will see to it? Across to your own house with you, now, and lie down before you fall down – my old mother used to say that and there wasn't a woman in the neighbourhood that had the brains she had, I'll tell you that, Brehon. You'll be a new woman once you've had a good rest.'

Scolding and chattering, Brigid tucked her arm into Mara's and led her along the short distance between the Brehon's house and the law-school enclosure. Mara drew in a deep sigh and began to feel better. Brigid had asked for no explan-ations, had offered no sympathy. Her housekeeper had a simple code. While Mara's father was alive, she and Cumhal had served him with the utmost devotion and unquestioning loyalty. After he died and Mara had become first the head of the law school and then the Brehon of the Burren; that loyalty had been transferred to the daughter. Whatsoever she did, whatever she thought, every decision that she made was right in their eyes. Though they had known her from babyhood, both Cumhal and Brigid always respectfully addressed Mara as 'Brehon' and only on rare occasions did an endearment like '*alanah*' steal out.

And, of course, Brigid, as always, was right. She was bone-tired and every fibre of her body seemed to ache. Once the housekeeper had left her, Mara went quickly into the small room at the back of the house. There was a big pump there and someone had already filled the wooden bath tub with icy water from the hundred-foot-deep well. It was her father that had the well dug and she blessed his memory every time she used it. It had never gone dry – in some way that Domhnall had endeavoured to explain to her, the streams that flowed down from the mountains filled a vast lake beneath the limestone of the Burren and the water was available to the inhabitants for the labour of digging a well.

Cumhal had lit the charcoal in the iron brazier; the place was gloriously warm. Mara took the large pot of boiling water from the iron grid across the top and poured it into the cold water in the bath, testing the water with her hand until the temperature was right. Then she noticed an iron cup, filled with a dark red liquid, standing at the back of the grid. Brigid's special elderberry cordial! She picked it up, drained it and felt the hot spiciness warm her right down to her toes. She shed her clothes and climbed into the hot water, lay back and closed her eyes. I can't help matters, she said to herself resolutely. Now is the moment to stop thinking and worrying. After her bath she would do as Brigid suggested. Go straight up the stairs, get in under the blankets made from the fleece woven from her sheep flock and just sleep for as long as she could.

Mara slept heavily, an exhausted, nightmare-filled sleep, and then woke when it was dark. There was a platter of oaten biscuits by her bed and a glass of milk. She ate and drank mechanically and wished that she had stayed asleep. Her mind had started to become very busy. Could she have done things differently? And yet she had acted in good faith and she could not wish her actions undone – just that she had never gone to Bunratty Castle. In the past the continuous battles, attacks and defence had been a different part of Turlough's life and not one that she had taken much interest or part in and now she desperately wished the past couple of weeks had never taken place. Her mind went around and around in circles and when dawn came she suddenly fell into a heavy sleep.

The noise of horse hoofs roused her. For a while she lay there feeling dazed and uninterested. Then she realized that this was a large party and sat up in bed. That could mean only one thing. Her heart skipped a beat. For a moment, she had thought that it might be her nearest neighbour, a local *taoiseach*, Ardal O'Lochlainn, but there were too many horses in the train for that. Ardal was a simple man, a man who normally rode alone or in the company of his steward, though perhaps it was possible that he had mustered a crowd of his shepherds and they were riding out to round up the sheep from his lands near the sea.

She got up, went to the window, pushed open the casement and leaned out. No, it was not Ardal. She had thought that there had been too many horses for that. The stately banners told their own tale – this was the King and his men. For a moment she felt almost like creeping out from the back entrance to her house and avoiding this meeting, but a moment's reflection stiffened her backbone and she went rapidly to the wooden press in her room and selected a gown dyed a cherry red and slipped it over a fresh starched linen *léine*. She combed her hair, braided it, fastened it with pins behind the back of her neck, checked her appearance in the mirror of burnished steel, slipped on a pair of soft leather shoes and went out of the bedroom and down the stairs. It took all of her courage to lift down her fur-lined mantle from the back of the door, to slip it on and to walk resolutely down the flagstoned path to the garden gate. There she waited calmly and courageously until the horses rounded the last bend in the road.

Despite the recent events, Turlough rode with only his usual small band of guards in front of him and his two personal guards behind him. Riding beside him, though, one on either side of him, were a pair of young people and lagging behind the guards came two small figures on ponies.

'Enda!' exclaimed Brigid, rushing forward to greet one of the former pupils of the law school. Mara was glad to see how eagerly the golden-haired young man jumped from his horse and hugged her elderly housekeeper. Enda had always been a favourite with Brigid, even when she had deplored some aspects of his adolescent behaviour.

And then the scholars burst from the kitchen house, each with a half-eaten oat cake in hand.

'*Iontach!* Are you coming to stay with us,' shouted Cormac rushing forward and beaming exuberantly at the MacMahon twins. 'Brigid, this is Cael and Cian – they will have a marvellous time here. Are you staying for long? Come and see my wolfhound. You didn't believe that I have a real, live wolfhound puppy, all for myself, did you?'

Chattering wildly, Cormac escorted the twins to the stable and followed by the other boys they rushed over to the stables and released the puppy who immediately jumped up on the twins, his paws, still muddy from his early morning run. Once Cormac had greeted his father exuberantly, he, the twins and the other scholars took off across the road and began running across the limestone clints, Smoke barking and leaping and making circles around them.

When the noise died down a little, Mara looked up at the dark-haired girl beside Enda and said impulsively, 'You are very welcome, Shona. I hope you will stay here for a long time. I will love to have your company. Brigid, we can have a room for Shona in the guesthouse, can't we? Enda, you take her there?'

And then they were all gone, the twins and the scholars still running with the wildly excited, loudly barking puppy, Enda, with a protective hand on Shona's elbow, escorting her over to the guesthouse, Brigid, in her element, calculating her stores for a worthy meal for all of those unexpected guests.

And Mara was left gazing up at her husband Turlough Donn O'Brien.

'I thought this might be best thing to do with these poor children,' said Turlough apologetically. 'You don't mind, do you? You could try the two little ones in your school, they get on well with Cormac, you know. Clever as a pair of eels, they are; the two of them. You'll like them. I'll pay their fees, of course. And Enda wants to marry Shona – that will be all right, won't it? I'll give the dowry – you get him qualified as a Brehon and then they can settle down.'

He gazed around him with a smile of satisfaction. 'God, I'm hungry,' he said. Don't know why. We stayed overnight with Brad at Kilnaboy and he gave us a great meal, but I'd love a cup of wine now. Let's go inside and leave these youngsters to look after themselves.'

And that, probably, thought Mara, was all that was going to be said about that time in Bunratty. Turlough was a simple man who lived for the day and seldom looked back either in repentance or in anger. She tucked her arm into his and led the way back towards the house.

'You go in,' she said when they came to the door. 'I'll just find Cumhal to open a new barrel of wine.'

'Let's have the glass goblets that your father brought from Rome,' said Turlough and Mara smiled back at him before going across to the law-school enclosure. So this was going to be a celebration.

'Cumhal,' she called when she went in through the gate of the enclosure. 'Would you come and help me to open a new barrel of wine?' While she waited for him, her mind dwelt fondly on an unopened cask of the finest burgundy, imported from France by Domhnall's father, her daughter's husband. It had sat quietly in the cool, damp darkness of her cellar for over a year. Now was going to be the perfect moment to broach it.

'I'll just fetch a flagon and be with you in a minute, Brehon,' promised Cumhal, hurrying over to the kitchen. Brigid had left Enda to show Shona around and was calling orders to her assistant. Turlough would have a superlative meal in front of him with the greatest rapidity. Mara waited for Cumhal and then accompanied him down the steep steps to the cellar and pointed out the choice wine, lingering while Cumhal decanted it in his expert way and poured some into the flagon. She stood back and told him to precede her up the narrow staircase to the parlour in the Brehon's house.

There were going to be no recriminations, no demands for an explanation, she thought as she followed him up the steps. Her guilt had dissipated. '*Everything done in good faith*,' she quoted to herself from her law documents. Neither she nor Turlough would mention the matter for a while, she decided, and then the sting would have gone out of it.

There were voices from the front of the house, and she could hear Turlough's booming laugh. A sociable man, he must have got tired of sitting alone in her parlour and gone out to look for company. When she came out of the front door, she saw that Ardal O'Lochlainn had hastened over to pay his respects to his King. They were both laughing heartily over some joke.

And then she stopped abruptly, her eyes widening with incredulity.

'So there you are, Ardal,' came Turlough's voice, choked with laughter. 'That's the story. That's just the way that it all happened. I got my wrist well and truly slapped by my lady judge!'